THE LAST CONNECTION

Girls—innocent young girls like poor Alathea—
were being kidnapped, enslaved, murdered. Now
before me sat El Señor, who could give me the
monster's name. And before him sat a bottle.

"Drink, Mr. Axbrewder," he said softly—too softly.

I stared at the bottle. I didn't touch it. If I took
that drink, it wouldn't do any good to know the
name. I wouldn't be able to do anything.

"Sorry I bothered you," I muttered. "Should have
known better."

His goons hit me before I could move. Maybe I
could have taken them, but I didn't get a chance.
They caught my arms, jerked me down onto the
chair. One knotted a fist in my hair and hauled
my head back. El Señor picked up the bottle and
started pouring the contents down my throat.

Then I went blind with tears while the stuff burned
into my guts.

Also by Reed Stephens
Published by Ballantine Books:

THE MAN WHO RISKED HIS PARTNER

THE MAN WHO KILLED HIS BROTHER

A Novel by

Reed Stephens

BALLANTINE BOOKS • NEW YORK

To Barbi, James, and Deb—
none of whom are particularly
interested in mystery novels

Library of Congress Catalog Card Number: 80-66560

ISBN 0-345-33538-4

Manufactured in the United States of America

First Edition: December 1980
Third Printing: October 1986

PART I

Tuesday Night/Wednesday

Chapter One

I was sitting at the bar of the Hegira that night when Ginny came in. The barkeep, an ancient sad-eyed patriarch named José, had just poured me another drink, and I was having one of those rare moments any serious drunk can tell you about. A piece of real quiet. José's cheeks bristled because he didn't shave very often, and his apron was dingy because it didn't get washed very often, and his fingernails had little crescents of grime under them. The glass he poured for me wasn't all that clean. But the stuff he poured was golden-amber and beautiful, like distilled sunlight, and it made the whole place as soothing as sleep (which drunks know how to value because they don't get much of it).

It made the dull old fly-blown *santos* against the wall behind the bottles look like the saints knew what they were doing and it made the drinkers at the tables look peaceful and happy. It made the men playing pool in the back of the room look like they were moving in slow motion, flowing through the air as if it were syrup. It made José look wise and patient behind his stubble and his groggy eyes. It was one of those rare moments when everything is in the right place, and there's a soft gold light shining on it, and you feel like you're being healed. It never lasts—but you always think it will, if you just stay where you are and don't stop drinking.

By the curious logic of the drunk, I felt I'd earned it. After all, I'd been drinking most of the time for several days now, just trying to create that amber glow for myself. So when Ginny walked in the door—when every head in the bar turned to stare at her—I didn't know which to feel first, surprise or resentment. There wasn't any doubt she was looking for me.

I had a right to be surprised. For one thing, she had no business walking into the Hegira like that—especially

at night. The Hegira is down in the old part of Puerta del
Sol, on Eighth Street between Oak and Maple (cities are
like that: the old parts—where the descendants and coun-
trymen of the founders live—have street names like
"Eighth" and "Oak"; the rich white suburbs—half of them
built in the last ten years—have flashier names, names
like "Tenochtitlan" and "Montezuma"), and in the old
part of town women don't go into bars at all. When the
Chicano and Mestizo and Indian women want their men
to come out, they stand on the sidewalk and send in their
children.

As Ginny pushed her way through the door, scanned
the room, and came striding over toward me, the quiet
buzz of voices stopped. José's eyes went blank and empty
—you could tell if she spoke to him he was going to say
he didn't speak English. The men with the pool cues
stood very still, as if they were waiting to start a different
kind of game.

But I also had another reason to be surprised. This
wasn't the way Ginny was supposed to come looking for
me. She came looking for me often enough—I would've
probably drunk myself to death by now if she hadn't been
so faithful about it—but this wasn't the way. We had a
system worked out, and she was breaking it.

What the system did was let me get ready. She didn't
bother me in the morning, when I was taking those first
stiff drinks, trying to push the sickness back down my
throat where it belonged. She didn't bother me during the
day, when I was drinking slow and steady to control the
shakes. She didn't bother me in the afternoon, when I
started to hit the bottle harder because the stuff didn't
seem to be having any effect. She didn't bother me in the
evening, when I went to places like the Hegira looking for
amber and comfort. She didn't bother me when I left
whatever bar it was, and bought a bottle and wandered
away into the night to pay the price.

No, we had a system.

When I was ready for her, I knew where to go at night
with my bottle. One of the benches in a cheap little park
down on Tin Street. It was still in the old part of town,
which meant the city didn't water the grass and the cops
didn't roust drunks who spent the night there. And when
the sun came up I'd be sitting on that bench, waiting—
just waiting because I was too sick to be hoping. And then

I'd see her walking over to me. She always came from the east—the sun was always behind her, so I couldn't see her face. She always said, "Brew." (My name is Mick Axbrewder, but not even my enemies call me Mick.) I always said, "Ginny." And then she always said, "I need you."

That was when I knew I was going to get sober and go back to work.

(Sometimes I said, "What do you need me for? I'm a drunk." But that was just a variation. She never gave me a straight answer. I wouldn't have known what to do with a straight answer.)

So I was surprised when she walked into the Hegira looking for me. But I resented it, too. Because I was having one of those rare moments, and she took it away from me. And because I wasn't ready.

But Ginny Fistoulari is not the kind of woman who lets things like that stand in her way. She's tall (about the only time she doesn't look tall is when I'm standing beside her), maybe five years younger than I am (which makes her thirty-four), with the kind of lean and ready look about her you see in good racehorses. Her eyes are the same color gray as the .357 Smith & Wesson she carries in her purse, but other than that you wouldn't know she's tough as rivets unless you look at her up close. From a few feet away, she's just an attractive blonde with a nice mouth, delicate nostrils, and a perfect chin. Up close you can see her nose was broken once—broken the way a nose gets broken when somebody clips it with a crowbar. (The clown who did it didn't live to regret it. She shot him three times in the face. For that the commission almost took away her license.) She's tough the way you have to be tough in order to spend your time getting involved in the messy side of other people's problems. As a result, she's reasonably successful. Fistoulari Investigations can afford to refuse surveillance cases and domestic problems, even if it isn't making her rich.

Maybe she would've made more money if she hadn't insisted on dragging me back to work every time one of her cases got hard. Maybe in the long run she could've had pricier clients if that big goon working for her (me) wasn't always in trouble with the cops for carrying out investigations without a license. I don't know. When I was sober, I never asked her why she put up with me. I just did the work. She didn't have any use for my gratitude.

But this time I wasn't grateful. I wasn't ready. When I saw her striding straight at me as if the Hegira and all its patrons didn't exist, I wanted to tell her to go to hell. I could see from the way the men were watching her that I was never going to be welcome in the Hegira again. And I resented that—a bar where you can get amber and quiet is hard to find. The words were right there in my mind: *Go to hell, Ginny Fistoulari.*

If I'd said that, she probably would've turned around and walked away and never come back.

So it was a good thing I kept my mouth shut.

But I had to do something. I swung away from her and went back to my drink. The stuff was there waiting for me. It was the right color, even if the feeling was gone. I wrapped my fist around the glass and raised it in the direction of my face.

Ginny's hand came down on my wrist, slapped the glass back to the counter so hard the stuff spilled all over my fingers. Which isn't easy to do to me, even when I'm not expecting it.

If anybody else had done it—anybody at all—I would've taken their hand off. At the wrist. People don't do that kind of thing to me—just like they don't call me Mick.

Only this wasn't anybody else—it was Ginny Fistoulari. I couldn't even try to get her hand off me. I was doing everything I was capable of when I worked up enough energy to be mad.

"God damn it, Ginny—"

She came right back at me. "God damn it, Brew"— she had one of those voices that can do anything—melt in your mouth or tear the skin off your bones—"you're going to come with me, or I swear to God I'll let you have it right here." Right then she sounded like a pistol-whipping. She didn't shout—she didn't have to. When she used that tone on me, there was no question about which one of us was in charge.

So much for my being mad. I've never been able to be mad at her at the same time she was mad at me. Which is probably a good thing. But this time I didn't have the vaguest idea *why* she was mad at me.

I didn't want to have any idea. I wanted to drink. Without looking at her, I said, "I'm not ready."

Her voice practically jumped at me. "I don't give a flying fuck at the moon whether you're ready or not. You're going to come with me."

That reached me. Ginny doesn't talk that way very often. Only when she's furious. I turned, met her eyes.

She didn't look furious. The anger was just in her voice, not in her face. Instead, she was worried—her nostrils were flaring and pale, and there were lines at the corners of her eyes that show only when she's worried. And her eyes were wet. They looked like they might overflow any second now.

I couldn't remember the last time I'd seen her look so concerned. Concerned about me. All of a sudden my throat was dry, and I could barely scrape the words out. "What's the matter?"

Anybody else, and the tears would've been running down her cheeks. But not her. She was Ginny Fistoulari, private investigator. Licensed by the state to work on other people's misery. Human trouble and pain did a lot of different things to her, but they didn't make her cry. She just looked straight at me through the wet and said with all the anger gone out of her voice, "Your niece is missing."

I heard her, but something about it didn't penetrate. "Alathea?" Of course I had a niece, my dead brother's daughter. Her mother hated me. Alathea was another one of those people I was responsible for without being able to do anything about it. And on top of that I liked her. But I couldn't seem to remember what she looked like. "Missing?" I couldn't call up an image. All I got was her name—and a blank wall of dread. "What're you talking about?"

Ginny didn't flinch. "Lona Axbrewder called me today. I've been looking for you ever since. Alathea has been missing for a week."

I must've stared at her for another minute. Then it got through to me. Alathea was missing. Lona had called Ginny. Ginny had come looking for me. We had work to do.

There were things about it that didn't make sense. But right then they didn't matter. Not with Alathea missing—and Ginny looking at me like that. I fumbled some money onto the bar, got off my stool and started for the door. I didn't know how much I owed because I didn't know how much I'd had to drink, but José didn't even blink at me so I must've paid him enough—or else he was just glad to get a woman out of his bar without trouble. I stumbled once, then Ginny took my arm. I didn't even say good-bye to the Hegira. Together we went out into the night.

Chapter Two

Ginny took me back to my apartment to get me sobered up. I didn't have a car, and she'd left hers at my apartment, so we had to walk.

I live in one of those run-down apartment houses on the edge of the old part of town. The place is just far enough from the center to have been named La Cienga Apartments, but still close enough to be in danger of being torn down for urban renewal every time the city fathers feel like they have to make some kind of choice between "modern" and "quaint." (In Puerta del Sol those words are really two different names for *profitable*—the city is growing and people like to come for a visit, so it's just a question of whether money is going to be made from redeveloping real estate or from tourism.) Right then I didn't give a damn. They could blow up the place or sell tickets to my bedroom for all I cared. I was in one of those horrible "between" places any drunk can tell you about—too drunk to cope, not drunk enough to be anes-thetized. I was half blind with dread and my mind kept repeating, *Alathea, Alathea, Alathea.* I wanted Ginny to talk to me, tell me what was going on. But she just hung on to my arm and dragged me along and didn't say a thing.

The walk must've done me some good; she didn't have to carry me upstairs.

At least I was spared the embarrassment of being hauled into a messy apartment. I'm tidy enough when I'm sober, and I hardly ever visit my apartment when I'm drinking. So the place smelled musty and it needed dust-ing, but it wasn't a mess.

I was a mess. Getting sober is something I usually do for myself—it's not a pretty business, and you don't like having people watch. With Ginny there I kept noticing things that don't usually bother me—like the fact that I stank. (How many days had I been wearing these clothes? I had no idea.) And that I couldn't put one foot in front of the other. I needed a drink—and I didn't like having Ginny see it.

She didn't give me any choice. Before I could get past Alathea's name to try to do something for myself, she had me undressed (God knows how—when you're six foot five and two hundred forty pounds, other people usually can't just take your clothes away from you) and pried into the shower. She slammed on the water and left me there as if she wanted me to drown—but after a while she came back, scrubbed me, got me out of the shower and into an old bathrobe. Then she began pouring coffee down me.

That lasted for a while. Then the coffee and the other stuff started to do a little dance inside me, and I threw up for a while. After that I felt better. I was just about to tell Ginny about Alathea when I fell asleep.

It was dawn before she woke me up and began treating me again. Orange juice, coffee, toast, vitamin pills of all kinds. She's a vitamin freak—carries whole bottles in her purse, along with her .357. She even got me shaved. But it was close to nine before I was in any condition to go anywhere. All that time she didn't say a word. And I didn't ask any questions. I was too sick.

I was going to be sicker. Already I wanted a drink so bad it brought tears to my eyes—and this was just the beginning. Shame is an awkward thing to live with and having Ginny there, having her see me like this, made me ashamed on top of all the other remorse and responsibility. And there aren't very many cures for it. Sometimes work is one of them. But the only one you can actually count on is alcohol.

But Alathea was missing. When Ginny asked me if I was ready to go, I didn't answer right away. I went over to the dresser in the bedroom half of the apartment and got out my gun, a .45 Magnum—which is about the only gun I've ever found that doesn't feel like a toy in my hand. I checked it over, made sure it was loaded, then strapped on a shoulder holster and put the .45 under my left arm. Then I looked Ginny in the eye as steadily as I could and said, "Alathea is my niece. My brother's daughter. She's thirteen years old—and beside the fact she's one of those cute kids that makes you happy just to look at her, she also happens to like me. For some reason, Lona has never told her exactly what happened to her father. She thinks I'm just her nice old Uncle Brew. And besides that, she's solid as a rock. Half the time these days when things get too much for Lona, Alathea carries her —which is a hell of a job for a thirteen-year-old, and she does beautifully. It doesn't matter whether I'm ready or not. Let's go."

For a second there, Ginny almost smiled. The lines of worry around her eyes faded. She seemed to shake herself, and then it was as if she hadn't been up most of the night taking care of me—she didn't look tired anymore. "That's more like it," she said, mostly to herself. She handed me a jacket, and a minute later I was thudding my way down the stairs.

Talk is cheap. I wasn't ready, and it showed. I almost didn't make it down the stairs—my knees felt like mush, and the stairwell kept trying to stand on edge. There was a little voice in the back of my head saying, *You need a drink you need a drink you need a drink*. It wasn't easy to ignore, even with Ginny watching me.

But I didn't figure out why she was acting so much like she was worried about me until she took my arm to steer me toward her car. Of course she knew all about the connection between me and Alathea. Now she thought something serious had happened to my niece. She was afraid of what knowing that would do to me. She knew killing Richard had pushed me right to the edge. She was afraid whatever had happened to Alathea would push me over.

I wanted to ask her about that. (Ask, hell! I wanted to drag it out of her.) But I put it off. Just climbing into her Olds left me as weak as an old man. And I'd forgotten my sunglasses. Already the sun was beating down on the streets like bricks out of the dry thin blue sky. Made my eyes hurt. If it hadn't been for the tinted glass in the Olds, I might not have survived as far as Lona's house.

Lona Axbrewder, my brother's widow. I wasn't exactly her favorite person. There was one question I had to ask. When we parked in front of the house, I stayed where I was for a minute, trying not to hold my head in my hands. Then I said, "Why did she call you? You know how she feels about me."

"Ask her yourself," Ginny said. "I'm not a mind

reader." But her voice was stiff, and I'd heard that stiffness before. It meant she knew the answer and didn't want to tell me.

"Maybe," I muttered to myself. Maybe I would ask her. I was in no condition to know what I was going to do. I had enough problems just getting the door open and climbing out onto the sidewalk.

Lona lives down on Mission Street in a neighborhood that's only about two levels up from my apartment building. None of the houses for blocks in all directions are new, none of them look big enough to have more than two bedrooms, and none of them are out of spitting range from the houses next door. But it's a nice enough neighborhood, and the people don't spit. Lona's house is adobe, but that squat brown adobe look is softened by rose trellises that frame the top and sides of the front door. She must've watered those roses twice a day to make them look so nice.

I spent a minute standing on the sidewalk, looking around. Trees along the walk cut out a lot of the sun, and after the glare of the roads and traffic it was restful in a way to just stand there, looking. The whole place was restful—shade, trees, grass, tidy brown houses. It looked like the kind of place where nothing ever happens. I didn't want to move—didn't want to find out any different.

But Ginny took my arm again, and before I knew it we were standing in front of the door, and the door was opening, and Lona was telling us to come in. Then the door was shut behind us, and my retreat was cut off. I felt like I'd made some kind of fatal mistake. The voice in my head started to shout, *You need a drink!* It sounded desperate.

Dumbly, I let Ginny steer me. We followed Lona into the living room and sat down.

I couldn't see very clearly. The room was too dark—she had all the shades pulled down and didn't turn on any lights. That made the air dim and cool and comforting (which was nice—it almost seemed like she did it for my benefit, as if she had any reason in the world to give a good goddamn how I felt), but it didn't let me read her face. I wanted to read her face. I wanted to know how hard she was taking this thing. That would tell me a lot I needed to know.

The outlines I could do from memory. She was small and vague and somehow brittle, like most wives of cops I'd ever met. (They don't start out that way. It just happens to them because they're afraid of losing their husbands, and they can't share the danger—or even the strain—and they can't feel good about it because nobody loves a cop. It's like living with a man who has some kind of terminal disease.) She had medium-length brown hair, and a habit of pushing both hands through it, pulling it away from her temples as if she was trying to drag some horrible grimace off her face. Even before she lost her husband she used to make me nervous. Now she could've made me scream with no trouble at all.

She sat Ginny and me down on the Naugahyde couch across from the TV, then asked us if we wanted any coffee. Ginny said, "Yes, thanks," before I could even think about the question. Lona pushed her hands through her hair, and then left us alone.

I suppose I should've been thinking about Alathea—as a way of fighting off the need—but I was too strung out to have any control over what I was thinking. I was sitting exactly where I used to sit when Richard and I watched football together. I knew from memory that there was a picture of him sitting on top of the TV, staring at me with that lopsided grin of his. Richard Axbrewder, my younger brother. Rick and Mick. It was when he died that people stopped calling me Mick.

Died, hell. I killed him, and half the city knows it. The papers didn't exactly play it down. One of them had it right there on their front page: PRIVATE INVESTIGATOR KILLS COP. BROTHER SHOOTS BROTHER. There's no way I can pretend I didn't do it.

It happened five years ago, when Ginny and I were partners. I remember everything about it. I was sitting at a table by the window in Norman's, which is one of those downtown bars that caters to the business-man-getting-off-work trade. It just happens to be right across the street from the First Puerta del Sol National Bank. I was having a few drinks (exactly six, according to the testimony of the barkeep) and trying to make up my mind about whether I wanted (or had the nerve) to ask Ginny to marry me. Not an unpleasant kind of indecision, and I had enough stuff in me to glow while I thought about it. It was almost dark outside, but the streetlights hadn't come on yet so I couldn't see very well, and the air was dim and relaxed.

Then I heard gunfire. I snapped a look out the window and saw a man running away from the bank in my direction. He was carrying a bag of some kind and waving a gun over his shoulder, shooting at something behind him. There was a cop chasing him. I jumped to the conclusion he'd just robbed the bank.

I was out the door and on the sidewalk in no time. I had the .45 in my hand. I shouted at the man to stop. When he pointed his gun at me, I fired a couple times. He kept on running, but the cop chasing him went down.

It turned out the man was a purse-snatcher. Richard had already been chasing him for three blocks. If the snatcher hadn't had a gun, I would've been indicted for manslaughter. As it was, the commission read the results of my blood-alcohol test, charged me with "negligence," and took away my license. For good.

The cops were not amused. For a while, a bunch of them used to roust me every time we ran across each other. (I spent a lot of time in the drunk tank in those days, while bruises I couldn't remember getting turned black-and-blue on my ribs and face. Probably that was where I got in the habit of not letting anybody except Ginny touch me.) But after a couple years they let it ride. Then I got in trouble only when some cop got the bright idea I was working for Ginny without a license. But that's pretty hard to prove, because I was careful and I never got caught doing the kinds of things you're not allowed to do without a license. So far I've been able to get away with it.

So what? So now I don't drink in bars like Norman's anymore. I go down to the old part of town, where they don't care what I look like (or smell like) as long as my money's green and my Spanish doesn't sound like it came out of a textbook in some Anglo school. When I'm not working on a case for Ginny, I'm drunk. When I am working on a case, I'm sober. She's the one friend I've got, and everybody who remembers Richard hates me. Except Alathea. She doesn't know I shot her father.

Or at least she *didn't* know. Maybe she was missing because she ran away when she found out the truth—the truth her mother hadn't told her.

I was trembling deep down inside my gut. When Lona

brought the coffee, I had to hold the cup with both hands to keep from spilling it. While I drank it down, she stood right in front of me as if she was waiting until I finished to start screaming at me. But she just refilled my cup, then put the pot down where Ginny could reach it, and went to sit in the armchair beside the TV. Her hands she knotted in her lap, as if she was trying to keep them out of troubble.

When she spoke, her face was aimed at me, and her voice was brittle. "Will you take the case?"

"Of course," Ginny said smoothly. Her tone was sympathetic-neutral. Gentle but businesslike. The kind of tone she uses when she doesn't want a client to break down. "But I'll have to ask you a lot of questions."

"Yes." Lona sounded small and far away. The light was so dim I couldn't even see her lips move—her voice could've come from anywhere in the room. All of a sudden, I knew for a fact it was serious. Lona wouldn't have me sitting in front of her like this if it wasn't serious. She kept the room dark so I couldn't see the need in her face. The trembling was climbing up through my bones. I had to clamp my forearms between my knees to keep from shivering.

"How long has she been gone?" Ginny asked.

"Eight days." Her voice was as brittle as it could get. Brittleness was the only defense she had left. "Last week Tuesday—she went to school and didn't come home."

"Did you call the school?"

"Yes. That evening. First I called some of her friends —but they didn't know where she was. They said they hadn't seen her since P.E.—physical education. So then I called the school. She goes to Mountain Junior High — it's just five blocks up the street. They said that after fifth period she wasn't in any of her classes. Fifth period was P.E. They thought she must've gotten sick and gone home. But she didn't come home. She didn't." Lona was insistent. "I don't have anywhere to go on Tuesdays and I was here all the time."

"I understand," Ginny said. As smooth as Vaseline. "What did you do after you called the school?"

"I waited . . . I waited a while." Her hands were starting to twist in her lap. One of them went up to push at her hair, but she jerked it back down again. "As long as I could stand. Then I called the police."

"You called the police." Ginny was perfectly neutral-sympathetic.

I wasn't. Alcohol is a jealous comforter, and it doesn't like to let go. Right then my nerves had all the abstinence they could stand, and now they were getting even with me. I was going into withdrawal. I was shaking all over. My head was shivering on my neck—my brains were rattling in my skull. The need was using a vise to squeeze sweat out of my forehead. My jaws hurt because I was grinding my teeth, but I had to do something to keep from groaning out loud. I had to have something to hang on to, and the only thing in reach was Lona's voice.

"Yes," she said, in the same small brittle voice. "I talked to Missing Persons. Sergeant Encino. I've talked to him half a dozen times, but he doesn't help. He says he wants to help, but he doesn't. The first"—for a second her voice shuddered as if she was about to lose control, but she didn't—"the first time I talked to him, he said she'd probably be home in a couple days. He said kids are like that—they run away, and then they come home. He gets cases like that all the time. He said . . . he said it's department policy that they don't even start looking for runaways for three days. It's about impossible to find runaways because most of them are trying hard not to be found, and anyway most of them come home in three days. That's what he said.

"If I wanted the police to start looking for her right away, he said, I'd have to go down and swear out a complaint against her. File charges against her! He advised me not to do that. If I did, he said, the police would start looking for her right away, but if they found her they wouldn't bring her home. It's not against the law to run away and they couldn't bring her home against her will. They'd put her in some kind of juvenile shelter—he called it a 'JINS facility'—where she could run away again whenever she wanted, and I wouldn't get her back until a judge in juvenile court ruled on my complaint.

"I said, 'What if she hasn't run away? What if something happened to her?' But he just told me to try not to worry, and to call him when she came home."

She dug out a handkerchief and blew her nose. Then she went on. "So I did what he told me. I tried to wait. He's a police officer, isn't he? He works in Missing Persons, doesn't he? He knows what he's talking about, doesn't he?" She was talking to Ginny now, asking Ginny to tell her she'd done the right thing. But after a minute, she aimed herself at me again. "I tried to wait. But I couldn't. I called him again Wednesday, and Wednesday night. I asked him to check the hospitals. Maybe she was hurt—maybe she was in a hospital, and the doctors couldn't call me because they didn't know who she was and she hurt too bad to tell them.

"He told me I didn't have to worry about that. He said the hospitals always call the police when they have a patient they can't identify and they hadn't had any such calls recently.

"I wanted to call the hospitals myself, but I didn't. I waited. I used to do a lot of waiting when Richard was alive."

I was dripping sweat, and my head almost split open when she said his name.

"I tried to do it again, but it wasn't the same. He was a grown man. He was doing what he wanted to do. She's a child. A child!"

"What happened then?" Ginny asked. She might as well have been living in another world. Lona was talking to me. She and I were tied together in that dim room by fear and need. Ginny's questions were just cues, promptings.

"Thursday in the mail I got a letter from her." She didn't offer to show it to us. "It said, 'Dear Mom: I'm not going to be coming home for a while. I've got something to work out. It might take a long time. Don't worry, I'll be all right. Love, Al—Al . . .'" But she couldn't say the name. For a long minute she didn't go on. I could feel her eyes on me, but I wasn't looking at her. I was looking at the place where the sweat was dropping from my face onto my pants and sinking in, making a dark patch in the material—just watching the sweat fall and hanging on to her voice.

"What did you do after you got the note?"

With an effort, Lona got started again. "I . . . I called Sergeant Encino. What else could I do? I asked him to help me. He told me I'd have to file a complaint—even though she's just a child." She didn't shout, but the protest in her voice was so strong it almost made me lose my grip.

Ginny asked softly, "Did you do it?"

"No."

"You don't believe the note." It was just a statement of fact.

"No!" She was so vehement I looked up at her. "She wouldn't run away from me. Never!"

"I appreciate that, Mrs. Axbrewder—but it doesn't prove anything. Can you tell me why you're so sure?"

The question didn't faze her—she'd thought about it a lot since Missing Persons had asked her the same thing. "Because she wasn't the kind of girl who runs away from problems. If she had something bothering her— something she hadn't told me, which I do not believe— she wouldn't have run away from it. Her father taught her"—then she faltered, but only for a second—"her father taught her to stand her ground."

I believed her. I was in pain from head to foot—I wanted to pound my hands on my knees, just to distract myself from the hurting inside—but I believed her. If Alathea had run away because she found out about me and her father—found out her mother'd never told her the truth—then the note didn't fit. She would've been angry, and it wasn't an angry note. And I couldn't think of anything else in the world she would run away from. She wasn't the kind of kid who gets herself in trouble she can't handle—she had too much common sense.

Lona was right, the note didn't fit at all; there had to be something wrong with it. Something. But I was in no condition to figure out what. I wanted more coffee— wanted to try to trick my nerves into thinking the stuff was on its way—but I couldn't control my shakes enough to even pick up the cup. Something inside me was at the breaking point. If this withdrawal went on much longer, I was going to be a basket case.

Ginny must've been thinking along the same lines, because she asked, "What about the handwriting? Do you recognize it?"

"It's hers," Lona said carefully, "but it's different than usual. She has such neat writing—she's always gotten A's in penmanship—and this is so messy. It looks like she wrote it while she was riding in a car—over a rough road."

"How about the postmark?"

"Sergeant Encino asked me about that. It was mailed right here in town."

Suddenly I passed over the crest and the crisis began to recede. You never know if the first one is going to be the worst or the easiest, but this one was starting to let go of me. The pain was running out of me like dirty dishwater. It left me feeling like I'd been bedridden half my life, but at least I was able to get my voice back. Without looking at Lona—without unclenching myself at all for fear the need might turn around and come back at me before I had a chance to recover—I asked her, "How was the note signed?"

She didn't answer. I could feel the air of the living room pleading with me, raging at me, hating me, but she didn't answer.

My voice grated in my throat. "How did she sign her name?"

A long time passed. Finally Lona pulled herself together enough to say faintly, "Alathea."

Alathea. That was it. Proof this whole thing was serious—that there was trouble worse than just a runaway thirteen-year-old. It was a minute or two before I realized I hadn't said what I was thinking out loud. From somewhere, I mustered up the strength to say, "She never called herself Alathea. Everyone else did, but she didn't. She called herself Thea. That's what her father called her, and she never called herself anything else."

"That's right," Lona said. Just echoing what she heard in my voice. She knew it was true—it just hadn't occurred to her.

"All right," Ginny said. "I can accept that." Back-to-business-Ginny-Fistoulari. "We'll take the case on that basis. I don't know what all I'll need from you, but I'd like to start with a list of her friends. Names, addresses, phone numbers for everyone you can think of."

"Sergeant Encino asked that. I thought you'd want a copy." She got up, handed Ginny a sheet of paper, then went back to her chair. She never turned her face away from me the whole time. We weren't finished with each other yet.

But Ginny wasn't finished either. Maybe she didn't like being left out of the silence. She stood it for half a minute, then said, "I've just got one more question, Mrs. Axbrewder. Alathea disappeared last week Tuesday. Why did you wait more than a week before you called me?"

"Sergeant Encino told me to wait and try not to worry.

He told me she'd come back when she was ready. I thought I was doing what Richard . . . what Richard would want me to do. But then I read—in yesterday's paper—I read about that Christie girl." She was under too much strain—her brittleness was starting to crack. "Since she didn't come home, I've been reading the paper every day. Every word. I've been looking for some kind of news that would . . . tell me what happened.

"Yesterday I read about that poor Christie girl. Carol Christie. The paper said"—she was right on the edge—"she ran away from home three months ago, and Monday they found her body in the river. She was just thirteen, the same age as my Alathea." Her hands were jammed into her hair, pulling at the sides of her head as if that was the only way she could keep herself from crying. "The same age."

I didn't have anything else to offer, so I gave her something to get mad about—hoping it would help her hang on to herself. "But why us, Lona? Why me? If you have to have a detective, you could've called some of Richard's friends on the force. They would've referred you to somebody you could trust."

"Because you owe me!" Her sudden vehemence was as physical as a fist. "You took my husband away from me! You owe me my daughter back!"

"We'll do our best." Ginny came between Lona and me as if she was afraid we were about to start hitting each other. "There are no guarantees in this business, but we'll do everything we can. Which is more than the police are doing.

"Now." Ginny was on her feet and I joined her. Force of habit—I didn't actually feel strong enough to stand. And I sure as hell didn't want to be towering over Lona like that. It was a cheap advantage, and with her I didn't want any advantages. But I've been following Ginny so long now, taking orders from her, I hardly ever think about it anymore. "There's one thing we have to settle before we can get started. My fee."

"There doesn't have to be any fee," I said, ashamed money'd even been mentioned.

"Mrs. Axbrewder has to pay something," Ginny snapped. "If she doesn't, I can't call her my client. And if she isn't my client, I don't have any legal standing. Anybody who wants to can tell me to stuff it."

There was no help for it. Lona was looking at me, and I had to say, "She's right, Lona."

She didn't say anything for a long minute. When she found her voice again, she wasn't angry any more—just weak and helpless and at the end of her rope. "I don't have much," she said. "Richard's pension is so small. And my job—I work as much as I can, cleaning house for some of the neighbors—it's hardly enough to pay for clothes." Then she said, "I have a hundred dollars."

Ginny said, "Fifty will be plenty." Fifty bucks would just about pay three days' rent on her office. "If I get in trouble with the commission I can always tell them it was only an advance."

The commission frowns on private investigators who work cheap. The same kind of argument doctors and lawyers use; people who work cheap are presumed to be shoddy and unscrupulous. Unprofessional. If I still had a license, I'd be in danger of losing it twice a day.

Lona shuffled out of the room and came back a minute later with the money. Ginny took it without counting it and gave her a receipt. Before I could think of anything else to say, Ginny and I were out on the walk again and Lona had closed the door behind us. In the whole time I hadn't had one good look at her face.

Ginny made straight for the car, but I dawdled along for a moment. Though the sun was getting hotter, in the shade of the trees it was still bearable. I wasn't eager to sear my butt on the vinyl of the Olds. And I wasn't satisfied, either; there were things I needed to know.

"All right," I said at Ginny's back. "Spill it."

She stopped, then turned around, looking blank. "Spill what?"

But she couldn't fool me with that. Her face has more than one kind of blank, and this wasn't the right kind. Besides, she'd turned around too quickly—like she was expecting me to say something.

"You know what I'm talking about."

She came back toward me a couple of steps. "When you've been drinking I never know what you're talking about."

That was a cheap shot, and she knew it. As soon as she said it, she winced in regret. But I sloughed it off. It just confirmed she knew something she wasn't telling. So I said, "The hell you don't. You're scared of this case,

Fistoulari. You're scared of it because of me. You're afraid something about it is going to get to me. I want to know why."

"You heard her." Ginny nodded at the house. "She didn't tell me any secrets."

"Yeah," I growled. "First you're worried about me, and then you won't tell me why. If you've got so goddamn little confidence in me, why didn't you just leave me out of it? You don't need me to find a runaway."

Now she came close and looked right up at me. "She's your niece. You've got a right to be involved. Besides, I thought you'd want—"

"Don't say it. Of course I want to help find her." For a minute I glanced around the neighborhood, looking for suggestions. Then I locked on to her again. Something about that broken nose of hers did funny things to my insides. Sometimes I wanted to kiss it so bad I had to grit my teeth. Now I wanted to hit it. "Maybe I'm asking the wrong question. Let's be professional about it. It's just a case. Like any other case. There's just one thing wrong with it. You don't do missing persons. You've never done missing persons. Why start now?"

"She's your—" But I didn't let her get to the word "niece."

"Don't do me any favors."

That got through to her. All of a sudden, her eyes went cold and narrow, and her nostrils flared. Just for a second, her voice had the soft hot sound of an acetylene torch. "That's cute, Axbrewder. All right—you want it? You got it. I read the papers, too. I read about Carol Christie. There's one little fact your sister-in-law neglected to mention. According to her parents, Carol Christie was an excellent swimmer."

An excellent swimmer. Oh, hell. You don't have to be an excellent swimmer to be safe in the Flat River. If you're half as tall as I am, you don't have to know how to swim at all.

"When the reporter asked the cops if there was any reason to think she might've been killed," she went on, "they did not deny it."

I scanned the neighborhood one more time. It still looked like the kind of place where nothing ever happens. It was too tidy—and there was too much sunshine.

I turned my back on it and followed Ginny to the Olds.

Chapter Three

While she started the engine I pulled down the sunshade to give my aching head what little protection was available. Then, more to let her know I was still with her than to satisfy my curiosity, I asked, "Where do we go from here?"

She glanced over at me. "How long has it been since you had a full meal?"

That was the kind of question she usually asked me. I shrugged. She didn't need an answer.

As we pulled away from the curb, she muttered, "You ought to be more careful. If you don't get regular meals, it'll stunt your growth."

I suppose I should've at least grinned; she was just trying to clear the air. But I didn't have the energy for it. The little strength I had I was using to think about thirteen-year-old girls who end up dead in the river for no good reason. As far as I knew, there was zero connection between Carol Christie and Alathea, but just knowing something like that could happen to my niece gave me a cold pain in the stomach.

And maybe there was a connection. In this business, things like that happen all the time. Accidents happen by themselves—crimes have a way of tieing themselves together. I was in no mood to grin at bad jokes, even when I knew why Ginny was making them.

We didn't have to go far to find food. In a few blocks, we were in one of those small business sections that look like somebody just dropped a bunch of white concrete bricks out of the sky and ran away before anybody could catch him and make him clean it up. Pawnshops, grocery stores, insurance offices, and gas stations stood facing every which way. With all that sun on them, they were blinding—I could hardly tell them apart. But Ginny's eyes handle brightness better than mine and after a couple minutes, she pulled into a Muchoburger that was just opening up. We went inside, ordered cheeseburgers and about a gallon of coffee, then sat down at one of the tables.

We didn't talk while we waited for the food, and after

that I was too busy eating half-raw hamburger and the vitamin pills that Ginny handed out to me like my life depended on them. When she'd had enough to eat, she got down to business.

"The first thing we ought to do is talk to this Sergeant Encino. Since your sister-in-law always talked to him in the evenings he probably doesn't come on duty until mid-afternoon, which gives us five or six hours to do our homework. I suppose we could start with this list of Alathea's friends, but I'd rather wait until they get home from school, so they can't check-out what they're saying with each other—just in case there's something going on that they want to keep secret."

I nodded. My stomach didn't much like what I was putting in it. But I liked it better than dread.

"Any suggestions?"

She was just being polite. She knew what our choices were as well as I did. But she was usually polite to me when we were just starting a case. That was usually the only time when she wasn't way ahead of me. As soon as she had a handle on what was happening, she wouldn't waste time being polite.

Anyway, I owed her some politeness myself. And if she was giving me a choice, I wanted to use it. There were some things I wasn't ready for yet, so I said, "We might as well go to the school while we're out this way. It's closer than your office."

That must've been what she wanted to do herself. She said, "Good enough," and went to pay the check. I finished up, drank down as much of that coffee as I could stand. Then we got in the car and drove to Mountain Junior High over on the corner of Mission and Natividad.

It wasn't the best junior high in the city (the best ones are all called middle schools), but it was far enough from the old part of town to be better than the worst. It didn't look like a converted warehouse, and it wasn't cramped into a plot of ground too small to hold that many kids, and it didn't have a chain link fence around it. In fact, it had several buildings built around one another; there was a small gymnasium and a ragged playing field. It was the sort of place where some kids would be perfectly happy—and where some would get started on drugs.

We went in and found our way to the main office, where Ginny showed her ID to a secretary and asked to see the principal. The secretary informed us the principal was "out." But when she found out why we were here, she told us the vice-principal was really the person we ought to talk to. Vice-Principal Rumsfeld was "in."

She was a taut little woman with a severe hairstyle and an air of being very tired, worn out by burdens. You could tell by the tension compressing her lips she was responsible for "discipline" in the school, and had long since used up whatever tolerance she had been born with. Her office suited her. It was stark and forbidding and the chairs were uncomfortable. Probably in her career she'd seen thousands of kids squirming on those chairs. Probably Ginny and I didn't look much different to her than those kids did.

"You want to know about Alathea Axbrewder." She sounded like a blunt instrument. "There's nothing I can tell you. She came to school last week Tuesday, but did not attend any of her classes after fifth period. That was physical education. She hasn't been here since. In the old days, we used to have truant officers who tracked down runaways, but now the police are supposed to handle it. They do a poor job."

"What about Alathea herself?" At times like this, Ginny was a model of diplomacy. She could be firm, even insistent, without sounding pushy or irritating the people she was talking to.

"What do you want to know about her? She was a good student—bright and pleasant. Her teachers liked her, and she didn't get into trouble. She seemed more grown up than most girls her age. That happens quite often when a child loses a parent. The added pressure forces them to mature more rapidly."

"She doesn't sound like the kind of girl who runs away."

Vice-Principal Rumsfeld's lips got tighter, and her hairdo suddenly seemed even more severe. "What kind of girl is that, Ms. Fistoulari? All kinds of children run away."

"At thirteen?"

"They run away because they are in pain. No one is immune to pain—not even children."

The stiffness in her voice made me revise my opinion of her. She wasn't the wicked witch of the west. She was tired because she was the school disciplinarian, and she didn't like her job. I said softly, "That bothers you."

"It *concerns* me, Mr. Axbrewder. A society that cannot care for its children is in very serious trouble. I do what is in my power here, but I'm a poor substitute for a healthy family or a constructive sense of life. When a child like Alathea runs away, she places herself entirely beyond my reach."

"Ms. Rumsfeld," I said, "Alathea didn't run away."

She looked at me sharply. "Do you have some reason to believe that?"

"She's my niece. I know her pretty well."

"Your confidence is misplaced. Alathea is not the first young girl to run away, and will not be the last. I admit that it used to be that most runaways were boys, —perhaps because they were boys, they believed they were expected to be adventuresome. But in recent years, there have been more and more girls doing the same. Twelve-and thirteen-year-olds, Mr. Axbrewder."

"How recently is that?" Ginny asked.

"I can't say—I've only been aware of it for the last year or so. Fortunately, Alathea is the first from our school, but other junior high and middle schools in the city have had more than their share."

"Can you give us any details?" Ginny was groping—but that's normal. At the beginning of a case, you have to look under every rock you find.

"I don't have any," Ms. Rumsfeld said. "I don't see what possible use they could be to you, but if you feel compelled to look for them, the school board may be willing to help you." She was dismissing us. "In a case as serious as a runaway, the board receives copies of all reports as a matter of course. In fact, they have copies of all our files on every student."

Ginny and I stood up. Ginny thanked her for her time, and turned to open the door. I said, "When we find out what happened to her, we'll let you know."

"Don't find out what happened to her," the vice-principal snapped. "Find her. Bring her back."

"We'll try," Ginny said. She ushered me out the door, and we went back to the Olds.

Sitting in the car, she said, "Maybe she did run away."

I said, "Maybe none of them ran away."

After a minute, she said, "Right." She put the Olds in gear, and we headed in the direction of her office.

Fistoulari Investigations is in the Murchison Building, one

of the three buildings in Puerta del Sol that stands more than five stories tall. It's on the other side of the city from Mountain Junior High, but the new beltway made it fairly easy to get to. We had the Olds parked in the basement garage and were on our way up in the elevator before noon.

We hadn't been working on it very long—but so far I had the distinct impression we weren't getting anywhere. If something had happened to Alathea, it was a secret, and we didn't know who to ask. So the next thing for us to do was start trying to eliminate the obvious. That was why we were going to Ginny's office.

The Murchison Building isn't cheap, but it isn't as expensive as it looks. It sits in the middle of what used to be the business center of Puerta del Sol; it's a good three miles down Paseo Grande from the ritzy real estate where the banks live these days. The owners of the building have always had trouble attracting people, and even now the place isn't more than two-thirds occupied. Which is why Ginny (and at least two other agents, a handful of half-reputable lawyers, some chancy doctors, and a few insurance companies that may or may not have any assets) can afford to operate there. The elevators and halls are carpeted, but the lighting is bad so you can't see that they don't clean very often. Too many of the walls have the kind of smudges you'd expect to find in places where people get arrested regularly—the kind sweaty palms make while the rest of the body is being frisked.

But Ginny's office is in good condition. FISTOULARI INVESTIGATIONS is neatly lettered on the door, and inside the air-conditioning works. The front room—the waiting room—has only three chairs to go with the plastic potted plant and the side table covered with old magazines. But three chairs is about all it needs—most people won't even bother to wait in a private investigator's office if somebody else is already there. And the office itself is at least comfortable. It has room for Ginny's desk and files, a large sofa, a couple roomy chairs, two phones, and a picture window looking out toward the valley of the Flat River. The carpet is clean because Ginny keeps it that way. The walls are bare except for a couple framed diplomas (all part of making the place look "professional") and the display copy of Ginny's license.

Fortunately, there was no one waiting in the outer room so she didn't have to try to juggle clients. We went into the office and I started up the electric coffeepot (caffeine isn't alcohol, but my nerves had to have some kind of substitute) while she went through her mail. After she'd read it all—and thrown most of it in the wastebasket—we went to work.

On the phones.

Ginny called the school board and got us an appointment to see the chairman the following afternoon. Then she went down the list of Alathea's friends, getting the parents' permission to go to their homes and talk to their kids (calling for permission is a nice touch, when you can afford it—forestalls a certain number of potential complaints to the commission). I used the other phone, and worked on eliminating some of the obvious.

Didn't take either of us very long. I'd never worked on a runaway before, but I knew of a place that was in the business of telling people like me where to look. Tel-a-Help. Basically, it's a referral agency for all the social services in San Reno County, including state and federal bureaus. I called them, and they gave me five different numbers—the State Bureau of Children's Services, the National Runaway Hotline, the National Drug Abuse Hotline, the San Reno County Crisis Hotline, and the police. I thanked them very politely before crossing the police off my list.

I wanted to cross off the National Drug Abuse number, too—but I didn't. Couldn't afford to. It was one of the obvious possibilities I had to check, and I had a sick feeling about it. So I did that number first. It's one of those toll-free 800 numbers. The way my head felt, you'd have thought I was about to pass out from anoxia—but I gave them my spiel and listened to their answer: "We're a confidential information service, Mr. Axbrewder. We can't give out the names of the young people who call us. But we always urge runaways to call their parents, and no reputable drug treatment facility or social service agency in the country would accept a thirteen-year-old girl without making some effort to contact her parents." When I hung up, I was practically gasping for breath.

The Bureau of Children's Services and the Crisis Hotline gave me variations on the same answer—confidentiality, always urge runaways to get in touch with their parents, etc. In five minutes, I was starting to understand Lona's outrage at the new laws and public machinery that exist for the "benefit" of runaways—which seems to mean, "protect them from their parents."

But the National Runaway Hotline—another 800 number—was an improvement. They said they too were confidential—but part of their business was to pass messages back and forth between kids and parents. And whenever possible they got the name of any runaway who called, so they could at least assure the parents their child was safe. All the names and messages were fed into a computer, so they could be retrieved instantly.

No one named Alathea—or Thea—Axbrewder had ever called the National Runaway Hotline.

I almost hung up—but I snatched back the receiver and asked, "Did you ever get a call from a girl named Carol Christie?"

That was the wrong thing for me to say. All at once, the voice at the other end of the line turned distant and suspicious. "Why do you ask, Mr. Axbrewder? Is she a relative of yours?"

I didn't have any other way out, so I said, "She's dead. I'm worried about Alathea, and I'm trying to find some kind of pattern."

The voice was silent for a minute. Then it said carefully, "There's no Carol Christie in the computer."

"All right," I said. "It was a dumb question. Tell me this. Out of all the kids who run away—how many call you? What percentage?"

"We don't have any reliable figures, but our best estimate is only about twenty percent. We're not as well known as we need to be."

"Thanks."

I hung up the phone, looked at Ginny. In spite of the air conditioner I was sweating. But I wasn't due for another crisis yet—and if one was coming there wasn't anything I could do about it anyway, so I just tried to shove it out of my mind. When Ginny put down her phone, I asked, "What've you got?"

She pushed her list away from her. "We're going to be busy this evening. How about you?"

"Nothing." I surprised myself by sounding so disgusted.

"Relax," she said. "If you found her this fast, you wouldn't know what to do with yourself for the rest of the day." She was jollying me—but her eyes had that worried look in them again. She gave me the impression she was asking herself how long I could hold out without a drink.

I got up, went and faced her across the desk and said, "I don't like it when you look at me like that. Let's go talk to Carol Christie's parents."

I was half hoping she had something better in mind. I wasn't feeling any readier to visit those parents than when the idea first occurred to me. It was like calling the Drug Abuse Hotline—something in me was afraid of it. But we had to do it. We were looking for some kind of pattern, and we wouldn't know if there was any connection between Carol Christie and Alathea unless we checked it out.

Ginny knew that as well as I did. She said, "Good idea," and pushed herself out of her chair. She looked in Tuesday's paper for the names of the Christies, then got their address out of the phone book. Five minutes later, we were back in the Olds.

The Christies lived quite a ways out—in what they call the North Valley. Puerta del Sol lays down its inhabitants horizontally instead of stacking them vertically, so it's a sprawling place. And the way the population's growing these days there are suburbs and even industries sitting on ground that used to be just neglected desert ten years ago. The city sprawls in all directions, but mostly north and south along the valley of the Flat River, where water is a little easier to come by.

Mr. and Mrs. Christie lived all the way out at the northern tip of the sprawl. Where the cowboy-money lives. Half the people out there wear old Stetsons and plaid shirts and faded jeans and dusty boots, and if you meet them on the street you wouldn't know they're solid gold on the hoof. Most of them probably get their money from things like real estate—but the way they dress and live you would think they get rich just by looking and acting so by-God western. Before we were within five miles of the Christies', every house we passed was an ersatz ranch, with a split rail fence, three acres of ground, and two horses.

When we got to where we were going, we found the Christies ran a stables, complete with riding lessons, trails, and about thirty of the mangiest-looking horses I'd ever seen. They used a converted horse trailer for an office.

When we went inside, we found Mary Christie there, working on a set of books.

She looked up as we came in and said, "Howdy, folks. What can we do for you-all?" Her cowboy-twang was stretched pretty thin over an accent that sounded like it probably came from Boston. But she was dressed right— not-too-new, not-too-clean, let's-go-muck-out-the-stalls clothes, with a red bandana knotted around her neck.

Ginny said, "Mrs. Christie?" Her professional voice made it seem like she had every right in the world to be standing there asking personal questions. "I'm Ginny Fistoulari." She flipped her ID out of her purse and showed Mrs. Christie the photostat of her license. "This is Mr. Axbrewder. We'd like to ask you and your husband a few questions."

It didn't take much to make Mary Christie forget about horses. Ginny's ID was enough. She practically jumped to her feet, went to a window behind her and jerked out, "John!" There was an edge in her voice that sounded like panic at first, but I put it down to strain. It was only two days ago that her daughter had turned up dead. Then she came and stood in front of us with her arms clutched across her stomach as if she was trying to hide something. "Questions about what? What do you want?" Her twang had deserted her.

Ginny said evenly, "We'd like to talk to you about your daughter, Carol."

"Why?" She was as jumpy as a hophead. "What has it got to do with you?" Then she was at the window again. "John!"

Now I knew it wasn't just strain. Mrs. Christie was afraid of something.

From outside, a man's voice—real cowboy, this time— answered, "Ah'm comin'!" Ten seconds later he was in the trailer with us.

He was tall and rangy, like a cowboy is supposed to be, with a grizzled and weather-bitten face and a cigarette stuck in his teeth. His battered old hat was pulled down tight on his head—probably so it wouldn't fall off when he was riding. He scanned Ginny and me, then asked slowly, "Now, what's all this-here ruckus about?"

"They want to know about Carol," Mary Christie said quickly—too quickly. "They want to ask questions about her."

At that, her husband's eyes narrowed until he was practically squinting at us. Deliberately, he took the cigarette out of his mouth, threw it through the doorway. Then he said, "Naw, they don't want to ask no questions. They was just leavin'." If he was worried about the fact I was three inches taller and seventy pounds heavier than he was, he didn't show it.

But I didn't need Ginny to tell me this was no time for muscle. I just stood my ground and let her handle it.

She said, "We have good reason for asking." If it came down to a bluff, she could match John Christie any day. "We don't want to pry into anything that doesn't concern us, but we're working on a case that's remarkably similar to Carol's." Remarkably similar, hell. Both girls were thirteen—period. "If you help us, we might be able to prevent the same thing from happening again."

She made it sound practically inevitable. But Mr. Christie wasn't having any. "You said one thing right," he drawled. "You ain't goin' to pry. There ain't no 'case' on Carol. She was a good little girl, and you ain't goin' to dig up no dirt on her. If other folks want to let their young'uns screw around, it ain't no concern of mine."

Ginny faced him squarely. "Nobody said anything about dirt. That was your idea." Then she asked harshly, "If Carol was such a good swimmer, how did she happen to drown?"

Christie felt that. For a second, his eyes went out of focus. His hands twitched as if he was getting ready to swing at Ginny. I shifted into position to block him. But instead of moving, he just said in a dead voice, "Get the hell out of here."

Ginny considered him for a moment, then turned to Mary Christie. The woman was staring back at her with something like nausea in her face. Sharply, Ginny said, "All right. Let it happen to other girls. Why should you care? There's just one thing I have to know." She knew how to be tough. "Did she write to you at all after she ran away? Was there a note?"

John Christie barked, "Mary!" For a minute, she just stood there, squirming with indecision and grief. Then, abruptly, she jerked open one of the desk drawers, fumbled for a sheet of paper, and handed it to Ginny.

Ginny gave it to me without looking at it. If John

Christie wanted it back, it was safer with me. I put it in my pocket.

"Thank you, Mrs. Christie," Ginny said softly. "I hope you won't regret helping us." Then she went to the door. "Come on, Brew. Mr. Christie thinks we should leave."

I followed her out, half expecting Christie to jump me as I went past him. But he didn't. He slammed the door behind us, and a second later we heard him yelling, "God damn it, woman! You want the whole fuckin' world to know?" We could hear him until we got into the Olds and shut the doors.

I didn't say anything. I just took out the note, and we looked at it together.

It said, "Dear Mom and Dad: I have to go away for a while. I have a problem, and I have to take care of it myself. It might take a long time. Don't worry about me. Love, Carol."

It was written on half a sheet of good twenty-pound bond, but the handwriting was a mess.

Chapter Four

We didn't say anything. We didn't have to. We both knew what to do next. Ginny started up the Olds, and we headed back into the city. Hurrying. We wanted to get to Lona.

It was after four o'clock when we reached her house, so we didn't waste any time. Ginny was better at this kind of thing than I was so I waited in the car while she went to talk to Lona.

Even that way, it took a while. Lona didn't want to let go of her note. It was the last tangible thing she had from Alathea. But we had to have the original—a copy wouldn't do us any good. I was relieved to see it in Ginny's hand when she came back to the Olds.

With her sitting beside me, we compared the notes. The similarity of the wording made my stomach ache, but Ginny was looking at other things. She compared the writing quickly, pointed out that the ink and scripts were different, then started to examine the paper.

Lona's note was written on half a sheet of twenty-pound bond.

Both sheets had been neatly torn—not cut—along one edge.

When Ginny held them up to the sun, we could see they both had the same watermark.

I said, "Sonofabitch." Something deep in my chest was trembling. I was overdue for another withdrawal crisis.

"This doesn't prove anything," Ginny said stiffly. "There's a lot of this kind of paper around. It's a big company. It doesn't prove anything unless these notes came from the same sheet." She put the notes up against the sun again, then said, "No chance. Look what happens when I put the torn edges together."

I looked. The watermarks were facing in opposite directions. The top third of the mark on Lona's note was cut off—and it wasn't completed anywhere on the other sheet.

"Terrific." I could taste bile in my mouth. The lining of my stomach wanted alcohol—wanted to be numb. "Two thirteen-year-olds run away from home and write notes that say almost exactly the same thing on the same kind of paper, with the same kind of bad handwriting. Of course it's just a coincidence. Why didn't I think of that?"

"I didn't say it was a coincidence," she replied with elaborate patience. Just letting Axbrewder know she wasn't senile yet. "I said it wasn't proof." Then she grinned. It was a shark's grin—eager and dangerous. "That's the difference between us and the police. We don't need proof." She threw the Olds into gear. "Let's go talk to Encino."

We were on the trail now—I could see it in her eyes.

I left it to her. I was thinking about the Christies. They were scared about something—and anything that could worry John Christie would probably frighten Lona to death.

We went down Mission a ways, then crossed over on Gypsum until we hit Paseo Grande and turned right. A couple miles down Paseo Grande we came to the new Municipal Building—the pride of the mayor, the joy of half a dozen construction companies, the flower of a couple architects, and the treasure to whatever bank it was that floated the loan. I didn't know anybody else who liked it.

From the outside, it looks like a country club for millionaires. An ordinary citizen can no more walk in there and feel comfortable than fly to the moon. All those fountains and flower beds might've been a good idea—but unfortunately the main part of the building hangs over the fountains and flowers and walkways. This square mountain of white concrete leans on the back of your neck—from some angles you can't even see what holds it up—so by the time you get to the doors and start climbing to wherever you have to go, you're already feeling intimidated. And of course there's no parking. Official cars have a private garage—ordinary citizens have to scramble for what they can get.

We were lucky—we only had to walk a couple of blocks.

Inside, there isn't a scrap of carpet or one warm soft color in the whole place. It looks like a brand-new abattoir. Since there aren't any windows, and that blank fluorescent lighting is always the same, you can't tell whether it's day or night.

I suppose I should've been used to it—the Municipal Building wasn't so new I hadn't been in the City Jail, up on the top floor of the police department wing, a couple times. But I was always at a disadvantage here. I could never remember the names of the cops who rousted me when I was drunk. I could never remember anything about them, except they always looked short. They knew who I was, but I didn't know them. The whole situation gave me a definite paranoid feeling.

But I figured I should be pretty safe in Missing Persons. They didn't have any reason to know who I was. So I just kept my coat buttoned and my hands at my sides, hiding the .45 under my left arm, and followed Ginny—trying to ignore the fact I could feel another withdrawal attack coming on.

The sergeant at the front desk issued us passes (for security—the cops don't want anybody walking around their home turf unidentified) and told us where to go in the dull mumble of a man who'd spent too many years repressing a secret yen to *really* tell people where to go. We did what he told us, and a couple corridors later we were at a glass door. The glass was safety plate with steel mesh sandwiched into it and it said MISSING PERSONS across the top. We went in.

Inside, there was a Formica counter so close to the entrance that the door almost hit it when it opened. Behind the counter there were four desks and a row of file cabinets. That was all. Missing Persons wasn't a very big item in the police budget.

Three cops sat at the desks, two women and a man. The man was a sergeant—the women were just policewomen. After making us wait for a minute (cops always make you wait as long as they can—it's all part of being a good officer of the law), one of the women, Policewoman Rand, asked us what we wanted. Ginny asked for Sergeant Encino, using her "I'm-an-important-citizen-don't-mess-with-me voice. The man didn't look like he was hurrying, but he was off his butt and standing in front of us faster than he wanted to be.

He was short (if he looked straight at Ginny, he got a good look at her clavicles) and Chicano. He had dark olive skin that complemented his dark blue uniform, and his close-cut black hair was so tidy you'd think he trained it with a whip. His moustache was assertive but not aggressive. And he had Chicano eyes—sad, world-weary, and arrogant. Sure enough, both the name-tag pinned over his left shirt pocket and the ID clipped to his right shirt pocket said, "Sgt. Raul Encino, Missing Persons."

Ginny introduced herself, flashed her license, mentioned my name. Encino looked back at her with his face blank (that's another part of being a good law officer—treat everybody as if two of them and a sandwich would be just about right for lunch). "What can I do for you?" He had just enough accent to make what he said sound more interesting than it really was.

"Information," Ginny said crisply. "We're trying to find a young girl named Alathea Axbrewder. Her mother reported her missing eight days ago."

Encino's expression was perfect—as noncommittal as a rock. "Mrs. Axbrewder chose to make no complaint. We are looking for her daughter, of course. Each patrol officer in his briefing is given a description. But without a complaint . . ." He gave us a delicate Chicano shrug. "You understand, it is not a breaking of the law to run from home. The girl is a minor, so we have our eyes open for her. But in a city so big as Puerta del Sol to have our eyes open will be unlikely to find her. Also she has possibly left the city. The sheriff's office we have informed. What more is your desire?"

With just a hint of sarcasm, Ginny said, "You assume she ran away."

"For why not? As I am saying, the city is big. Many girls run from their homes each week. Do you wish to think she has been kidnapped? I say to you, no. What is the purpose? There has been nothing said of ransom."

That was true enough. If there'd been any kind of ransom demand, this whole thing would've been different. There aren't any cops anywhere who don't take kidnapping seriously. But that didn't faze Ginny. In the same light-acid tone, she said, "I don't know whether I'm talking about kidnapping or not. I haven't gotten that far yet. What I'm interested in right now is thirteen-year-old girls who disappear and then turn up dead." She was trying to irritate Encino, nag him into defending himself. Maybe spring loose some spontaneous information.

I could see the muscles along his jaw tighten, but he didn't change his ground. "Is the daughter of Mrs. Axbrewder dead?"

"The daugher of John and Mary Christie is."

He blinked. As far as the rest of his face was concerned, he was sound asleep. "Of what interest is Carol Christie to you?"

"There's a connection between her and Alathea."

"Are the parents of Carol Christie then your clients?"

Ginny could've refused to answer that. She had a right to protect her client. But I guess she didn't see any point to it. She said, "I've been retained by Lona Axbrewder."

"Then the death of Carol Christie is of no concern to you."

"I said there's a connection." Ginny let herself start to sound angry. She took out the notes and put them down on the counter in front of Encino. "Both Alathea and Carol wrote to their parents after disappearing. If you look at them, you'll see that they were written on the same kind of paper. The sheets were torn in half the same way. What they say is almost identical, and the handwritings are similar."

"That is most ingenious." Encino didn't even glance at the notes. "Unhappily, I must repeat myself. The death of Carol Christie can be of no concern to you. The rights of your client do not reach so far. Mr. Christie and his wife require to be private."

"Says who?"

"Their wishes were made known to Detective-Lieutenant Acton in his investigation."

Investigation, huh? Ginny was getting somewhere. Now we knew there was enough wrong with Carol Christie's death for the cops to be interested in it.

But she didn't stop to chew it over. She had Encino backing up, and she kept at him.

"That's wonderful. The Christies don't want people to know what really happened to their daughter, so the cops clamp a lid on it. Having money is good for something after all. I just wonder what you and Acton are getting out of it."

Encino's composure snapped for a second. *"Hija de la puta!"* Before he could get it back, I had my fist knotted in the front of his nice blue uniform. I was about to shake him up good, but Ginny stopped me with an elbow that almost caved in my ribs. I let him go, stepped back. I could feel blood pounding in my face.

The sergeant straightened his shirt. He had his blankness back in place, but he couldn't keep the rasp out of his voice. "Now go from this place. You Anglos—you are every one of you the same. A girl runs from home and is later found to be dead. There is an investigation and everything is kept with great propriety, even from the papers, so that there will be no distress to the family. Detectives are employed, and because they are unable to do their work they come and speak bitterly to the police. It is so in all places. And for why? Because the girl is white. Anglo. Let a girl of my people be gone from her home, and let the mother go with weeping and fear to desire help, and then behold how the Anglos lift their shoulders and say, 'What do you expect? Look for her in the brothels.' And if that girl of my people should become dead, then behold how the papers will print all the ill that can be heard of her, true or false." His sneer twisted his whole face. "Go from here. You prevent my work."

My pulse was still racing, but I heard him. I picked up the notes, pulled open the door, said to Ginny, "Come on." But she was really mad now. She was leaning over the counter, thrusting her face at Encino. "I work for whoever asks me," she said very softly. "I don't have any control over who asks. I just take whatever they ask, and give it my best shot. That's *my* work."

Encino jerked his head contemptuously. *"Muy bravo."*

I took Ginny's arm, dragged her out into the corridor and shut the door behind us. She threw off my hand. Stalked along for a minute in silence. Then she said, "That sonofabitch."

I said, "He has a point."

"He has orders. Somebody told him to put a lid on Carol Christie. It's not my fault he doesn't like it." Then she asked, "How come you're so sympathetic all of a sudden? Two minutes ago you wanted to take his head off for him."

I didn't have any good answer to that, so I just said, "I spend a lot of time in the old part of town. Probably he's a good cop."

"A good cop!" she snorted. She didn't say anything more until we got into the elevator. Then she muttered, "You big ape, you've got to learn to keep your temper."

"Dear God," I said. "Did I lose my temper? I'm pitifully sorry. It's never happened to me before."

She said, "Aw, shut up." But she didn't sound so angry anymore. After a minute, she asked, "What was that he called me?"

" '*Hija de la puta.*' Daughter of a whore."

She considered that briefly, then grinned. "It's probably true." When the elevator doors opened, she led the way out.

Following her toward the exit of the Municipal Building, I had a wild urge to put my arms around her and kiss the back of her neck. But when we walked out into the late afternoon, the sun hit me in the eyes like a hammer. Suddenly my head was reeling for a drink. It was coming, and there was nothing I could do about it. Except get a drink. My nerves were pleading for the stuff. *Get a drink get a drink get a drink.* Feel the alcohol flow like bliss through the sore lining of my stomach straight into my blood.

Usually when I go sober, I have three big withdrawal attacks—along with half a dozen or so smaller ones—before my body gives up on pain and starts looking for other arguments. So far this time I'd only had one. One coming on, and after that at least one more to go. With the sun in my eyes, and my brain aching, I didn't think I was going to make it.

I didn't realize I was just standing there with my fingers

clamped over my face until Ginny came back for me. She put her hands on my arm. "It's that bad?"

"All of a sudden. Doesn't usually come on this fast."

She said, "Is there anything I can do?" but she knew there wasn't. She'd done everything anybody could do when she came looking for me in the first place.

I said, "Take me home."

She shook my arm. "No chance. We've got all those friends of Alathea's to go see, remember? We're late already."

I said it again. "Take me home."

"Brew," she whispered at me, "I don't want to leave you alone."

With an effort, I pulled my hands off my face. I must've looked pretty fierce, because she winced. "I want to be alone. It's bad enough when I'm alone. This morning was easy. It's going to get worse. Do you think I like having you watch me fall apart?"

That reached her. It didn't ease the tight worry in her face, but it got me what I wanted. She took me home.

By the time she got me up to my apartment, the pressure in my skull was squeezing sweat out of my face like beads of thirst. I was shaking like a cripple. It was all I could do to get across the room and sit down on the convertible couch I use for a bed.

This one was going to be a sonofabitch.

Had it ever been this bad before? I couldn't remember. Probably not. Every time is always the worst.

Ginny sat down beside me for a while. She looked like she wanted to hold my hand. "Are you going to be all right?"

From somewhere, I dredged up the energy to say, "There's nothing here. I never keep the stuff in my apartment."

"That isn't what I asked. I asked you if you're going to be all right."

I said, "You go on." If she didn't leave soon I was going to scream. "Talk to Alathea's friends. I'm going to sit here—as long as I have to. Then I'll get something to eat. Then I'll go to bed. Pick me up in the morning."

"All right." She didn't like it, but she swallowed it. "I'll make sure the answering service knows where I am." A minute later she was gone.

A minute after that, I wanted to cry out, *Ginny!*

But this mess was one I'd made for myself, and I was going to have to live with it. So I just sat where I was, and watched the sunlight in the room get dimmer.

Soon there were red-hot bugs crawling along my nerves, ticks and chiggers and cockroaches of need, and at one point I thought I could hear high-pitched mewling sounds coming from somewhere in the vicinity of my face. But I just sat where I was—and waited. Waited for the sun to set. Waited for night. There was a cure for this, and I was going to go get it. Never mind what I had told Ginny. I was going to go as soon as it was dark. A soon as I recovered enough control over myself to move.

I hung on for the sake of the dark. After a while there was no more light in the room, and the pressure eased a bit. Not much—this was going to be a long one. But enough so I could tell my arms and legs what to do with some hope of having them listen to me.

I lurched into the kitchen, and drank what felt like about a gallon of water. Then I left my apartment, struggled down the long stairs to the street, and went shambling in the direction of the old part of town.

Looking for that cure.

Chapter Five

The cure I had in mind was to find a Mestizo named Manolo.

Somewhere in the old part of town, he would be sitting alone in the corner of a bar, sipping a glass of anisette. Looking for all the world like the last remains of some long-dead grandee's noble family. He'd be sitting there like a sleepwalker, and if you saw him you'd be afraid to wake him up for fear the shock might fuddle what was left of his wits. But all the time he'd be as alert as a cat, soaking up little bits and hints of rumors, facts, information, as if he took them in through his pores. He knew a world of secrets. And if you asked him the right questions—or if you asked them the right way, or maybe if he trusted you for some reason—he'd tell you one or two of them.

There was a good chance he'd be able to tell me the secret of Carol Christie, and I knew how to ask.

I had an idea in my head that made my nerves crawl as bad as the DT's, and this was the only way I knew of to check it out.

I'm not like Ginny—I'm not a puzzle solver. For instance, it might never have occurred to me to compare the watermarks of those two notes. My brain doesn't work that way. I get where I'm going—wherever that is—by intuition and information. In a city like Puerta del Sol, there are a lot of information dealers (I'm not talking about stool pigeons—they're just punks who shill for the cops) and I know at least half of them.

Like most independent businessmen, old Manolo is a specialist. Next to el Señor himself, Manolo knows more than anybody in the city about who's doing what to whom and how in the grubby world of drugs. The cops could put away most of the pushers in the state if they just knew what old Manolo knows.

I was doing my best not to think too much about Alathea. I didn't dare. I was already too jittery—if I stopped to think about what I was thinking, I might not be able to stop myself until I ended up at the bottom of a bottle somewhere. No, all I wanted to know was how a good swimmer ends up drowning in the Flat River.

It was the kind of question you have to ask at night. People like old Manolo don't exist during the day. When the sun comes up, they evaporate somehow, and all you can find of them is what they leave behind—a rank and sodden body snoring away like a ruin on a pallet full of fleas somewhere, as empty of answers as an old beer can.

But I didn't get the chance to ask. I wasn't more than five blocks away from my apartment, just turning onto Eighth Street on my way toward the Hegira and all the other bars where Manolo might be drinking his anisette, when things started to get out of hand.

Down from the corner of Eighth and Sycamore, there are a couple abandoned buildings with a long dirty alley between them. They're close enough to the old part of town so even the cops don't walk into an alley like that unless there're two of them and more on the way.

I was just about to cross in front of that alley when the screaming started. A woman screaming. Terror and pain. Somewhere back in the semi-darkness of the alley.

My body is faster than my brain, and by the time the

woman screamed again, before I'd even thought about it,
I was headed toward the sound as fast as I could run.

Probably I should've had the .45 out where I could use
it, but when you're as big as I am, you get in the habit of
thinking you don't need a gun—half the time I forget I
even have the thing with me. Anyway, I had good reason
not to trust the way I handle a gun.

This time—for once—it turned out I was doing the
right thing. The only reason the woman didn't get hurt
worse was because I got there so fast. The man had already torn off most of her clothes, and he had her on her
back in the dirt. She was fighting like fury, but he was
much too strong for her.

He should've heard me coming—I'm not exactly light
on my feet—but he must've been too far gone in what he
was doing. Holding her down, he sprawled himself between her legs and started to thrust at her.

I was moving too fast to land on him without hurting
her, so instead I caught hold of the back of his shirt with
both hands as I went past and used his weight to help me
pivot to a stop. I was ecstatic with rage; the pressure inside me was exploding. Frustration and dread and all the
long pain of trying to fight my way off the stuff came to a
head in a second and I went happily crazy.

The man wasn't small—but for all the good it did him
he might as well have been. My momentum lifted him
bodily into the air, and when I pivoted I swung him
around and slammed him into the wall of the building.
When he bounced back off the wall at me, I saw he had a
switchblade, but even that didn't slow me down. I blocked
it aside, grabbed him again, wheeled, and threw him face
first against the other wall as if I was trying to demolish
the building.

Before he could turn and bring his knife around, I got
him. With a long swing that came all the way up from my
shoes, I hit him in the small of the back, just on the left
side of his spine.

A gasp of pain broke out of him. His knife skittered
away into the dark somewhere. He spun around and then
flipped forward. He fell on his face, then jerked onto his
side, arching his back as if he was trying to get away from
the pain. His legs went rigid, and he kept pushing with
them, slowly skidding his body around in a circle.

There was a high keening noise in my ears, like the

sound of blood rushing through my head, and I had a terrible urge to haul off and kick him. I wanted to so badly I could feel the jolt of my toe hitting his back. But I didn't do it. He'd had enough.

I turned away from him and went to see about the woman.

She was huddled, sobbing, against one of the walls. She had her knees pulled up tight in front of her and she clutched the remains of her clothes about her desperately, as if those scraps were all that was left of her. Her face was pressed against her knees; she didn't look up when I spoke to her.

I hunkered down in front of her. Not knowing what else to do, I put one hand on her arm.

She flinched away so violently I had to draw back. But at least the movement made her lift her head. I saw she was Chicano. It's hard for me to tell the age of a young Chicano woman—when they first stop being kids they look too old for their years, and later on they look too young—but I didn't think she was more than seventeen. Not pretty, but beautiful. Either the bad light or the tears made her eyes look dark as bruises.

"Hush, child," I said to her gently in Spanish. "The harm is past. I am Señor Axbrewder. My name is known in many places. Are there injuries?"

She didn't say anything. But she made an effort and finally managed to swallow back her sobs. In answer to my question, she shook her head.

The man on the ground behind me groaned.

Her eyes jumped fearfully toward him, but I said, "Do not have fear. The harm he wished for you has fallen upon himself." This time when I touched her arm she looked back at me and didn't flinch.

"That is well," she said in English. Strength was starting to come back into her face. There was a dignity in her tone, perhaps in the way she spoke English, that touched me more than any amount of crying. "He is a pig, and I spit on him."

I liked her English so much I switched to it also. "We'll do better than spit on him," I said. "The rape laws around here are pretty tough." That's one of the advantages of living in a state where some of the old Spanish traditions and values still carry weight. "We'll put him in jail, and he won't get out until he's too old to even think about doing something like this again."

She nodded her head once, sharply. "Yes."

"Good."

I got up to check on the man. He was groaning louder and moving around a bit now, but he wasn't going anywhere. He was a white dude—an Anglo all dolled up in the kind of "cowboy-tourist" finery no self-respecting westerner would wear. That made him a hit-and-run rapist, the kind that never gets caught because by the time the cops go looking for them they're already in some other part of the country, bragging about how the "Mex girls" couldn't get enough of them. "Not this time, ace," I muttered at him. Then I went back to the woman and asked her her name.

She said, "Theresa Sanguillan."

"Well, Theresa Sanguillan." All of a sudden, I was trembling—reaction, I guess—and I had to sound fake-hearty to keep my voice from quavering. "I'm afraid you've got a long night ahead of you. We'd better get on with it."

She didn't respond. The brief look she cast down at her clothes said more than enough.

I groped mentally for a second, then shrugged off my jacket and handed it to her.

Her eyes snagged momentarily on the butt of the .45 sticking out from under my left arm, then she took the jacket. I turned my back and went to look for the knife. I found it a few feet away, snapped it closed and dropped it into my pocket. Then I started trying to rouse the dude.

While I was shaking him to his feet and she was getting herself covered as best she could, I asked her how she'd happened to run into this clown.

I liked her—she had spunk. Now that her fear was over, she was just mad. But it was a controlled mad, cold and vehement. I was glad about that, because it meant she wasn't going to back out on me, refuse to press charges. In a tight, even voice, she told me she worked as a domestic out in the Heights, where a lot of professional people live. She was on her way home to her mother and two younger sisters, but the bus she had to take doesn't go into the old part of town, so every evening she had to walk this way home in the dark. The Anglo had been on the bus with her, and when she got off he followed her, and then started giving her some sort of speech about how girls weren't safe on the streets alone at night. It only took him three blocks till he started treating her like a hooker, and when she gave him to understand he was mistaken (I grinned at that—I could picture just how exactly she gave it to him to understand) he turned nasty.

The whole thing made me want to hit him again. While I was getting him up, I saw his organ was still hanging out of his open fly. I was tempted to leave him that way. But on second thought, for the dignity of Theresa Sanguillan I tucked him in and zipped him up. Then I lifted him to his feet and dragged him along. The three of us went out to the street.

In that part of town, you can't find a prowl car at night unless you go looking for it with a bloodhound. I didn't feel much like lugging the dude all the way back to Cuevero Road in hopes of spotting a cop or a working phone booth, so we went on down Eighth Street and turned in at the first bar we came to. The few lethargic drinkers in the place looked at us with only momentary interest despite our far-from-tidy appearance. The barkeep knew me and let us use his phone. First I called the cops. Then Theresa called a friend who had a phone, so the friend could take a message to her mother. Then we went back outside to wait for the cops. It would've been nice to sit down in the bar for a rest but, considering the shape I was in, I didn't want to stay in such close proximity to all those bottles.

It was an easier decision than it should've been, almost twenty-four hours since my last drink. I was wearing my white armor—knight rescues maiden—which helped. But that was only part of it. Vanity is no match for alcohol—if it were, half the distilleries in the country would go out of business. No, the main thing was that I was working; doing something I believed in. While we stood out there on the sidewalk there were even six or eight times that I didn't regret I wasn't back in the bar having a drink.

I passed the time by shaking the dude up every time he started to fade on me or shutting him up whenever he started to groan too much and by asking Theresa questions—simple questions, the kind she could answer without having to forget she was mad. After about five minutes the cops showed up. There were two of them in the cruiser, and they drove up quietly, trying not to attract attention.

Once they had heard what had happened they didn't seem very eager for our business. They inspected Theresa and the dude and me, and shuffled their feet and asked us a bunch of questions without writing any of the answers down, generally making it clear they wanted us to forget the whole thing. I suppose I could understand their situation—in this city, Anglo versus Chicano was every cop's nightmare. But I wasn't having any. Theresa Sanguillan and I were citizens; the dude had committed a crime and we had a right to have him arrested. I handed over the knife and finally the cops gave in. They piled us into the back of their cruiser and took us over to the Municipal Building.

The building is just as bad at night as it is during the day. Inside, it's always disorienting. During the day, you have the impression that the sun set hours ago—and at night, you end up thinking it's noon outside. But this time I didn't think about it. As long as Theresa had her chin up, I didn't intend to let anything get in my way. I knew it could turn out to be messy, but I didn't care.

The so-called "arresting officers" took us to the duty room where all the detectives had their desks (the person who designed that room was either a drunk or a real joker—the place looked like the embalming room of a mortuary) and for a while we were ground along by the usual routine of police work. The arresting officers made a statement to one of the detectives. He tried to ask the dude a few questions, but the dude was hurting too bad to make sense so the detective put him in the tank to wait for a doctor. Then a couple detectives took Theresa and me to opposite sides of the room—so we couldn't check our answers with each other—and made us tell our stories a few times. After that, we were given the opportunity to sit around and wait.

The cops do stuff like that on purpose. They try to put pressure on the people who're filing the charges. Most of them don't actually want the people to back out, but from a cop's point of view, if a victim is going to back out, the sooner the better—saves wasted effort and frustration later on. So they give you a chance to reconsider. A long chance.

While we were waiting, we saw the doctor come in. He

examined the dude, then went away muttering to himself. A few minutes later, two ambulance-guys arrived with a stretcher and carted the dude off on it. Theresa watched them go, but the anger in her eyes stayed.

After another half hour or so, a different detective came over to us and introduced himself as Captain Cason. He was a short fleshy man with hands like shovels and eyes so flat and pale from the side they looked like the eyes of a blind man. His voice had a particular kind of rasp I was all too familiar with—the hoarseness of a man who does a lot of interrogating. He took Theresa across the duty room into his office and shut the door.

They were in there for a long time. When they came out, she looked shell-shocked, like she was about to faint away right there on the floor. I had a sick taste in my mouth as I hurried toward her to get a closer look.

Cason tried to stop me. He put himself between me and her, steered her over to a nearby desk and told the detective there to arrange a ride home for her. Then he took my arm and tugged me in the direction of his office.

I slapped his hand off and stepped around him. For one second Theresa looked straight at me. Her face was as pale as if she was bleeding internally, but there was a hot red spot of color on each cheekbone and her lips were tight. Her dark intense eyes didn't flinch; half her anger was aimed at me.

Cason barked, "Axbrewder!" But I ignored him long enough to say to her as fast as I could in Spanish, "I will put him in prison by myself alone if you do not choose to speak against him." Then I turned away from her. Cason was getting ready to try to muscle me and I didn't want that to happen. I said to him, "Tell your detective I want my jacket back." Then I strode straight into his office and dropped myself into one of the chairs.

He followed me in, shut the door and sat down. He put his hands on the desk and kept them there as if they were too heavy for him to carry around—or maybe he just didn't want me to forget how strong they were. With that harsh rasp of his, he demanded, "What did you say to her?"

The bad taste in my mouth was getting worse, but I made an effort to keep my vocabulary polite. "The opposite of what you said."

"Huh?"

"You told her I wasn't going to testify for her." That was what I'd seen in her eyes; I didn't need her to explain it to me. "You tried to scare her off this by telling her she'd have to carry it alone in court. You must've had a fine old time telling her how ugly a rape trial can get."

"Is that so?" Cason growled. But for a second there he didn't sound quite so sure of himself. Then he rallied. "Well, I've got news for you, smartass. You aren't going to testify."

"How do you figure that?" I said, hoping there wasn't something important about all this he knew and I didn't.

"You're a known alcoholic. You were in the part of town where you always do your drinking. The arresting officers found you outside a bar. Who's going to believe a thing you say?"

"That's cute." The taste in my mouth made me sound like him. "The only problem is I'm sober."

"Is that a fact?" he drawled. "How do you propose to convince a jury?"

I almost laughed at him. "You're wasting my time. I'll call you as a character witness. Even you won't be able to explain why you didn't give me a blood-alcohol test." He blinked at that a couple times, but didn't say anything. "Come on, Captain," I went on. "You're playing games with me. Why don't you cut out the bullshit and tell me what's really going on?"

His fingertips began to touch each other lightly. "The man's name is Charles Saunders and he's from Cleveland. We're trying to get in touch with his wife. The doctor says he may have a ruptured kidney." Then his hands jumped into fists. "Goddamn it, Axbrewder! Haven't you ever heard of minimum force?"

"Minimum force?" I said. "What's that?"

"He could sue you for every penny you ever had!"

"Is that a fact?" Deliberately imitating his tone.

"We can probably get you off the hook if you let this thing drop."

I felt like it was my turn to get angry, but I held back. "So let him sue me. That's my problem. I don't give a shit what he does, as long as he does it in jail."

"Smartass!" Cason barked. "I wish you still had a license, so I could get it ripped off you for this."

"Yeah, well, I appreciate your consideration. But I'm just a private citizen. I saw a crime being committed, and

I intervened. I went in hard because there wasn't time for anything else. He had a knife. I didn't have a chance to ask him if he was going to use it." I was trying not to sound too angry, but I couldn't swallow all of it. "What the hell's the matter with you, anyway? You like rape? You want clowns like this Saunders running around loose?"

"Shut up, Axbrewder," he said softly, "or I'll stuff it down your throat."

"Just what we need around here," I shot back. "More police brutality."

"All right." He was furious. "That's enough. You want to be cute? I'll give it to you straight. This Sanguillan"— he made her name into an insult—"is just another Mex chippy who tried to back out when she didn't get enough money. It happens all the time. That's why she was out on the street alone at night. Saunders just got sucked in. He's a tourist here, and he deserves an even break. A ruptured kidney is a hell of a price to pay for not having enough cash on him. It isn't going to go any further. You're not going to testify."

"Because he's Anglo," I said carefully.

"If that's the way you want to put it." His hands were flat on the desk, as if everything was settled.

I got to my feet. "Theresa Sanguillan has a perfectly respectable job as a domestic in the Heights. That'll be easy to prove. She was on the street at night alone because that's the only way she can get home. But even if she is 'just another Mex chippy,' it doesn't make any difference. She was being *raped!*" I couldn't stop myself. I hammered my fist onto the top of his desk so hard a couple files fell off onto the floor. "If you try to sit on this, I'll go straight to the DA." District Attorney Martinez was notoriously unsympathetic with racist cops. "He might like to see if he can find out how many rape investigations you've dropped since you got your promotion."

Captain Cason was standing behind his desk, and his hands were twitching, and he was saying, "You sonofabitch, you—!" But I wasn't listening. I'd had enough of him. I threw open the door and went out into the duty room.

I'd been in there longer than I thought. Theresa wasn't there and my jacket was sitting on the corner of his desk. Everybody in the duty room was looking at me, but I ignored them. I shoved my arms into my coat, moving fast to try to hide the way I was shaking. Then I stalked out of the room.

I was in no mood to be interfered with, so when some woman in the corridor behind me called my name, I didn't pay any attention. No, thanks—not interested. I've had enough. But she was determined. "Mr. Axbrewder!" I could hear her hurrying to catch up with me. Oh, hell. I gritted my teeth, shoved my hands in the pockets of my jacket so she wouldn't be able to see them tremble, and turned to face her.

Policewoman Rand, from Missing Persons.

"Mr. Axbrewder," she repeated. "Sergeant Encino wants to see you."

Encino—just what I needed. He was a racist, like Cason only on the opposite side of the fence, and I didn't feel like putting up with him. I had my mouth open to tell Policewoman Rand to tell Sergeant Encino to stuff it when my right hand found a piece of paper in my jacket pocket. I shut up long enough to take out the paper and look at it.

It was just a scrap of paper. On one side there was something in Spanish, that looked like a grocery list. On the other side, in awkward childlike handwriting it said, "I am much thankful to you. Theresa Maria Sanguillan y García."

That made a difference, somehow. All of a sudden, Cason didn't seem to be worth the emotion I was spending on him. I folded the note neatly, put it back in my pocket. Then I asked Policewoman Rand, "Where is he?"

She nodded back down the corridor. "In the office."

"All right," I said. "I'll go see him."

She didn't come with me, but continued on the way I'd been going. Maybe it was time for her coffee break; I went back to Missing Persons alone.

Encino was the only one there. As soon as he saw me come in, he got up from his desk and came to stand at the counter, facing me. We stared at each other for a minute across the Formica, then he said. "It is said that you have stopped"—he made it sound like *estopped*—"a rape tonight."

That took me by surprise. I nodded stupidly.

His sad eyes didn't waver. "It is said that the woman is Chicano."

I didn't say anything to that either. Something was going on here I couldn't even guess at. As a way of answering him, I took out my scrap of paper and let him see it.

"Ah." He read it, then looked back up at me. He was too good at hiding his emotions—I couldn't find anything in his face. After a moment, he said, "So it is that you have spoken with Captain Cason."

For the sake of not acting like an idiot, I mustered up enough voice to growl, "Yeah."

Carefully, Encino asked, "What have you said to him?"

It was none of his business, but I was glad to tell him anyway. "I told him to blow it out his ass."

Suddenly, his whole face smiled. He was so happy even his hair looked like it was grinning. He was serious again after a few seconds, but by then everything between us was different.

"Señor Axbrewder," he said formally, "I have been unjust with you. Such men as he"—he obviously meant Cason—"have been a bitterness to me. Bitterness causes the eyes to close when they are needed to remain open. I am giving you apologies."

Before I could try to respond, he went back to his desk and picked up a stack of manila folders and brought them over to the counter.

"Yet even before the matter of Señorita Sanguillan I have been ashamed for my hard words to you. You say there is connection between Alathea Axbrewder and Carol Christie. I have done much reading in the files. For two years back. These I found." He tapped the stack of folders. Then he shrugged. "Investigations were done not by Missing Persons. Connection was not found."

He didn't let me interrupt him. "It is not permitted for you to read among these files. But"—he sighed eloquently —"I must depart this office for a short time. Who can say what has taken place when none are there to see it? Please make use of my desk." Five seconds later, he was gone, and I was alone with his files.

Now I was more than just surprised. But I didn't have time for it. I wanted to read those files, and I didn't know how long the office would be empty. I grabbed hold of the stack, pulled it around in front of me, and got started.

There were seven folders. Carol Christie's was on the top, and I took it first.

Before I finished it, I was feeling so weak I was afraid I was going to fall down. I couldn't help myself—I had to go sit in Encino's chair.

After Carol Christie's, I read the other six files straight through. Then I went back to the beginning and started over again. This time I took notes. Halfway through, Sergeant Encino came back—but he was alone and I didn't stop.

By the time I was done, I was dripping sweat on his blotter; my shirt was soaked and sticking to my back, along with most of my jacket. I didn't ask Encino's permission to use his phone—I just grabbed it, and dialed as well as I could with my hands shaking like cowards. I held on while Ginny's answering service tried to track her down. When she answered, they patched me through to her.

"Brew," she started, "what's wrong?"

I brushed past her anxiety. "I'm at Missing Persons. You've got to get down here."

"Why? What's happened?"

"There are seven of them," I said. "Not counting Alathea. I don't care what the cops say—this is no accident."

"Make sense, Brew! Seven what?"

"Seven thirteen-year-olds. No, five. Two of them were twelve." I knew I wasn't getting through to her, but I couldn't help myself. I was too upset to pull it together.

"What the bloody hell are you talking about?"

I pushed the phone against the side of my head as hard as I could, trying to make that damn inanimate plastic steady me. I wanted to shout, but I couldn't get enough air into my lungs to do it. "Carol Christie didn't drown because she couldn't swim. She didn't drown. She died from an overdose of heroin. And that's not all. Before she drowned, she . . ." But I couldn't say it over the phone. Carol Christie was only thirteen—just like Alathea. There are some things you can hardly say out loud at all.

"I'm on my way," Ginny said. "I'll be there in fifteen minutes." Then the line went dead, leaving me with nothing but an empty phone to hang on to.

PART II

Wednesday Night/Thursday

Chapter Six

Ginny made good time, but it was long enough for me to get a grip on myself. I couldn't afford to fall apart just because this case had turned messy all of a sudden. Alathea needed help in the worst way. So I muttered curses at myself for a while, then finally managed to give Sergeant Encino his desk back. By the time Ginny arrived I was standing at the counter where I belonged.

She came in so fast she almost hit me with the door, then stopped. Her eyes jumped back and forth between Encino and me, trying to figure out what was going on. She was on the alert and ready to explode if either of us tried to play games with her. But I didn't say anything for a few moments. I was so glad to see her I wanted to hug her. Just having her there made me feel steadier; she'd know what to do, know how to cope.

"All right," she panted, out of breath from hurry and anxiety. "What's going on?"

It was still a tough question, but I was in better shape to handle it now. "After we talked to him this afternoon, Sergeant Encino went through his files for the past couple years. He found six more young white girls like Carol Christie who ran away from home and later turned up dead. All seven of them were heroin addicts. In one way or another, they all died as a result of overdoses." I faltered for a second, groping for courage, then went on. "According to the medical examiner, they all showed signs of 'intensive sexual activity'." That was the way the coroner put it in all his reports. In each case, he'd concluded these twelve- and thirteen-year-old girls supported their addictions by prostitution.

Ginny took it in like a sponge. Whenever she's listening really hard she doesn't react to what she hears—she just concentrates on absorbing it. When I stopped, she asked in a flat voice, "Have you got the details?"

I showed her my sheaf of notes.

She nodded sharply, then turned to Encino. "Were these cases investigated?"

"Of course. Yes."

"And?"

He shrugged. "Connection was not found."

"No connection?" she snapped. "They're identical!"

If he resented her attitude, he didn't show it. "Drugs, yes. Prostitution—the running from home. But drugs are to be found in many places. For a young girl to purchase drugs, how can she obtain money? Especially heroin has much cost. It is a common thing. Many girls do such a thing. Where is connection to be found?"

I said, "He's right." I didn't agree with him, but he had a good point. "These seven girls lived in all different parts of town. They went to five different schools. According to their friends, none of them knew each other. Their parents don't have anything in common." When I thought about it, the individual investigations looked pretty thorough. "None of them went to the same church or belonged to the same club or had the same family doctor."

Ginny didn't even glance at me. "Who did the investigations?"

"Detective-Lieutenant Acton."

"All of them?" she demanded.

He nodded.

"Is he a good cop?" I asked.

Encino thought for a moment before he said, "He is Anglo—but not such a one as Captain Cason. There is no liking in him for drugs. He seeks to find the pushers who supplied these children."

Ginny started to ask another question, but I stopped her with a nudge. Policewoman Rand was coming through the door behind us. I didn't know which racial or political faction she belonged to, but she probably wasn't on Encino's side and I didn't want to risk getting him in trouble for helping us. In Puerta del Sol, the police department is like the city—it's so fragmented and so broken up into groups that can't stand one another, it's a wonder they can agree enough of the time to get any work done at all. About the only time I've ever seen the cops stick together is when one of them gets killed.

I guess my hunch was right, because there was a sudden change in Encino's tone as he said, "No, it is impossible. For you I have done everything I can. I will give no more apologies."

Two hints were more than enough for Ginny. "If that's the way you want it," she sighed in her aggrieved-citizen voice. "We will get a subpoena if we have to." That was a nice touch. Nice enough to keep Sergeant Encino in the clear as far as Policewoman Rand was concerned. I liked it so much I almost made the mistake of grinning. "Come on, Brew. Let's get out of here."

We turned to go, but the door was already in use. A short dried-up little man came practically running into the office. He had thin gray-and-black hair sticking up in all directions, a stiff moustache covering his mouth, and a face that looked like it'd been redesigned long ago by a pair of cleats. His eyes were bulging as if they were about to fall out. He didn't recognize us—I don't think he even saw us—but I knew who he was. One of Ginny's less-successful competitors—a private investigator named Treddus Hangst. Mostly because he didn't have any choice about it he worked in the grubby world of "domestic relations," spying for people who were jealous enough to pay him. I seemed to remember hearing somewhere that his wife had run off and left him a few years ago.

He almost jumped the counter to confront Sergeant Encino, as he thrust half a sheet of paper at him. His hands were shaking. "See! I told you she didn't run away!"

Ginny and I froze.

There was no triumph in his voice—just urgency and fear. "Read it!"

Sergeant Encino scanned the paper, then turned his sad eyes back to Tred. "It says that she has run away, Mr. Hangst."

"She didn't run away!" he insisted. "This proves it. Listen." He held the note trembling in front of his face. " 'Dear Dad: I won't be coming home for a while— maybe for a long time. Don't worry about me. There's something I have to work out. Love, Mittie.' " He slapped the paper down on the counter. "See?"

Without inflection, Encino repeated, "It says that she has run away."

"No!" His whole body was twitching with frustration.

"Mittie didn't write this. It says, 'Dear Dad.' She never called me Dad. She always called me Pop. That proves she didn't write this. She didn't run away. She was kidnapped!"

"For what purpose kidnapped?" the sergeant asked. "Not for ransom. Then why?"

"I don't know." He was close to crying. "It doesn't make any sense." Then he recovered his determination. "You've got to help me find her. I can't get anywhere alone. There are too many things that could've happened. I can't do it alone."

Encino leaned closer to Tred. "Mr. Hangst, I have sympathy for you. We of course will seek for your daughter. The importance has been made clear to us. But no promise is made. It is of great difficulty to find one who has run from home"—he stopped Tred's protest with a short gesture—"or fallen among troubles." Then he looked past Tred at me. "For now, it would perhaps be well for you to speak to Mr. Axbrewder."

"Axbrewder?" Tred turned, saw Ginny and me. "Oh." He nodded at us, swallowing hard. "Brew. Ginny."

At once, Ginny said, "We're working on a case that sounds a lot like what happened to your daughter. We'd like to talk to you about it."

Tred said, "Oh," again, weakly. He looked back at Encino. But before he could say anything, Ginny took his arm and started him toward the door. "Sergeant Encino knows why we think this is so important," she said reassuringly. "I'm sure he'll do everything he can to help."

Policewoman Rand was taking in all of this, so I didn't try to thank Encino. I just followed Ginny and Tred out into the corridor and closed the door behind me.

"Where shall we go to talk?" she asked me over the top of his head.

"Somewhere where we can eat." I hadn't had any food for close to fourteen hours and I was feeling it.

Tred didn't resist. He looked like he'd used up all his energy or resolution just going in to see Encino. Now he was mumbling along beside Ginny like an empty shell. So we took him with us, out of the Municipal Building into the night.

The streetlights are bright in that part of town, so you don't see many stars. But streetlights don't fool anybody; the lights just made the shadows look more dangerous.

The people on the streets—there are always a few—moved as if they had secrets they were trying to hide. The cars that went by were going either too slow or too fast. Night is the only time when I feel like I understand the city.

We went to a twenty-four-hour diner. After we'd ordered a good-sized pile of food, Ginny asked Tred to show us his note. He took it out without even a question—he looked like he was numb with shock. She scanned it, held it up to the light, then handed it to me.

It was a half sheet of good twenty-pound bond, neatly torn along one edge. The handwriting was scrawled every which way. I held the paper up to the light and looked through it. I saw part of the same watermark that was on the two notes in my pocket. I dug them out and gave them to Ginny.

She compared them from several angles, studied all three of them against the light, then she handed Lona's and Tred's notes back to me.

With the torn edges together, they matched perfectly. Tred's note held the top third of the watermark missing from Lona's. There couldn't be any doubt about it; both these notes came from the same sheet of paper.

Sonofabitch! It was all I could do to contain myself. Fortunately, the food began to arrive. I shut myself up by shoveling things into my mouth while Ginny told Tred about Alathea.

Just to look at him, you wouldn't have thought he heard a word she said. But when she asked him, "How long ago did Mittie disappear?" he blinked suddenly, and tears started running down his cheeks. It was hard to watch. His eyes were gushing, but he didn't let out a whimper. A couple minutes passed before he finally answered faintly, "Three days."

Five—no, six—days after Alathea turned up missing. For no reason in the world I was aware of, I found myself thinking, *The bastard's getting greedy.* There had always been more time between the disappearances of those other seven girls.

Then Ginny asked, "How old was she?"

He had to struggle to make himself audible. "Thirteen." A moment later, he covered his face with both hands. "She's all I have."

When Ginny looked over at me, her eyes were glittering the way they'd glittered after she'd shot the punk who broke her nose. "I'm ready to hear the details now," she said to me. I glanced at Tred, but she answered evenly, "He has a right to hear this too."

He must've been paying attention. He pulled out a dirty handkerchief, blew his nose hard. Then he fixed his watery eyes on me and didn't let go.

I put my notes on the table beside my plate and started to recite.

The basic facts were simple enough.

Two years ago, Marisa Lutt, a seventh-grader at Ensenada Middle School up in the Heights, failed to return home from school. Her parents filed a runaway complaint almost immediately. Five days later, they reported having received a letter from her, asking them not to worry. Her description—"very attractive"—was given to all patrol units. A detective spoke to her friends, her parents, and their friends, but was unable to trace her. Three months later, she was killed by a truck while walking in the middle of the southbound interstate. The M.E. found evidence of massive heroin addiction, which he described as being of recent origin. He also found evidence of intensive sexual activity. The coroner concluded she had turned to prostitution to obtain money for heroin. Death accidental as a consequence of an overdose. Investigation in progress to determine where she obtained her drugs. She was thirteen years old.

Twenty-two months ago, Esther Hannibal, a seventh-grader at Matthew Pilgrim Junior High down in the southeast part of town, failed to return home from school. Her parents reported her missing, but refused to file a complaint and did not call again. Her description—"very attractive"—was given to all patrol units. Five months later, she fell off the roof of an abandoned building in the old part of town and died a few hours later of internal injuries. The M.E. found evidence of massive heroin addiction, which he described as being of recent origin. He also found evidence of intensive sexual activity. The coroner concluded she had turned to prostitution to obtain money for heroin. Death accidental as a consequence of an overdose. Investigation in progress to determine where she obtained her drugs. She was thirteen.

Eighteen months ago, Ruth Ann Larsen, a sixth-grader at North Valley Middle School, failed to return home from school. Her parents were frantic initially and did not hesitate to file a runaway complaint. Four days later, however, they withdrew the complaint. Her description —"mature for her age"—was given to all patrol units. Three months later, she was found dead in the bottom of a construction pit out on the east side of the city. The M.E. was getting in a rut. Ditto the coroner. And the investigation. She was twelve.

Sixteen months ago, May-Belle Podhorentz, a seventh-grader at South Valley Junior High, failed to return home from school. Her parents reported her missing but were unwilling to file a complaint at first. However, three days later they received a letter from her, asking them not to worry. They asserted the letter did not fit their daughter, and must have been written under duress. They then filed a complaint. Her description— "lovely"—was given to all patrol units. A detective spoke to friends—and so forth and so on—with no success. Six months later, she crashed in a hang glider at night and was killed instantly. M.E. and coroner as usual. Investigation as usual. She was thirteen.

Eleven months ago, Rosalynn Swift, a sixth-grader at Matthew Pilgrim Junior High, failed to report to school after missing half her classes the previous day. The school reported her to the police. When questioned, her mother said she had not come home from school the previous day. Her mother described her as "a no-good chippy who's only interested in boys" and refused to file a complaint. The school filed a complaint. Her description— "cute and well-developed"—was given to all patrol units. Investigation went nowhere. Six months later, her body was uncovered by a plow in the city dump while sanitation workers were redistributing garbage. The M.E. reported death by suffocation about a month previously. The rest of the report was as usual. She was twelve.

Seven months ago, Dottie Ann Consciewitz, a seventh-grader at Alsatia Junior High, failed to return home from school. Her parents filed a complaint immediately, claiming she had been kidnapped by her uncle in Detroit. Three days later, they received a letter from her, asking them not to worry. This they showed to the police as evidence her uncle had kidnapped her. They claimed she could not have written such a letter without his help. She was described as being "beautiful." The Detroit police were unable to locate either her or her uncle. Five months later she was found in an apartment on the south side of the city. Death by electrocution. Bad wiring on an electric hotplate. The M.E. and the coroner had nothing new to say. The investigation went nowhere. She was thirteen.

Three months ago, Carol Christie, a seventh-grader at North Valley Middle School, failed to return home from school. Her parents reported her missing. They appeared distressed and her father filed a complaint without her mother's approval. Her description—"healthy and pretty" —was given to all patrol units. A detective—and so on— without success. Her father called the police frequently to complain. Several times he made vague threats against the police. Three months later—Monday this week—her body was found floating in the Flat River. Although she had apparently been in the water for several hours, the M.E. found little or no water in her lungs. The cause of death was a heavy overdose of heroin. The rest of his report was the same as the other six. Likewise the coroner's findings. Investigation still in progress. She was thirteen.

Ginny didn't react to any of it—she was just absorbing data. But a change came over Tred while he listened. Gradually he went rigid. Before I was finished, he had turned so pale I was afraid he was going to have a coronary. He looked like a man whose whole life was falling apart. So he surprised me when he said in a tight flat voice, "You tell it as if all those girls were tied together— as if this is some kind of sick conspiracy. I don't know about that. What does it have to do with Mittie? She isn't a junkie. And she isn't a wh . . ."—for a second, he couldn't get the word out—"a whore."

"Neither is Alathea," I growled.

"We don't know for sure that there is any connection," Ginny said. Her voice was abstract, and she didn't look at either of us—she was just thinking out loud. "All we know for sure is that both Mittie's and Alathea's notes came from the same sheet of paper—which happens to be the same kind of paper Carol Christie's note was on. Those three notes say almost exactly the same thing. If there were anything more solid than that, the cops would've found it by now. Obviously, there are a lot of differences. But there are a lot of similarities, too. They were all in the same kind of trouble before they died.

They all overlap by about a month—each one dies a month after the next one disappears."

Except for Alathea and Mittie, I said to myself. But I didn't want to interrupt her.

"And they all disappeared from school. None of them ran away at night, or after school, or over the weekend, or during the summer. And none of them seem to have been on the stuff for very long."

"Three to six months," I agreed.

"I didn't know it was that easy to get," she muttered. "I didn't know a kid could buy enough of it to actually kill herself in three months—or even six." Suddenly, she was angry. "Who the bloody hell supplies children like that?"

I was about to say that that was what Detective-Lieutenant Acton was supposed to be trying to find out, but Tred distracted me. He didn't look like he'd heard what Ginny just said. He was fumbling for his wallet. He got out a picture, showed it to Ginny and me. "They were all cute."

He was right about that. I could vouch for Alathea. And Mittie looked very nice in her picture. It was hard to believe she was actually Tred's daughter.

For a while, none of us said anything. Ginny was staring at a burnt-out light bulb in the ceiling and I concentrated on eating. Judging from past experience, this would probably be the last food I could hold down until after the next withdrawal crisis. I didn't know when it was going to come—but it sure as hell was going to come. After that maybe being sober would start to get a little easier for a while.

Tred didn't eat anything. He was fidgeting under the silence. Finally, he asked in a thin voice, "What're you going to do?"

Ginny's thoughts came down off the ceiling with a jerk. "The first thing we're going to do is try to get a look at some more notes."

Tred nodded. For a moment, his lips trembled. Then he said, "I want to help."

"I'm counting on it." The glitter was back in her eyes. *"If* Mittie and Alathea really are tied in to Carol Christie and the rest of these girls, we need to move fast. Where did Mittie go to school?"

"Alsatia Junior High."

"All right. You take the Consciewitz girl. Give him the address, Brew." I got out a pen and wrote down the address on one of the napkins. When Ginny starts to give orders, she doesn't kid around. "The report on her mentioned a letter. I want that letter—the letter itself, not a copy. I want to know when they got it. I want to know where it was postmarked. I want to know why they think Dottie Ann didn't write it.

"Then go to the school. I'm not sure what I'm looking for there, so ask them about everything you can think of. Try to find out exactly where and when Dottie and Mittie left school. When you've got all that, call my answering service. We'll figure out where to go from there."

Watching him, you'd have thought she'd just given him a transfusion. A little blood came back into his face, and some of the rigid way he held himself relaxed. It was just what he needed—somebody to give him orders, make him feel like he was doing something to help Mittie. But there was something else going on, too. There was something distant in his eyes that didn't match the rest of him. For just a second, he gave me the distinct impression he had ideas he wasn't telling us. Then he was away from the table, over at the counter paying his bill. A minute later, he'd left the diner. The impression faded as soon as he was gone.

I turned back to Ginny. "You found out something from Alathea's friends."

"Maybe." She started getting money out of her purse. "I'm not sure. I want to take another look at her school. She disappeared after fifth period, P.E.—right?"

"Right."

"Well, her sixth period class was Home Ec. Apparently, she was the only kid in that P.E. class who had Home Ec. afterward. So she was always alone when she went from one to the other. The gym and the Home Ec. classroom are on opposite sides of the school and she didn't have much time to get from one to the other, so she always took a shortcut outside the buildings. As far as her friends know, she's the only one who took that shortcut between fifth and sixth periods."

"So whatever happened to her happened on that shortcut."

Ginny nodded. "Seems that way. We'll check it out tomorrow." Then she got to her feet. "Right now I'm going to take you home. You need sleep. If your eyes sink any farther back in your head, you might swallow them."

I couldn't argue with that. I'd been running on nothing but nervous tension for hours now—I did need sleep. And I always have an easier time relaxing when Ginny is in one of her take-charge moods. Spares me having to make decisions for myself. I waited for her to pay the bill, then followed her out to the Olds.

By then it was after midnight, and the night was darker than ever. But that suited me, too. It's hard to work on cases like this during the day—sunlight makes everything about them seem unreal. At night there's always some-body somewhere who knows the secret. It's just a question of finding the right person and asking the right questions. And something else kept me from feeling quite so scared for Alathea. The other girls on that list took at least three months to end up dead. Alathea had only been missing for nine days.

On the drive back to my apartment, I told Ginny how Sergeant Encino had happened to change his mind about letting us see his files. That must've made a difference to her, because when she said good-night she didn't look anywhere near as worried as she had earlier. She looked like a woman who knew she was on the right track.

Chapter Seven

The next morning, the phone pounded me awake around eight. It took me a long time to get to it. As soon as I sat up in bed, I had a blinding headache and every muscle in my body hurt as if I'd just gone fifteen rounds with a brick wall and lost. That told me something, but for a while I couldn't remember what it was. All I could re-member was the fine sharp taste of whisky. Remember it, hell—I wanted it. For a while there it was worth more to me than love or money.

That explained why I hurt so bad. I'd slept through the first half of a crisis. My muscles ached from clenching, and my poor sodden brain was yowling with thirst. I was drenched in sweat.

The phone went on hammering away at me, but I ignored it. I lumbered into the kitchen, thanking all the

gods who watch over slobs like me that I'd had enough
foresight to make up a jug of frozen orange juice before I
went to bed. I drank about a quart of that while the phone
went on ringing. Then I answered it.

"Brew?" It was Ginny. "Are you—no, forget that. Did
I wake you up?"

That was an old question, and I answered it by force of
habit. "No, I had to get up to answer the phone anyway."
I didn't have enough brains with me to think of anything
original.

She didn't even pretend to laugh. "How soon can you
get ready to go? We've got work to do."

"Come pick me up," I said. "I'll be ready by then."

"We don't have time for that. We've got six sets of
parents, five schools, and a school board to talk to.
You'll have to rent a car."

"All right." Her tone was infectious. Just listening to
her made me feel like she and I actually lived in the same
world. "What do you want me to do?"

"There's no point in your going to any of the schools. If
they have any sense, they wouldn't talk to anybody unless they see a license. Why don't you start with John
and Mary Christie?"

"They'll never forgive me."

"I don't give a good goddamn. I want to know more
about that note. I want to know what they're so edgy
about."

I said, "They'll tell me." People generally tell me what
I want to know—one way or another.

"They'd better," she said. Then she went on giving me
orders. "When you're through there, go see that other
family up in the North Valley—the Larsens. If you finish
early, call my service. Otherwise, I'll meet you at the
school board at one. We've got an appointment to talk
to the chairman."

"Right." It sounded simple enough. It even sounded
good to have her give me things to do alone. A big improvement over having her worried about me. "Anything
else?"

"Yes. I need the addresses of those two girls who went
to Matthew Pilgrim Junior High. I'll concentrate on the
southeast—try to see the parents and talk to the school
before I meet you."

I left the phone to dig out my notes, then gave her

the addresses for the Hannibals and Mrs. Swift. A moment later, she said, "That leaves two."

"Marisa Lutt and May-Belle Podhorentz."

"Maybe we can check them out this afternoon."

She made sure I knew where the school board was. Then she hung up.

Work. I had work to do. I spent a minute trying to stretch some of the soreness out of my muscles. Then I went and got dressed.

The rest of the orange juice and a decent breakfast did a lot to soak the worst of the pain out of my head. By a quarter of nine I was practically functional. More out of duty than conviction, I strapped on my shoulder holster and checked over the .45. Then I made sure I had all the right papers with me—my notes and *the* notes—grabbed up my sunglasses and went out to start batting my head against the morning.

As it happens, there's a cheap rent-a-relic agency about ten blocks from my apartment. By the time I walked the distance, I was feeling steadier physically, and they were open for business. I ended up with a middle-aged Torino. It wasn't very comfortable (some cars just aren't designed to fit the human body, no matter what size it is), but it had four wheels and an engine, which was all I needed. Before long I was on my way out toward the North Valley again.

I avoided what was left of the rush hour traffic by taking old roads up along the river, but still it took me quite a while to get out to the horsey area where the Christies lived. By then I was sweating in the heat. The sun had a way of beating down on me that was almost an insult—which didn't do anything for my mood, either. When the Torino bounced into the parking lot for the Christies' riding stables, I was ready to be as tough as necessary to get what I wanted.

I went through the office door fast, aiming to take John and Mary by surprise. But the only one I surprised was Mrs. Christie. Her husband wasn't there.

When she saw me, she almost jumped out of her shirt. But she didn't yell for John. Instead, she asked me, "What do you want?" and her voice trembled. Which told me Mr. Christie was somewhere out of range—maybe out on one of the trails, or doing business in town. In a way, that was too bad—I was primed to throw my weight around, and it wasn't going to take any weight to make Mrs. Christie talk. Nerves or fear or whatever was already putting enough pressure on her.

So I sat down in a chair by the desk, crossed my legs, and said in the least threatening voice I could muster on such short notice, "I want to ask you a few questions about Carol."

"Go away." She had to hug herself to keep from shouting. "I can't talk to you. John doesn't want me to talk to you. He'll be back any minute. I'll call the police."

The way her eyes groped around the room as if she was praying for some kind of miracle told me she was lying about her husband coming back. So I gave her a lie of my own. "The cops know I'm here. They know we're working on this case."

"I don't want to talk to you." Somewhere she found the determination to sound defiant. "I don't have to talk to you."

I said, "That's true, Mrs. Christie." Calm, unthreatening. "But if you'll listen to me for a minute, I think you'll find you want to talk. You're afraid of something, and it isn't going to go away until this case is solved. It may be hard for you to believe, but I'm trying to help you.

"You see, I know what happened to Carol. I know she didn't drown. I know she died from an overdose of heroin. I know how she earned the money to buy heroin." Abruptly, Mrs. Christie dropped into a chair and put her hands over her face. "So there's no reason why you shouldn't answer my questions."

I gave her a minute to absorb that. Then I went on. "Carol isn't the only one, Mrs. Christie. For two years now, the same thing has been happening to twelve- and thirteen-year-old girls everywhere in the city. Right now, it's happening to my niece. That's why I need to talk to you."

She didn't look up, but slowly she took her hands away from her face. I could tell by the way her shoulders sagged she was giving in. She was under too much strain to fight me and her fear at the same time.

Very gently, I eased her into it. "How long after Carol disappeared did you get her note?"

She took a deep, shuddering breath. "It was three days. We were worried sick."

"I can believe it. Did you happen to notice the post-mark?"

"John did. It surprised him. It was mailed here in town."

"Why did that surprise him?"

"He—we both thought that Carol had gone some-where else. She has a lot of friends living in other parts of the state. We thought she must've gone to visit one of them."

"I understand. Mrs. Christie, did anything about the note bother you? Anything that didn't seem right, some-how?"

"No," she said. Then, a moment later, "Yes—sort of. Carol didn't write letters. We used to send her away to camp every summer, and she never wrote to us. And when she got back she didn't write to her friends. She didn't like to write. She liked to use the phone—she liked to call people. But she wouldn't write. One year she got in trouble at camp because the counselors wanted her to write a letter home like the rest of the girls, and she wouldn't." Finally she looked up at me. Her face was full of distress. "She loved us—that wasn't it. She didn't write to anybody—she didn't like to write."

I wanted to tell her I understood, believed her. But the way she was looking at me gave me a chance I didn't want to miss. "Mrs. Christie," I said softly, "what're you so afraid of?"

"I . . . we . . ." For a moment, she choked on it. But by now it was too late—she couldn't stop herself. "John says that we might lose our business. He says that if people find out what happened to Carol, they'll think we had something to do with it and they won't come here any-more. They won't bring their children here anymore. But he's just saying that. He doesn't care about that. Carol was a good girl, and he wants people to remember her the way she was, before . . . before she ran away."

I waited a moment, then said, "But that isn't it, either."

"No. No. We're both so . . . so ashamed. We don't want anybody to know. We failed her somehow . . . there must've been some way we could have been better par-ents . . . so she wouldn't have had to run away. That hurts. I keep wanting it to go away, and it doesn't.

"And that . . . that policeman—Detective Acton?" She looked at me, expecting me to recognize the name.

"He th . . . threatened us. He said that somebody is supplying drugs to young girls—all through the city—and the parents are the first suspects. He said he wanted to believe we were innocent—but he wanted to keep what happened quiet, out of the papers and everything so nobody would know about it, and if we told anybody, talked to anybody, he would know we were deliberately interfering with his investigation. He was . . . awful. He looked like he liked hurting us. I haven't been able to sleep for nights. I keep having this nightmare that Carol is drowning and screaming for help, and I'm running frantically to try to get to her, but before I can get there Detective Acton comes out of the water and pushes her head down, and all the time he has the most terrible grin." Again, she covered her face. "Oh, my baby!"

I didn't say anything. There was nothing I could say. The world's full of pains no stranger can comfort. The only thing I could do for her was try to find out the truth about Carol.

And keep my eyes open for a chance to give Detective-Lieutenant Acton what was coming to him.

I left the trailer, closed the door quietly behind me, and went back to my rented Torino.

As I eased myself into the seat I almost scalded my back on the vinyl upholstery. The sun had made it hot enough to fry eggs. I spat a few curses, but that didn't accomplish anything. The heat was just another item on a long list of things I couldn't do anything about. I started the engine, then tramped down on the accelerator and went slewing out of the parking lot onto the road. For a few minutes I concentrated on speed, trying to build up enough wind to ventilate the car. Then I settled back, got a better grip on myself and started looking for the place where the Larsens lived.

It shouldn't have been hard to find, but I didn't know the North Valley very well, and for some reason Lujan Street didn't seem to be where I thought it was. Finally I had to stop at a small corner grocery store (the kind of glittering artificial place you find in moneyed neighborhoods—the kind of place that stocks more caviar than macaroni) to ask directions. Sure enough, Lujan Street turned out to be just about where I thought it was. The problem was I wasn't where I thought I was.

So it was late in the morning when I finally parked in

front of the Larsen mansion. It wasn't new—it had the Victorian look of a converted funeral-home—but it sure as hell was big. I had to hike up the walk onto the porch to ring the doorbell, past five or six kids' bikes standing to one side—and about that time the name "Bjorn Larsen" began to sound vaguely familiar to me. A solid matronly woman—who turned out to be Magda Larsen—invited me into the house.

The front hall was only a couple of times larger than my apartment and it was decorated (if that's the right word) with four massive iron sculptures as tall as I am. Two flanked the door, one stood beside the staircase, and one opposite the entrance to the living room. That explained it. Ruth Ann Larsen's father was Bjorn Larsen, the famous sculptor—one of Puerta del Sol's few certifiable claims to being an "art center."

Magda Larsen steered me into the living room and a few moments later we were joined by her husband. He was as thickly built as she was and as brawny as a steeplejack. He had a pair of welding goggles pushed back on his head and wore an asbestos apron over his T-shirt and jeans. The contrast between his clean hands and grimy forearms showed he'd just taken off his work gloves.

"This is Mr. Axbrewder," Magda Larsen said. "He wants to talk to us about our daughter." Virtually a repeat of what I'd told her at the door. Her tone was noncommittal, almost distant, but her husband stuck out his hand as if he was prepared to welcome anybody she let into the house. "Pleased to meet you, Mr. Axbrewder. Have a seat?" He waved me toward an overstuffed sofa that looked like it ate people for lunch. All the furniture in the room was like that—deep, sturdy, and made to last.

I sat down at one end of the sofa. Mrs. Larsen joined me at the other end, and Mr. Larsen took a chair near her—unconsciously courteous about placing himself so I could talk to both of them at once. "Which daughter did you have in mind?" he asked directly, "Risa or Natalie?"

Their openness made me hesitate. Neither of them had the vaguest notion what I had to say—and neither of them was the least bit afraid of it. I had a sudden desire to just tell them I'd made a mistake and walk away. Somehow, the complete frankness in their eyes made me feel like a child molester—me with all my grim, guilty secrets. I had to make an effort to say, "Ruth Ann."

In a way, that announcement didn't make any difference. Mrs. Larsen gave a faint gasp and went pale. Blood flushed through Mr. Larsen's face. But neither of them made any attempt to hide their reactions—or to attack me with them. When Larsen spoke, he didn't sound either embarrassed or hostile. "Ruth Ann died a miserable and senseless death. Magda and I will never understand it. What is your interest in her?"

Now that I was started, it was easier to go on. "I'm a private investigator. My niece has disappeared and I'm trying to find her. It's possible she's going through the same thing that happened to your daughter. If you'd answer some questions for me, it might help me find her."

Bjorn Larsen looked at his wife. She was shaking her head. He turned back to me. "Ruth Ann has been dead for more than a year—fifteen months now. What do you think our daughter and your niece have in common?"

That was tough to answer. His politeness was harder for me to handle than almost any amount of hostility. After groping for the right words for a minute, I said, "It works better if I don't tell you. If I tell you precisely what I'm looking for, I'd be putting ideas in your head and anything you tell me after that might not be completely candid, because you'll be reacting to what I said."

"I see." He folded his arms across his chest, and considered me gravely.

"That policeman"—Magda Larsen was talking to her husband—"that Lieutenant Acton—he told us not to say anything to anybody."

He nodded. "You see our problem, Mr. Axbrewder."

"Yeah." I saw it, all right—and I didn't much like what I was seeing. "But that was fifteen months ago. We know things now Acton didn't know then. Look." My voice was rougher than I intended, but I had to appeal to them somehow. "I didn't find out about this from the papers. I know exactly how miserable and senseless Ruth Ann's death was. What I'm trying to do is prevent the same thing from happening again—to another vulnerable little girl."

Again, Larsen looked at his wife. She'd produced a Kleenex from somewhere, and was using it to wipe her eyes. "Ah, Bjorn," she sighed, "tell him. We . . . *we* should be willing to do anything to prevent such things from happening."

Larsen accepted that without argument. "Very well, Mr. Axbrewder. Ask your questions."

"Thanks. I won't take much of your time." But then I had to pause for a few seconds, pull my scattered brains together. The living room was starting to get hot, but neither of the Larsens looked like they felt it. Both of them were watching me, curious to see what sort of questions I'd produce. I took a deep breath.

"When Ruth Ann didn't come home from school that day, you were very concerned."

"That's true," Larsen said. "She was always a very responsible child. If she were going to a friend's home after school—if she were to be late for any reason—she was very faithful about letting us know."

"So when you realized she was missing, you called the police and filed a complaint."

"Yes. We were reluctant to file the complaint—but we were very concerned, and the police didn't seem to be taking the situation seriously enough. We filed the complaint to try to make them take action."

"Then four days later you withdrew the complaint."

"Why, yes." He seemed momentarily confused. "Yes, we did."

"Why was that?"

"Well, you see—as I say, she was a very responsible girl. We felt that she wouldn't run away without . . . very good reasons. Four days after she disappeared, we received a letter from her. Really, it was just a short note. She assured us that she was all right, and said that she would come home as soon as she had dealt with some problem bothering her. Under the circumstances, we felt it would be a violation of her privacy if the police were to 'capture' her and bring her home against her will. So we withdrew the complaint." He said this with such unselfconscious dignity I couldn't argue with him. It was on the tip of my tongue to say twelve-year-old girls have more important needs than privacy—but I didn't.

He must've seen some of what I was thinking on my face, because he added, "Children have the same rights as any other person. So many children grow up to be spoiled, irresponsible, or unproductive because they are treated 'like children'—which means that their parents are more interested in their own desires for power than in their children's rights."

That shook me up. Ruth Ann Larsen turned into a prostitute to support her drug habit, and her parents hadn't even tried to look for her. But my expression didn't make a dent on her father. He believed in his own integrity. For some reason, so did I. So I didn't shout at him. I just said, "All right. There's only one thing that really matters. Do you still have her note?"

"I will get it," Mrs. Larsen said. She climbed out of the sofa, left her husband and me staring at each other. I didn't much care for the view, so I spent my time looking around the room until she came back.

She handed me an envelope. It had a clear Puerta del Sol postmark. Inside, there was a half sheet of good twenty-pound bond, neatly torn along one edge. The handwriting on the note and the envelope was scrawled all over the place.

It said, "Dear Mom and Dad: I have to be away for a while, but there's nothing to worry about. I'll be fine. I have a problem to work on. I'll be back when I'm done. Love, Ruth Ann."

Sure enough, the paper had the same watermark as the other notes.

All of a sudden, my throat was so dry I could hardly swallow. I needed a *drink*. It took me a while to work up enough moisture in my mouth to ask, "Is . . . is there anything about this that . . . seems unusual to you? Out of place? Does it sound like her?"

Mr. Larsen said immediately, "Of course. It's her writing."

But Mrs. Larsen didn't hesitate, either. "No. In a way, that is not like her. It says, 'Dear Mom and Dad.' Our children do not call us by those names. Since she was a little girl she called us 'Bjorn' and 'Magda'."

I was cold and shivering inside. Whoever was dictating those notes hadn't even bothered to get them right.

I didn't ask the Larsens if I could take their note with me. I just took it, and left. What else can you do with parents who trust their children too much to try to protect them?

Chapter Eight

I still needed a drink. Sometimes being sober is like drowning; after a certain point, you know you're going to have to breathe, no matter what. But you don't—not until you pass out. I didn't go to a bar; I went to meet Ginny.

It was a long drive back to the middle of town, but when I got near Central High, where the school board has its offices, I was still a few minutes early so I stopped to grab a quick bite of lunch. That made it 12:45 when I pulled into the Central High parking lot.

Central isn't the newest high school in the city, but it is sure as hell the biggest and most bewildering. You could hide a football field in there and never be able to find it again because it was built in huge square sections that interlock and form a maze. They had to make it a high school because nobody younger than a freshman could find their way around in it. It was lucky I hadn't gone to school there; I've never been very good at mazes.

A couple minutes later, Ginny wheeled her Olds into the lot and parked it a few spaces down from my rented Torino. I was glad to see her. The sun on all those parked cars gave the day a glare of futility—everybody in the whole city could go crazy, rape each other and drop dead, and it wouldn't make one damn bit of difference to the sun. Ginny was a good antidote for that kind of thinking.

I walked over to join her. Maybe it was just wishful thinking, but I thought she looked glad to see me, too. I caught her making a sneaky effort to check my breath—then her face relaxed into a smile. For a second there, I almost hugged her; sometimes her smile does funny things to me.

Then she said, "What've you got?" and we were back to business.

I showed her the Larsens' note and told her about my morning. I didn't leave anything out—if anything, I got carried away about good old Detective Lieutenant Acton. That didn't do my blood pressure any favors, but I've never worried much about my arteries anyway.

She absorbed what I had to say, considered it for a couple minutes. Then she told me what she'd come up

71

with: "Mrs. Swift is a real charmer. I must've gotten her out of bed—the wrong side at that—and she came to the door looking like the wrath of God, wearing one of those polyester bathrobes—turquoise-and-pink paisley. Gave me a headache just to look at her. She acted like she'd invented bitchiness all by herself. All she could say about her daughter was that she was 'no good'—ungrateful chippy, running off and leaving her poor mother all alone like that. I had to lean on her to get anything else out of her."

I grinned. "Wish I'd seen that."

"It wasn't fun—and hardly worth the effort. She finally admitted getting a letter, though, sometime after her daughter ran away. She doesn't remember when, and she doesn't remember what it said—she tore it up as soon as she read it. She does remember the cops coming to see her, especially after Rosalynn turned up dead—but she claims she doesn't remember who they were or what they wanted."

She paused, then said, "I don't know, Brew. Maybe Rosalynn Swift doesn't fit the pattern. If I'd been her, I'd have run away from that woman seven days a week."

"Yeah, but don't cross her off the list yet—she went the same route as the others."

She thought a minute before she said, "Right."

"What about the Hannibals?"

"Better." She made the transition with a jerk. "*Much* better. I caught them both at home—he works the evening shift down at the paper mill, so he was just having breakfast when I got there. He's a feisty little man who likes to fly off the handle, but his heart's in the right place. Mrs. Hannibal is as steady as a rock, so she keeps him in line. At first they didn't want to talk. Some cop told them not to—they don't remember his name, after all it was a year and a half ago. But after I explained what we were trying to do, they changed their minds.

"Judging from what they told me, I'd say that when Esther disappeared they were nearly paralyzed—torn between anger and fear. Furious at her for running away, and at the same time terrified that something had happened to her. It was all they could do to report her missing —they just couldn't bring themselves to swear out a complaint. Mr. Hannibal probably spent half his time shouting and the other half in a cold sweat. Then they got a letter from her telling them not to worry, she was all right. That gave them an 'out'—an excuse to do nothing.

"Looking back on it, they're pretty bitter about themselves. Esther's death gave them a real shock, which probably explains why they were willing to help me in the end. They say they've changed their whole attitude toward their other children. To prove it, they gave me Esther's letter." Ginny handed it to me, envelope and all.

It had a local postmark; the handwriting was barely legible. The note was on a half sheet of good twenty-pound bond, neatly torn along one edge. It said, "Dear Mom and Dad: I'm not going to be coming home for a while. Maybe for a long time. I've got something to work out. Don't worry, I'll be all right. Love, Esther." The watermark matched the others.

While I studied it, Ginny went on, "I asked them if there was anything about this that bothered them. At first they couldn't think of anything, but then they said there was one thing—one of the many things that made them ashamed of themselves. Esther always came home from school for lunch, which she always complained about because all her friends ate in the school cafeteria. But the Hannibals only live about three blocks from the school and anyway they couldn't afford school lunches.

"The day she disappeared, she didn't come home for lunch. The Hannibals didn't think much about it—they assumed a friend gave her lunch or she bought her own out of her allowance. Now they feel like they let her down —failed her by not realizing something was wrong. As if there was anything they could have done." Abruptly, her voice went stiff with anger. "Heaven help the bastard who's responsible for this when I get my hands on him."

I knew how she felt. But we have a reciprocal relationship—when one of us gets mad, the other tries to stay calm. I said, "If Tred doesn't get to him first." Which wasn't much of a contribution, but it was all I had. "How's he doing, anyway? Has he called in?"

She calmed herself down again so fast it was almost scary. "He called while I was at the Hannibals. He didn't want to talk about it over the phone—he just wanted me to give him more to do. I told him to check out May-Belle Podhorentz and South Valley Junior High. He's supposed to meet us back at the office in a couple of hours."

It was one o'clock when we headed into Central High's monster building and began hunting our way toward the school board wing. The kids must have all been in class, because we saw only one or two. As we walked along the hollow corridors I asked Ginny if she'd learned anything at Matthew Pilgrim Junior High.

"It probably doesn't mean anything," she said, "but both Rosalynn Swift and Esther Hannibal disappeared at times when they were always alone. Esther was there for her last period before lunch—and gone afterward. As for Rosalynn—apparently, she was frequently in some kind of trouble. Nothing serious—just a way of getting attention. So as a form of punishment she was assigned to clean up one of the classrooms—the math room—every day right after lunch, while the other kids were free. Alone. She'd been doing it for about a month—and doing a good job of it, according to the math teacher—when she disappeared. Just didn't show up for her next class. Nobody saw her leave, which isn't surprising since the math room is in the corner of the building farthest away from the playground and the cafeteria.

"The people I talked to were fairly helpful, but they made it clear that I ought to be talking to the school board instead of bothering them. They kept assuring me the board had all the information I needed. I got the impression they want the board to decide for them whether or not we have any legal right to pry into all this."

"Sounds familiar," I muttered. Vice-Principal Rumsfeld, at Alathea's school, had given me pretty much the same impression.

Then we found what we were looking for. A frosted-glass door in the middle of a blank wall. The lettering on the glass said, PUERTA DEL SOL BOARD OF EDUCATION— PAUL M. STRETTO, CHAIRMAN/JULIAN Z. KIRKE, SECRETARY. Ginny pulled open the door, and I followed her in.

The rooms inside reminded me of the Municipal Building—no windows, no comfortable colors, everything artificial. Beyond the counter in front of us was a room that looked too small for the ten or twelve desks and thirty or so huge file cabinets squeezed into it. Most of the desks were being used—women in various stages of energy or desperation were hacking away at typewriters, scrawling on files, answering phones. Two or three of them in particular had an air of being frightened, as if someone was standing over them with a cat-o'-nine-tails.

We found out why. Before we had time to introduce ourselves to the secretary who did double duty as receptionist, a man came out of an office at the back of the room. He had light blond hair, sleepy eyes, and a mouth so sharp and strong it looked like he ate steel for breakfast every morning. He wasn't in a hurry, but somehow he gave the impression he was pouncing.

He said, "Sondra." His voice wasn't loud, but it cut through all the work noise in the room, and a woman two desks away from him flinched. She was young and pretty. After I'd noticed that, I saw that all the secretaries who looked particularly miserable were young and pretty. He went over and held a sheet of paper in front of her. He handled the paper gently enough, but in some strange way his manner made the movement look like an act of violence. "Type it again," he said. "This time, get it right." His tone was sarcastic enough to draw blood.

He had started back to his office, when he noticed Ginny and me standing at the counter. He turned toward us. "It looks like Sally is asleep on the job again." The secretary-receptionist flushed, and bit her lip. "What can I do for you?" the man asked.

"I'm Ginny Fistoulari," Ginny said. "This is Mr. Axbrewder." If you didn't know her, you would've thought she hadn't felt a thing. But I could hear the underlying bite in her voice. "We have an appointment with Mr. Stretto."

"He's expecting you," the man said. "This way." We made our way around the counter and followed him toward a door in the opposite corner. As we crossed the room I caught a look at the tag on the door of the man's office. It said "JULIAN Z. KIRKE, SECRETARY."

Then we were in a corridor that ran between more offices and ended up in a big place that looked like a corporate boardroom. Long dark wood table, heavy matching armchairs. Soft indirect lighting. Picture window along one wall overlooking the glare of the parking lot. A far cry from the sweatshop where those harried secretaries worked. Kirke guided us into the room and introduced us to Chairman Paul Stretto.

He looked like the kind of man the Republicans wish they could run for president. Strong lines in his face, a

mane of silver hair, resonant baritone voice, just a hint
of well-earned fat on his tall frame. He was sitting at the
head of the table as if he had been born there. For a second, I couldn't figure out what he was doing in a lowly
job like Board of Education chairman, when he could've
been elected mayor tomorrow—with a little help from
TV. But as we shook hands I got a closer look at him.
He was younger than he seemed and if my eyes weren't
tricking me, the fine silver of his hair came out of a jar.
Probably he was saving mayor for later. After which
he'd take a crack at governor.

He gestured Ginny and me toward chairs as if he was
offering to knight us. He asked Kirke to stay. "Things always run better around here," he explained, "when Julian
knows what's going on."

No doubt. I was already sure Paul M. Stretto was just
office-sitting on his way to better things. Kirke was the
man who actually ran the school board.

When we were all seated around the head of the table,
Stretto said, "Now, what can we do for you?" He
sounded full to the gills with professional bonhomie.

"Mr. Stretto," Ginny began, "we're private investigators." She showed him the photostat of her license.
"We've been retained to find two young girls who ran
away from home early last week. In the process, we've
learned that quite a few girls of junior-high age have run
away recently—in the past two years, to be more exact.
Some of those cases bear a striking resemblance to the
ones we're working on. It might help us to find these girls
if we could see some of your files."

"I see." She'd taken him by surprise (most people
don't expect visits from private investigators), and he
made a great show of thinking hard about it. Which led
him to the unsurprising conclusion he was out of his depth.
"What do you think, Julian?" Before Kirke could answer,
Mr. Stretto said to us, "Julian is the expert on our files.
We're in the process of making a major overhaul of our
record system. Our goal is to computerize the files completely so that each school in Puerta del Sol will have a
terminal tied to a central computer complex here. Everything will be available at the touch of a button anywhere
in the system.

"But," he smiled warmly, "that's a few years in the
future. Right now, Julian is busy getting our files ready

for the computer. It's a huge job. First he had to get copies of everything from each individual school. And now he has to put all that data in a usable form. Fortunately, he's an expert at it. That's why the board hired him."

Kirke listened to all this without any particular show of respect—but at least he didn't interrupt. On the other hand, he didn't waste time when the chairman finally finished his little speech. Right away, he asked Ginny, "Do you have consent from the parents?"

"Not in writing," she said evenly. "We've spoken to them—that's all."

"We'd be violating the confidentiality of our students if we opened our files to you without some kind of written permission."

"That's right," Stretto said. But nobody even looked at him.

"In any case," Kirke went on, "I don't think it would be worth your trouble." There was just a hint of a sneer in his voice. "What could you possibly find? From our point of view, all runaways are the same—and every one is different. They're all having trouble of some kind. They all miss school for a while. If some of them have something in common, you wouldn't find it in our files."

As innocently as sugar, Ginny asked, "You don't keep any record of the runaways who end up dead?"

"Dead?" Stretto demanded. "Are these girls dead?"

Now she let some of the bite in her voice show. "In the past two years, seven junior-high girls in this school system have run away from home—and died."

"But"—the chairman was groping—"what does that have to do with us?"

"Somehow, those seven girls are connected. And they're also connected to the girls we're trying to find. We want to find them before the same thing happens to them. We can't afford to overlook anything—and one of the possibilities is that there are facts buried away in your files that could help us."

"This is very upsetting." Stretto looked upset. "Of course we want to do anything we can to help." Probably because he didn't have any better ideas, he latched on to what Kirke had said earlier. "If you'll get written consent from the parents, we'll show you everything we have."

"We don't have time to do all that again," Ginny

snapped. "Those seven girls died as a direct result of whatever it was that made them run away. The process has already started for two more." She was laying it on thick. "Every delay could be fatal." I wanted to applaud.

"I'm sorry, Ms. Fistoulari." If you could trust his face, Paul Stretto really was sorry. "There's nothing else I can do." But if he wanted us to believe him, he blew it a second later by turning to Kirke and asking, "Is there, Julian?"

Kirke said, "No." He made the word sound like he'd chewed it out of pig iron.

Ginny considered for a moment. Then she said, "Give me the notes, Brew."

I dug them out and handed them over.

"Mr. Stretto," she said grimly, "we have reason to believe that these girls didn't just die. They may have been killed. Murdered." She stressed the word. "Each girl sent her parents a note. I have some of them here and I'd like you to read them." One by one, she put the Christie, Larsen, and Hannibal notes in front of him.

He was confused, but her tone didn't leave him any choice. He read them, then read them again.

"Now please read these two," she said. "They were written by the girls we're trying to find." She gave him the other two notes.

He read them too but he seemed to be struggling to understand what they said.

"They're all written on the same kind of paper," Ginny said roughly. "The watermarks are identical."

The next minute, I was surprised to see a change come over Mr. Paul M. Stretto, Chairman of the Board of Education. All of a sudden, he didn't look like a man who just happened to have a lucky face anymore. He looked like he had a right to that face. "Julian," he said in a completely different tone, "get Martha and Astin in here."

If all this made any impression on Kirke, he didn't show it; he just got up and left the room. A moment later, he came back with a man and a woman in tow. The man looked worn out, like a pencil that's been sharpened too often, but the woman bristled with energy.

Stretto introduced us. The man was Astin Greenling, Curriculum Vice-Chairman for the board. The woman was Martha Scurvey, Budget Vice-Chairman. Aside from Stretto and Kirke, they were the only full-time members of the board—all the other elected officials served part-time.

Stretto gave a quick summary covering most of the facts, then handed the notes to Greenling and Scurvey.

Neither of them seemed to grasp the significance of what they were reading. Greenling muttered, "You'd think we didn't teach penmanship at all." Scurvey gave a sigh that puffed out her cheeks. "If this kind of thing gets made public, we're going to have even more trouble than usual sneaking our budget past the voters."

"I didn't call you in here for your opinions," Stretto rapped out. If he wasn't a secretly decisive man under his hair-paint, he was doing a damn good imitation. "I just want witnesses so there won't be any confusion. These notes have convinced me that Ms. Fistoulari is right. As of now, I'm instructing Julian to give her everything she wants. I don't know what's happening to these girls, but I want it to stop."

There was silence in the room. Then Scurvey said, "Wouldn't it be better to call the police?"

"Leave that to me, Martha," the chairman said. Finally I figured out what he was doing. He was putting on a show for two influential—i.e., voting—members of the board. A display of power—probably as a way of consolidating his position. When a diplomat does it, it's called statesmanship. But it was a gift horse, and I didn't look it in the mouth. All I cared about was getting to see those files.

Stretto dismissed us. I picked up the notes, and we followed Kirke back down the hall to his office where I gave him the names of all nine girls. Mostly because I didn't like him, I watched to see if any of those names meant anything to him, but for all he cared I had got them out of the phone book. He wrote them down, then left us in his office. He came back with the files fast enough to prove he knew his job, but he didn't leave us alone while we read them.

It took us about half an hour to go through them all. It irritated me to admit it even to myself, but as far as I was concerned, Kirke was right—they didn't do us any good. I took some notes—the girls' schedules on the days they disappeared, the names of their teachers, things like that —but they didn't tell me anything. Ginny didn't say anything either, but I didn't expect her to—not with Kirke standing there.

When we were finished, she thanked him—which I thought wasn't called for—and led the way out of his office. As we were going out the door he stopped me. He stood up close and whispered so Ginny couldn't hear him, "Do you always follow her around like that?"

"Like what?"

He shook his head, dismissed the question. "You're wasting your time. By the time they reach junior-high, all the girls in this town are nothing but little whores. There's nothing special about the ones that run away. Did you know that we're practically having an epidemic of V.D. among the junior-high boys?"

I wrapped my left hand around his upper arm and dug in my fingers until his face turned white. Then I whispered back at him, "Watch your mouth. You're talking about my niece."

I gave his arm a little extra squeeze to remember me by, then I went to catch up with Ginny. I was grinning, but I wasn't amused.

Once we were outside the office, and on our way back to the parking lot, Ginny asked me, "What was that all about?"

"Kirke didn't much like the way he got overruled."

She nodded sharply. "Sonofabitch."

I agreed with her. But the main thing bothering me was the feeling it was all wasted. We weren't getting anywhere.

Chapter Nine

We didn't talk about it. Ginny had that pinched look between her eyes—the one that meant she was thinking hard. I had no idea what she was thinking about, but I learned long ago to leave her alone when she looks like that.

I didn't even ask her where we were going. She headed straight for her Olds, opened the door and got in. I just wedged myself into my Torino and decided to follow her.

We ended up at Mountain Junior High, where we had another session with Vice-Principal Rumsfeld. Ms. Rumsfeld wasn't exactly overjoyed to see us again, but this time Ginny had a much clearer idea of what she wanted to know, and the vice-principal wasn't the kind of woman who could turn us down if there was any chance at all of helping one of her students. She took us to meet Alathea's P.E. teacher, and the two of them showed us the shortcut Alathea had used between her fifth and sixth periods.

"We don't normally allow our students outside the school buildings unsupervised," Ms. Rumsfeld said sternly, "but I understand that this was something of a special case."

"Alathea had an awkward schedule," the P.E. teacher said. "She had a hard time getting from the gym to her next class before it started. She asked my permission to take this shortcut. I didn't see any reason to turn her down. She was a very dependable girl."

Very dependable. Yes. That's what I had to keep in mind. I didn't know any of the seven dead girls—for all I knew, every one of them might have been a raving lunatic. But I knew Alathea. She wasn't crazy, or on drugs, or a whore.

With the vice-principal and the P.E. teacher guiding us, it took us about five seconds to see why Alathea had wanted to use the outside route. For someone in a hurry, it was a big improvement over going through the buildings. But it was also a perfect place to disappear from, if that was what you had in mind. The buildings stood close to the street, and on that side most of them—the gym, the auditorium, one end of the library—didn't have any windows. Alathea hadn't just been alone—she'd been out of sight.

Which fit with what Ginny'd learned about Rosalynn Swift and Esther Hannibal. But it really didn't mean anything to me. If you wanted to run away from school, would you do it when you were surrounded by kids and teachers, or when you were alone?

But Ginny seemed satisfied with whatever it was we'd found out. She thanked Ms. Rumsfeld and the P.E. teacher, told them we wouldn't bother them again if we could help it. Then we left.

This time she led me all the way down Paseo Grande to the Murchison Building. Back to her office.

Tred was there waiting for us. He looked like he'd spent

the day in a dryer at the Laundromat—he looked hot, thirsty, and about two sizes smaller. But his eyes weren't bulging the way they had been last night. They were sunken and sizzling, as if they were being cooked from inside by whatever he was thinking.

He didn't say anything until we were settled in Fistoulari Investigations' back room. Then he confronted Ginny. Standing in front of her with his hands on his hips, he looked like the losing end of a cockfight—plucked half to death and still ready to peck anything in sight. "You're wasting my time," he said.

That surprised her. She looked at him hard. "I thought you wanted to help." Even sitting down, she was almost as tall as he was.

"I want to find Mittie. This way isn't getting me anywhere."

Well, off and on I'd been thinking the same thing myself, but for some reason it irritated me to hear him say it. Sometimes I seem to feel nobody but me is allowed to disagree with Ginny—which makes even less sense when you think about it. But I didn't get a chance to argue with him. She was working on what he said faster than I was. "Why not? Didn't you get anything?" she asked.

"Oh, I got what you wanted, all right." He took two halfsheets of paper out of his pocket and tossed them on the desk. "I know we're in a grubby business, but it isn't supposed to be this bad. Nailing people who're screwing around, and clearing people who aren't—that's what we're supposed to be doing. Not this. It was bad enough talking to those Consciewitz people. They're completely loony—all that stuff about an 'uncle' in Detroit'—but they miss their daughter so much it's making them sick. They were practically desperate to let me take their note. They say it proves she didn't run away—I don't know how, their explanations didn't make any sense to me. Believing she didn't run away is about the only way they can keep themselves from going crackers with guilt.

"But May-Belle Podhorentz' parents—my God, Ginny! I practically had to extort that note out of them. It's the only piece of her they had left. After what happened to her they had to put up with some halfwit cop who gave them a bunch of shit. They spent ten months being eaten alive by fear and shame and God knows what else. Then

I came along. Next time, just ask me to rape the rest of their kids. It'll be easier."

Ginny still hadn't even glanced at the notes on her desk. But if Tred made her mad, she kept it to herself. She just held her eyes on him and asked, "Did they say if they thought May-Belle's note was written under duress?"

"They didn't say, and I didn't ask. I was too ashamed of myself."

She considered for a moment, then said, "All right. I don't really need that. What about the schools?"

"Nothing," Tred rasped. "May-Belle Podhorentz and Dottie Ann Consciewitz were just like Mittie—they disappeared when nobody was watching them."

Ginny sat up straighter in her chair. "What do you mean?"

"What do you think I mean? None of them walked away from their friends or disappeared in the middle of a class or snuck out the back way during lunch. They all waited until they were alone. May-Belle was a piano student. One of the practice rooms was assigned to her during her third period. She didn't show up for her fourth-period class. Dottie Ann liked P.E., and she had a special job in the gym during fifth period—she sorted uniforms and equipment for her teacher. Alone. She didn't make it to sixth period. And Mittie—it was the same goddamn thing with Mittie!" He was starting to shout. "What the hell do you care? What does all this prove? We're not getting anywhere, and you know it!"

Ginny never flinched. "I think that what we're doing is pretty obvious. What else would you suggest?"

That stopped him. But not because he didn't have ideas of his own. His expression reminded me of the way he'd left the diner the night before. He was thinking about something, all right. Whatever it was, he stopped because he didn't want to say it out loud.

"Spill it, Tred," I said softly. "We're all in this together." He didn't move a muscle. I went on, "And you need us. You don't have a client. As far as the commission is concerned, you can't hire yourself to look for your own daughter."

Then he turned to face me. His cheeks were as pale as frostbite. "I don't give a shit about that," he said. "I don't want any of this to be true."

I held his eyes.

Thickly, he said, "What do you think about . . . about prostitution? Where does that fit in?"

"Isn't it clear?" I was trying to guess what he was really thinking. "That's probably the only thi͟ ͟ ͟e coroner was right about. They have to get money for drugs somewhere. How else? If they couldn't ͟ ͟ him the pusher wouldn't make any money. He wouldn't be doing this in the first place."

Something like a spasm of rage or disgust jumped across Tred's face. He turned on his heel and left the office.

Ginny stared after him for a long time, frowning grimly. Then she picked up the notes he'd left on her desk. She read them, studied them, checked the watermarks, then handed them to me.

They fit the pattern exactly—paper, watermark, torn edge, handwriting, everything. When I compared them with the notes we already had, I saw May-Belle Podhorentz' note was word-for-word identical with Mittie's.

After all, sixteen months is a long time for whatever bastard dictated these notes to remember exactly what they said.

"I should've told him what we've got," Ginny said. Still thinking about Tred.

"He didn't want to hear it." That was my first reaction, then I said, "Besides, we haven't got anything."

"That depends on what you're looking for," she replied in a musing tone. "Things are starting to fit together."

"Oh, good." Being sober doesn't do much for my temper. "Now if the fit just made sense, we'd be getting somewhere."

It was her turn to stay calm. "We are getting somewhere. If Marisa Lutt's parents have a note like these, we'll have a case that can stand up under any kind of pressure—even if Detective-Lieutenant Acton tries to get us out of the way."

"That isn't what I meant." Even I couldn't help knowing how important those notes were.

She looked at the ceiling for a moment, then said, "I take it you didn't notice anything interesting in what Tred told us—about how Mittie, May-Belle, and Dottie Ann disappeared."

"It's the same story as Alathea," I said sourly. "I knew all that already. I read it in Kirke's files. So what?"

"I'm going to have to check it out with the other schools —this is too iffy to take chances with—but I think there's something important in those files. According to what they say, these girls didn't just run away from school— they ran away *during* school. Never after or before— during. And every one of them was alone at some point in the school day on a regular basis. Being alone didn't happen by accident on a particular day."

"What does that prove?" She was on the edge of something—I could feel it, but I didn't have the dimmest notion what it was. I was like Tred—I had ideas of my own, and they didn't seem to have anything to do with what Ginny was thinking.

"I don't know yet. Files don't always give a very clear picture of what really happens."

That was true enough. But it still didn't mean anything to me. Even if the other files checked out with the schools themselves, that still didn't prove anything except that every one of the girls had a regular chance to run away. Opportunity, that's all. I used to know some cops—back in the days when there were some cops I was on speaking terms with—who believed opportunity creates crime. People do things for the simple reason they get the chance. Wives shoot their husbands because there's a gun in the house. Kids become junkies because drugs exist. Responsible executives take money out of the till and blow it in Las Vegas because Las Vegas is there. Opportunity. Those cops used to talk about preventing crime by getting rid of opportunity.

I think that's a crock of manure. In my opinion, people commit gratuitous crimes (crimes they aren't forced into, the way a starving man sometimes feels forced to steal, or a woman whose husband is cheating on her sometimes feels forced to shoot him) for the sake of power. If they can get away with it, it puts them on top of the world.

But right then I wasn't so sure of anything. If Ginny wanted to blame it on opportunity, I wasn't going to argue with her. I didn't have anything better to offer. Instead, I said, "There's plenty of daylight left. What do you want me to do while I've still got wheels?"

"Marisa Lutt," she said without hesitation. "Let's make sure we've got everything. I'm tempted to call Sergeant Encino—ask him to go further back than two years. But I'm half afraid to find out if there are any more of these cases. And I got the impression that he's going to be working on it anyway. Maybe he didn't know about the notes before, but he does now. He'll probably call us himself if he finds anything we need to know."

I agreed with that. "You're going to do the rest of the schools?"

"Yes. Ensenada and North Valley. I think that covers it, doesn't it?"

I made a quick mental check. "That's it."

"OK." She got to her feet. "Call my answering service when you're finished—and then you might as well get rid of that clunker."

"Yeah." I heaved myself up out of the chair. Collected all the notes and stuffed them in my pocket. This time, I went out first. I wasn't trying to prove anything—no matter what Kirke had said. It was her office, and she had to lock up after me.

Alone again, I dug the Torino out of the garage and headed in the direction of the Heights. The Lutts lived in one of those newish development-suburbs where all the houses look nice even though they're crammed together on lots you can hardly lie down crosswise on and all the streets (and sometimes even the development) have cute names that don't have anything to do with anything. The Lutts' development was called Sherwood Forest (in this part of the world, of all places), and they lived on Friar Tuck Road in between Little John Street and Maid Marian Lane. As first impressions go, it didn't raise my expectations about Carson and Lillian Lutt, but I suppose with real estate prices being what they are you pretty much have to live wherever you find a house you can afford. If I wasn't mistaken, Sherwood Forest's big selling point was that the houses were less expensive than they looked. That, and a chance to send your junior-high kids to Ensenada Middle School.

I parked in the street, even though that left precious little room for the rest of the traffic, and went up the walk to the Lutts' front door. Paint and trim aside, their place was identical to every fourth house in the development. And they had one chest-high piñon growing out of their front lawn, just like every other family on the block. But you can't tell what's going on inside a house from the outside. When Carson Lutt opened the door, it took me just one second to be sure he was drunk.

He looked me up and down blearily, as if I was some kind of obnoxious consequence of his drinking, then said, "What the hell do you want?" His voice was smeared around the edges in a way that showed he wasn't really very good at drinking. It takes practice—a lot of it to learn how to speak clearly when you're full of the stuff.

Unfortunately, the smell of his breath made me as thirsty as a dog. Besides that I was already in no mood to put up with a belligerent drunk; I had to make a special effort not to sound too hostile myself. "My name is Axbrewder. I'd like to talk to you about your daughter."

"That punk?" he snorted. "What's she done now?"

"Nothing, as far as I know."

"Oh." That seemed to surprise him. For a minute, he forgot he was trying to be angry at me. "Come on in." He waved me into the house and shut the door. "Have a drink."

"No, thanks." The living room looked better than I'd expected. Whoever decorated it had spent enough money to make the atmosphere soothing and the furniture comfortable—but had stopped before the place looked like those nauseating pictures in home decorating magazines. It was the kind of room where you'd expect a quietly successful businessman and his wife to give quiet parties for friends they actually enjoyed. Well, Lillian Lutt was sitting there on the couch quietly enough—but if she'd looked any more miserable you could've stuck her head on a pole and used her to ward off evil spirits. She had a tall glass in her hands—the kind you use for heavy drinking. It took me a couple seconds to pull myself together enough to add, "I'm on the wagon today."

Carson Lutt peered at me. "Did I hear you say no?"

"Offer him a drink, Carson," Lillian Lutt said from the couch. "I hate to drink alone."

"You're not drinking alone," he said. "I'm drinking with you."

"That's nice," she said. She almost smiled.

"Have a drink," he said to me. "I'm serious."

I said, "So am I. I don't want a drink. I want to talk about your daughter."

"What's she done now?" Mrs. Lutt asked. The pain in her face was terrible to look at.

"Nothing," I snapped. The smell of all that alcohol made my nerves jumpy. My control wasn't as good as it should've been. "She's been dead a little too long for that."

That took a minute to sink in. She gave me one straight look as if she was about to scream, then got up and walked out of the room.

"All right, you . . . whatever your name is." All of a sudden, Mr. Lutt's voice was clear and sharp and determined. "Get out of here."

"Tell me about Marisa first."

He didn't even blink. "You're a lot bigger than I am, so I probably can't throw you out, but I'm going to try. And I'm going to keep trying until you"—his voice jumped into a shout—"get the hell out of here!"

I didn't have anything to say to that. I had no intention of fighting him in his condition. So I shrugged, and let myself out the front door. I didn't leave—I just went and sat down on the front porch, and tried to think of a way to handle the situation.

Part of me wanted to go back and accept his offer. I had a feeling he'd tell me everything I wanted to know and more if I just had a few drinks with him—people who aren't used to being drunk are like that. But I wasn't ready to pay that much for the answers to a few questions. Because I knew once I got started I wouldn't stop. On the other hand, all the strain I was under made me want to go back into the house and pound on him for a while.

I was still thinking about that—more wishful than serious—when a kid came up the driveway toward the house. She looked to be about nine or ten—a cute kid with straight blond hair, braces, and one of those loose-jointed tomboy bodies that promises a lot of future development. She stopped in front of me, studied me seriously for a long minute.

Not having any better ideas, I said, "Hi."

"Hi," she said. Then, abruptly, "Are they drunk again?"

That sounded like a dangerous question, and I was leery of it. But the seriousness in her child-face demanded some kind of honest answer. Finally, I said, "I think so."

"Oh, damn." She made *damn* sound as innocent as sunlight. All at once, she dropped herself onto the porch beside me, and put her chin on her knees. "They're going to blame it on me."

"Why would they do that?"

"I'm late. When I'm late, they always use it as an excuse. They say they're worried sick about me." Her sarcasm only underlined the hurt in her voice.

I waited a moment. Then I said, "But you don't think that's the real reason."

"Of course not." This time I heard real bitterness. "I come home late because I know they're going on one of their binges. I stay away as late as I can."

I nodded. "It must be rough."

"Yeah." She stared in front of her as if her whole future was a desert. "They think I'm going to turn out like Marisa."

All of a sudden, the Lutts went *click* in my head, and started to make sense. Now I knew what they were going through—I'd seen a lot of it in the last two days. Your thirteen-year-old daughter suddenly runs away for no reason in the world and when she turns up dead months later you're told she's a junky whore. So who do you blame? It must be your fault—she's a little too young for you to pin it all on her—but to save your soul you can't think what you did wrong. So pretty soon you start to think you did everything wrong. You can't trust yourself anymore—and that means you can't trust anybody. Not even your ten-year-old.

"That's why they drink," I said quietly. "Because of what happened to her."

"Yeah," she assented. "And then that pig-cop came. At first I thought you were him. He was big, too. I didn't hear what he said, but when he was gone Mom was crying and couldn't stop, and Dad looked like he was going to be sick."

I was thinking fast now—and what I came up with disgusted me. I felt rotten just considering it. But I didn't see any other way. After a minute, I said, "My name is Brew."

She looked over at me, made an effort to smile. "I'm Denise."

"Denise," I said carefully, "I'm a private investigator. I'm trying to find a girl who ran away from home—just like Marisa. Right now, it looks like there's a connection—the same thing is going to happen to this girl unless I can find her in time. But I'm not getting anywhere and

I need help. Your parents—well, they're too upset to understand why I need to talk to them."

She was looking at me intensely now. "You can ask me. I know all about it. They didn't want me to hear, but I listened at the door." She was eager to help. Probably her own self-respect wasn't exactly in great shape. She needed to do something—something that had something to do with her situation.

I gave her the best smile I could muster. "There's just one thing I need. After she ran away, Marisa wrote your parents a note. That's where the connection is—in the note. I need it."

For a second while she looked at me, her eyes brightened. Then she jumped up. "I know where it is." Before I could regret what I'd gotten her into, she hurried into the house.

She wasn't gone long. I heard shouts—it sounded like her parents were yelling at her. Then she came back out, and handed me a piece of paper.

A half sheet of good twenty-pound bond, neatly torn along one edge. What the messy handwriting had to say wasn't more than three words different from Alathea's note. By this time I was good at recognizing the watermark.

I got to my feet. Talking fast so I could finish before Mr. or Mrs. Lutt came out after Denise. "Now, listen. When your parents are sober, I want you to tell them about me. Tell them Marisa didn't run away. She was kidnapped. I don't know how or why—but I'm going to find out. I'm going to nail whoever did it. Your parents don't have any reason to hate themselves. And they don't have any reason to be worried about you."

If Ginny had been there, she would've been trying to stop me during that whole speech. I didn't have any business making promises like that, and I knew it. But I felt dirty about the way I'd used Denise—gotten her in trouble with her parents when she already had more than she could handle. I had to give her something in return.

If it turned out I couldn't keep my promises, I could always go back on the stuff. One shame more or less wouldn't make any difference. Alcohol doesn't care about details like that.

Chapter Ten

Rush hour traffic slowed me down, so by the time I'd returned my rented Torino and walked back down Cuevero to my apartment it was definitely time for some supper. I didn't feel much like cooking for myself, but in my neighborhood there aren't any restaurants that don't have bars attached, so I didn't have much choice. I fixed whatever was left in the refrigerator—which wasn't much —and ate as much of it as I could stand. After that, I called Ginny's service and left a message telling her everything I knew. Then I spent about an hour cleaning my apartment. Which is something I do whenever I'm feeling particularly grimy inside—and trying not to think about it. You'd be surprised how much cleaning you can do in a one-room efficiency apartment if you really put your mind to it.

By then it was dark outside. But not dark enough to suit me. Looking for chores to pass the time, I stripped the .45 and cleaned it. It didn't need much—in the past few years, I've probably cleaned the damn thing three times for every shot I've fired. But that's another job that can take a while if you go into it with the right attitude. After that, I took a long shower.

The night still felt too early, but I'd done all the waiting I could stomach. I got dressed, loaded the .45 and stuffed it into my shoulder holster, and went out.

Looking for Manolo, the information dealer.

I'd spent the whole day doing what Ginny wanted me to do. Now I wanted to check out an idea of my own.

Manolo was the man who could help me.

By this time most of the traffic had died out on Eighth Street. I could smell the alleys as I walked past them, and hear the jukeboxes in the bars. Women shouted at their children, husbands, loan sharks. Young studs swaggered in the road, catcalling at every girl they saw. Grizzled Indians, Chicanos, Mestizos, looking patriarchal, tried their best to walk in straight lines. Couples stood and necked in doorways and around corners. I didn't pass five Anglos between Cuevero and the center of the old city, where Paseo Grande would've continued on if it hadn't turned into a pitiful narrow thoroughfare called Coal Street. For the first time today, I felt like I knew what I was doing. Things can happen at night.

Not that what I was doing promised to be easy. Old Manolo was a man of regular habits—and he made it his regular habit to be wherever the listening was good. Which on any given night could be any one of twenty different places. Sometimes he seemed to be everywhere and nowhere—and you had to know the history and fate of every bottle of anisette in the city to find him. Not a very reassuring prospect, but I didn't see any way around it.

I was just trying to decide where to start when I got lucky. A kid came running toward me down the sidewalk, and I recognized him before he got to me. His name was Pablo, and I knew him because I'd met his whole family once two years before when Ginny and I had been working on a protection-racket case. He was in a hurry, and there was a strange bulge under his shirt—a packet of some kind tucked into the front of his pants. Which told me he was probably running for some kind of numbers racket.

I suppose you could say that's a relatively harmless way for a kid to hustle a few bucks. He was a messenger boy, that's all. And anyway it was none of my business. I caught his arm as he went past, and swung him to a stop. *"Hola,* Pablo. There is no dignity in such haste," I said in Spanish.

"I must run, señor." He didn't even look at me. He was trying to break my grip without making too big a deal out of it—he was probably afraid of attracting attention. "If I go and come swiftly, I will be given a dollar."

"A man does not run to do the bidding of those who are themselves not men enough to do their own running." Stern Uncle Axbrewder. If Ginny'd heard me, she would've had real trouble keeping a straight face.

Now he looked at me. *"Ay,* Señor Axbrewder?"

"It is I myself, Pablo."

Then he put on a whine. "Señor Axbrewder, my arm is being broken."

"An arm will mend, Pablo. When it is the self-esteem which is broken, mending is not done easily."

"Yes, señor. For why have I been stopped?"

Well, I could see I wasn't getting through to him. I got

down off my high horse. "I wish to have speech with old Manolo the drinker of anisette. Where is he to be found?"

"God knows, señor."

"That is very true. But a cunning boy like Pablo has surely taken thought on the matter."

He twisted against me for another moment. Then he gave up. "It is possible that he takes his anisette in the place of Juan Cideño."

I said, *"Gracias,* Pablo," and let him go.

He stared at me for a moment as if I was as crazy as all Anglos. Then he turned and started running again.

Like I said—lucky. Juan Cideño's bar wasn't more than a block from where I stood.

On the inside, it wasn't much different than the Hegira. Its major distinction was a life-sized poster of Raul Ramirez on the wall opposite the bar. The poster wasn't old, but stale air and smoke had stained it until Ramirez seemed like a champion from another generation.

Old Manolo was sitting in a booth at the back.

His eyes were closed—he looked sound asleep. Even knowing him the way I did, I half expected him to topple slowly to the floor and start snoring. But there was a small glass of anisette sitting on the table between his hands, and after a few seconds he picked it up delicately with his fingertips, tucked it under his gray walrus moustache, and took a sip. Then he set the glass down, swallowed, and went back to looking like he was asleep.

I glanced around the bar, just making sure there wasn't anybody nearby who might be offended if he happened to overhear me (none of el Señor's men, for example, would take kindly to the questions I wanted to ask). Then I went over to the barkeep. Old Manolo is like an oracle —there are ceremonies you have to perform if you want to get anything out of him. I got a bottle of anisette and took it with me over to his booth. Hoping he wouldn't try to make me drink it with him. Wondering what I was going to say.

He spared me the effort of finding an opening line. When I arrived at his booth, he said without opening his eyes, *"Hola,* Señor Axbrewder. Have you come to sit with an old man and tell him interesting tales? That would be very welcome."

His English was distinct. But I answered in Spanish. *"Hola,* Manuel Sevilla y Acclara de los Maestos." Speak-

ing Spanish with him was one of the ceremonies—like
knowing his proper name (or part of it, anyway). "Alas,
all my tales are poor things in comparison to your own
legendary knowledge." I was trying to figure out how he'd
known who I was without opening his eyes. "Yet I would
sit with you, and share speech, if I am not an intrusion."

He nodded as if he knew exactly what I had in mind.
"You bear with you a thing more precious than many
tales. Please to sit."

Huh? I said to myself. But then I figured it out. He was
talking about the bottle. He must've heard me buy it, and
recognized my voice. I kept forgetting just how good he
was at picking up on everything around him.

I said, *"Gracias,"* slid into the booth. Then I un-
screwed the cap of the bottle and refilled his glass. He
nodded again, smiling faintly under his moustache. But a
moment later his eyes opened and he looked at me with
an air of mild surprise. His eyeballs were a muddy color,
as if they'd been stained by all the secrets—some of them
pretty ugly—he carried around inside his head. "You do
not accompany me, señor?" he asked. When I didn't answer right away, he went on, "Perhaps tequila would be
of more pleasure to you. Not all are equally enamored
with anisette."

He was being perfectly magnanimous. But his gracious-
ness cut both ways. He was offering me a chance to get
out of being rude—and warning me I'd better take him
up on it.

"Unhappily, I must decline," I said carefully. "I am
like other Anglos—drink plays upon my wits discourte-
ously." That was like admitting a failure of manhood, but
I didn't have any choice. "The matter before me is urgent.
I must practice great sobriety if I am to speak clearly,
and to hear what is said to me without confusion." I
shrugged as eloquently as I could.

Old Manolo considered for some time. But he didn't
close his eyes. Finally, he made up his mind. "It is said of
you, Señor Axbrewder, that you suffer an infirmity of the
heart, arising from the greatly-to-be-regretted death of
your brother. Such things must be understood and accepted." Solemnly, he took a sip of his anisette.

Deep inside me, I gave a sigh of relief. He wasn't offended. The oracle was still open.

I didn't say anything—I knew better than that.

He didn't keep me waiting long. He scanned my face for a moment, then said, "You spoke of urgency. Is it permitted to inquire concerning this matter?"

"Señor Sevilla, the young daughter of my brother's widow has gone from her home."

"Ah," he said politely. "That is to be regretted. But many girls both young and old have gone from their homes, señor. The world has become corrupt in every place. Girls no longer honor their homes—nor the wishes of their parents. What can be done? The world pays no heed to the sorrow of parents."

"That is very true. But I have cause for thought that the corruption does not lie in this widow's daughter. Hear what I have learned in seeking her." Speaking formally, carefully, I told him about the seven dead girls. I described the connection between them and Alathea. When I was finished, I said, "Such evil does not befall so many young girls by chance. It is deliberately done. It is my thought that for each the corruption comes from a single source—from one supplier of drugs. I must find that one supplier if I am to save my dead brother's child."

Old Manolo had closed his eyes while I was speaking. Now he was silent for a long time. I didn't rush him. Information-dealing is a touchy profession. He was alive after all these years because he was cautious and selective. But by the time he decided to speak my knuckles were white from clutching the edge of the table.

"Señor," he said softly, not opening his eyes, "I think perhaps you have made the acquaintance of my son's wife's father's sister's daughter. You were not introduced properly—so few things are now done properly in the world—but her name will be known to you. She is Theresa Maria Sanguillan y Garcia."

He paused, and I said, "I have been given the honor of knowing her name."

"Then you will understand that I wish to assist you."

"I believe it." His family was in my debt. That meant something to him.

"Unhappily, I can offer you nothing. Indeed, the fate of these young girls has been known to me. But the supplier—he who works this evil—that one is not known."

I was trembling. "Señor Sevilla, it is said that no grain or gram of heroin passes from hand to hand in Puerta del Sol without your knowledge. In the matter of drugs, it is said that all tales come to your ears."

"I hear much," old Manolo assented. "No man hears all."

"Can it be that el Señor has such evil dealings, and there is no talk of them? Or that men talk of the dealings of el Señor, and you do not hear?"

At that, he opened his eyes. I half expected him to be offended, but he wasn't. There was nothing in his gaze but sadness. "Señor Axbrewder, the knowledge you seek is dark and mysterious. I can shed no light upon it. But I ask you to believe that no hint of this knowledge has touched my ears. That in itself is knowledge for you, is it not?"

When I didn't answer, he went on, "I will speak further. There are many drugs, and much passing among hands. But in the matter of heroin, all passing begins in the hands of el Señor. That is his pride, and the source of his great wealth. I do not speak this to mislead you. El Señor is a man of honor, placing great value upon his family, and his children, and the purity of his daughters. Such corrupting of young girls is a terrible evil, and he would in no way permit it."

"These girls are Anglo," I said. "Does el Señor's honor extend itself to Anglos?"

"In truth it does. He has no love for Anglos—that cannot be denied. But I speak absolutely. This corrupting of young girls does not come through him."

Well, probably that wasn't the whole story. If the bastard I was after was cutting into el Señor's profits, el Señor would've slapped him down long ago. So I could assume those profits weren't in any danger. Which fit with what old Manolo was saying. Apparently, Alathea's kidnapper was making his own clientele out of people el Señor didn't want. But that didn't help me any. I was still stuck. I couldn't keep the bitterness out of my voice as I said, "El Señor controls all heroin in Puerta del Sol—and yet he does not supply these girls. Still they die from heroin. What, then, can I do? My brother's widow's daughter will surely die also."

Manolo poured himself another drink, then recapped the bottle and stuck it in the pocket of his coat. He emptied his glass, and got to his feet. My audience was over—he was going somewhere else. But before he left, he bent close to me and whispered so nobody in the bar could overhear him, "Possibly you must go to el Señor himself. If you wish to have speech with him, you must know his name. It is Hector Jesus Fria de la Sancha." A minute later he was gone.

I stayed where I was. Go to el Señor for help. Sure. That sounded like a polite way of telling me to go to hell. El Señor was what the newspapers probably would've called "the crime-czar of Puerta del Sol"—if they'd known of his existence. A man of honor. Oh, absolutely. He would chew me up into little pieces and spit me in the gutter. No, thanks. I wasn't that desperate. Not yet.

So I didn't go looking for el Señor, even though I knew where to find him.

I left the bar and started for home. Feeling like shit. Because I'd failed Alathea. I'd played the only hand I had, and lost. Now the only thing left was to be Ginny's errand boy while she tried to crack this case her own way. It must've showed in the way I walked, because this time the *muchachos* felt free to notice me, which they don't usually do, even when I'm drunk. Most of the time I'm a little too big for them. Not tonight. They weren't exactly aggressive about it, but they whistled at me from across the street and muttered obscure Spanish insults at my back when I went past. The whole community seemed to know I hadn't been able to get what I needed out of old Manolo.

When you're in that kind of mood, it's hard to stay away from the stuff. Alcohol is the only magic in the world. When you're working, you're trying to change things around you so you fit into them better. But when you're drinking, the fit comes from inside. And if it isn't real, at least it's easier than batting your head against the wall trying to figure out puzzles when nobody'll tell you the secret. So on my way home that night I had a tough time staying out of the bars.

But I did stay out of them—for Alathea. Because the one thing alcohol would never do was help me find her. Until she was found, being Ginny's errand boy was better than nothing, and it was probably about all I was good for.

I ignored the bars. I ignored the *muchachos* and their

insults. I just lumbered my way up Eighth Street in the direction of home.

There was a long black Buick parked at the corner of a side street just on this side of my apartment building. All the lights were off, but the motor was running softly. I could see three men sitting inside.

Just when I got abreast of the car, its doors thunked open, and the three men got out. They were wearing neat businessmen's suits, with crisp businessmen's hats pulled down tight on their heads. At that time of night in that neighborhood, they might as well have worn sandwich boards saying, "Plainclothes Cops." They were all big, and the biggest one was a chunky individual a couple inches shorter than I am and maybe thirty pounds heavier. He said, "Axbrewder," in the kind of voice you'd expect if you taught a bulldozer to talk.

The two clowns with him stayed back and didn't say anything—and the light was bad, so there was a chance I might not recognize them if I saw them again. But the goon with the diesel voice I got a good look at. He had a jaw you could use to set rivets, a nose that could have moonlighted as a bottle opener, and a forehead that looked like it was made out of reinforced concrete. He flashed his badge at me (it looked like a badge—in that light, I wasn't sure) and said, "Detective-Lieutenant Acton."

But he wasn't trying to introduce himself, or even prove he was a cop. He was just trying to get close to me. As he started to put the badge away, his other hand came up to my chest and shoved.

I wasn't braced for it, and it wasn't exactly a gesture of undying friendship. He got his weight into it. It sent me backward, smacked me hard against the wall of the building.

I was already bouncing back at him when I saw that the two clowns behind him had their guns out. Acton was grinning like the blade of a plow, and suddenly in my mind I saw him writing his report: "Shot while resisting arrest."

I stopped with a jerk.

"Detective-Lieutenant Acton," I said, trying not to show how much breath he'd knocked out of me. "What a pleasant surprise. I've been wanting to talk to you."

"Is that a fact?" His hand came up again, but this time he just poked me with one finger. Trying to jab me in the solar plexus. Which is a nice way to hurt somebody when you don't want to leave any marks. "Well, I want to talk to you, too"—he poked again—"Mick."

Mick. Instantly, there was a wind blowing inside my head, and my balance shifted. Nobody calls me Mick. Nobody. Not since my brother died. The night seemed to congeal at Acton's back, and I lost sight of the two cops with the guns. My chest was so full of rage pressure it felt like my ribs were going to cramp.

"What's the matter, Mick?" Poke. "Don't you like being called 'Mick'?" Poke. Any second now, he was going to rupture something, and then I was going to take his face off with my bare hands.

But then the two other cops returned to my vision. They had guns. If I touched Acton, the best thing I could hope for was to still be in one piece when they threw me in jail. Ordinarily I wouldn't have cared much about being locked up, but if it happened now I couldn't help find Alathea. Right this minute, she was probably somewhere in the city prostituting herself to get money for drugs. If we didn't find her, she was going to end up dead.

Just holding that rage in hurt so bad I thought I was going to pass out. But I stood there. Let Acton do whatever he had in mind.

He must've seen me make the decision, because he eased off with his finger. "That's nice, Mick. That's a good boy. Swallow your pride. A drunk like you should be used to it by now."

I didn't say anything.

"Give me the notes, Mick."

The notes! That surprised me. Who the fuck told him about the notes? But I was already clenched, and I didn't show anything. I said, "I don't have them." Through my teeth. If I'd opened my jaws, I wouldn't have been able to hold my rage in anymore.

"Where are they, Mick?"

"The safe. Fistoulari Investigations."

"Ah, that's too bad." He never stopped grinning. "That means I'll have to get a warrant. What a shame. It's a good thing you're a liar, Mick."

I couldn't do anything about it—I had to stand there

while he searched me. When he found the notes, he glanced through them, counted them, then stuffed them into his coat pocket.

"Now, Mick." I wasn't looking at him anymore. I was staring into the darkness past his shoulder. That grin of his was going to give me nightmares. "I'm going to let you have a little friendly advice. Get off my case. Stay off it. I hate your guts, Mick, and if you get in my way I'll slap you down so hard you'll have to reach up to touch bottom."

Staring into the darkness was a good way to watch his shoulder muscles. If he was going to hit me again, I wanted to know about it. "Why?"

He laughed, but it wasn't because there was anything funny. "Dick Axbrewder was a good cop. He was also a friend of mine."

I shrugged. What else could I do? "How did you know about the notes?"

He stepped closer—I almost flinched. But he didn't hit me. His tone was soft and bitter as he said, "That bastard Stretto lit a fire under the commissioner. Now he wants my hide. I'm in trouble, just because I didn't make the connection with those notes. Now I'm warning you. This is the last time a punk drunk like you is going to make me look bad."

"I don't have to," I said. "Why did you scare the Christies like that?"

That did it. His shoulder bunched and he swung at me hard. I blocked it as best I could and managed to keep him away from my solar plexus. But his stiff fingers still dug deep into my gut.

I hunched over, staggered back to get out of the way of another hit. But he didn't swing again. He and his goons got back into their car and drove off, roaring the engine and squealing the tires—probably trying to convince me they meant business.

For a couple minutes, I stayed where I was, almost retching. Then I went the rest of the way to Cuevero Road, and struggled up the stairs to my apartment.

I felt a lot sicker than just one jab in the stomach. But there was no way around it—I had to face Ginny. So while I was still mad enough to make decisions, I yanked up the phone and called her service. She was at home, and they patched me through.

"Brew," she said. "What's happening?"

"I just had a little run-in with Detective-Lieutenant Acton. He took the notes." It was my fault—any half-assed idiot could have told me to take better care of the evidence—but I was too sick about it to apologize.

My voice must've told her most of what she needed to know, so she didn't ask me how it happened or how I could've been so stupid. She asked, "Are you all right?"

"I'm not in jail."

"Thank God for small blessings." She managed to make her tone just right for my mood. After a couple seconds, she asked, "How did he even find out about them?"

"Stretto. Acton said Stretto went to the commissioner. Apparently Stretto doesn't think the cops are doing their job."

"Surprise, surprise," Ginny muttered. "But I wasn't sure the illustrious Mr. Stretto had that much in him."

"Anyway"—I gritted my teeth, and said it—"I've pretty well blown it. Now we've got nothing."

"He's a cop," she snapped. "What could you do—eat the damn things?"

"I shouldn't have been carrying them around."

She dismissed that without hesitation. "Forget about it. That's my fault as much as yours. They were safe enough, we just didn't know Acton was going to get desperate. Anyway," she went on before I could object, "we don't need them now."

I said, "Huh?" I've always been a brilliant conversationalist.

"Acton won't destroy them. Too many people know about them. And I've already got what I need out of them."

"Which is what?"

"Brew, I finished checking out the other schools." My head must've been clearing—I finally started to hear the vibration of excitement in her voice. "I'll spare you the details—the point is that everything fits. Every one of these nine girls disappeared from school at a time when they were scheduled to be alone."

"You already knew that. It's in the school board files."

"Exactly!"

"Exactly what? It still doesn't prove anything. Why call attention to yourself running away when you've got a perfect chance to sneak off every day of the week?"

"Well, that's true, of course—if you look at it that way. Let me ask you a different question, Brew. Is there any proof in those notes—proof that the girls didn't write them, or wrote them under duress? I'm talking about hard evidence—the kind that stands up in court."

I thought about it for a long time. Then I said, "No."

"Damn right. As far as we know, they were all addressed correctly. But that's minor. The main thing is that all the notes were addressed to the right parents."

I said, "Huh?" again. It was getting to be a habit.

"Marisa Lutt wrote, 'Dear Mom and Dad.' So did Esther Hannibal. So did Ruth Ann Larsen. And May-Belle Podhorentz, and Dottie Ann Consciewitz, and Carol Christie. We don't know about Rosalynn Swift. But Alathea wrote, 'Dear Mom.' Mittie wrote, 'Dear Dad.' "

I saw what she was getting at, but it still didn't mean anything to me. "So what? Most kids know how many parents they have. If they've only got one, they can usually tell if it's male or female."

"Of course! That's the point!" She was hot on a trail I couldn't see. "Just look at it from the other side. We know those notes are wrong. We have good reason to believe they were all dictated by the same person. Well, nine girls who live in nine different neighborhoods and go to six different schools aren't going to end up having the same person dictate their notes by accident. So what does that tell you?"

"Kidnapping." I grated. I already knew that.

"Right! But if that's true, then the girls didn't run away at all. So it isn't a question of figuring out why the girls ran away while they were alone. The question is, how did the kidnapper know they were going to be alone? How did he know they were going to be somewhere that he could get at them without being seen? For that matter, how did he know he could get them to come with him? And how did he know their addresses? How did he know how many parents they had?"

I said, "Research?" Feeling like an idiot.

"Now you're beginning to get it. Tell me, Brew. If you wanted to research nine different girls in six different schools, and find out the answers to all these questions, where would you go?"

That was it. Finally I understood. "The school board. The files." She was right—I could feel it. The bastard we were looking for was getting his information from those files. It was the only answer that made sense.

Maybe he was even on the school board.

PART III
Thursday Night/Friday

Chapter Eleven

Of course, it all rested on the assumption the girls were being kidnapped. But that was fine with me. I was willing to make that assumption. The only problem with it was there didn't seem to be any payoff. No ransom demands. And anyway, half the families involved couldn't have scraped up a self-respecting amount of ransom to save their souls.

Which brought me back to drugs. Some pusher in town was hot for new business—a very particular kind of new business.

Some pusher old Manolo'd never heard of.

I didn't say anything to Ginny about that. I said, "That's going to be a hell of a job. How many people are in the school board these days—twenty?"

She said, "Fifteen."

"And then there are all those secretaries. And on top of that, maybe some people from the individual schools have access to the general files. You're talking about maybe thirty suspects. Where do we start?"

"By whittling down the list."

I said, "Oh." Heavy on the sarcasm. Maybe all this was making me feel a little better about Alathea—we were finally getting somewhere—but it didn't do much for my opinion of myself. "That shouldn't be too hard. We'll just call people up and ask them how they feel about stuffing dope down thirteen-year-old girls."

"So we're going to have to work at it," she said evenly. "Where did you get the idea it was supposed to be easy?" When I didn't answer, she went on, "There's a lot we can do, but to save time we'll start with the obvious—the full-time people. Stretto, Scurvey, Greenling, and the secretaries."

I couldn't argue with her, so I asked, "What about Acton?"

"I'm going to check on him tonight. Find out if he was lying about the commissioner. If he was telling you the truth, we'll have to assume he's in the clear—and Stretto, too, for that matter. Until we know more, anyway."

I couldn't argue with that, either. If Stretto was involved, he wouldn't have called the commissioner. As for Acton—if he was dealing drugs, he was in a real bind. As long as the commissioner knew about those notes, Acton wouldn't dare destroy them. *If* the commissioner knew. After chewing it around for a minute, I asked, "What do you want me to do?"

"Get some sleep," she said promptly. "At this point, there's nothing more we can do until morning. Get a cab and come to the office tomorrow early. By then I'll have something set up."

After that, it was too late to argue; I didn't have anything else to offer. It was her case now. When she hung up, I went to bed.

I went right to sleep (being sober makes you more tired than you'd expect), but I spent the whole night dreaming about amber, and the next morning I was up with the birds. My face ached, as if I'd been grinding my teeth for hours. But I ignored it, ignored the feeling of stupidity that filled the inside of my head, ignored the dry wish for alcohol in my mouth. Someday I was going to have to find a way to be proud of being sober, but right then I wasn't up to it. By eight o'clock I was out on Cuevero Road looking for a cab.

It wasn't a good time of day for cabs, but I finally found one. Then it wasn't long until I was riding up the elevator of the Murchison Building to Ginny's office.

She was there already and when I went into her back room, I found her on the phone. I dropped into a chair. Whoever she was talking to, it didn't take her long; when she hung up a couple minutes later, we had an appointment with somebody or other for nine-thirty.

"That was Dr. Sandoval," she said. "Camilla Sandoval, pediatrician. How long has it been since you voted?"

I shrugged. How can you answer a question like that?

"Well, you probably don't know that she represents your

district on the Board of Education. This is her fifth term
—she's very popular. One of the part-time members."
She looked at me sharply, as if she expected me to be surprised. "Sergeant Encino speaks highly of her."

If she wanted a reaction out of me, she was going to
be disappointed. We errand boys try to keep our opinions to ourselves. Especially when we're ashamed of our
own bitterness. I got out a penknife, and pretended to
clean my fingernails, letting her hang for a moment before I asked, "What else did he have to say?"

She frowned—but she didn't look serious about it. I
don't think I was fooling her any. "Not much about Dr.
Sandoval. But he told me a little something about Acton
and the commissioner. Apparently, Acton was giving it to
you straight. Encino wasn't there, but when the commissioner personally goes to see a lieutenant instead of
sending for him, and chews him out in front of half the
duty room, word gets around pretty fast. Stretto called
the commissioner, all right. We can count on it."

"Politicians," I muttered, mostly to myself. They know
how to talk to each other. If I'd gone to the commissioner
with those notes myself, I would've gotten in trouble for
"obstructing an official investigation." Paul M. Stretto
makes one phone call, and all of a sudden the air's full of
shit. "So scratch the chairman of the board. Put Acton on
the back burner. What's next?"

Ginny frowned again. This time she meant it. "We've
got a lot of ground to cover, and everything we do takes
time. I can't find Tred, so I bit the bullet and hired some
help—I called fat-ass Smithsonian."

All things considered, that probably shouldn't have surprised me. We had between ten and thirty suspects lined
up, and every day that went by put Alathea in that much
more trouble. But Ginny is an independent cuss and she
doesn't like farming out work to other agencies. And of
all the private investigators we know, Lawrence Smithsonian is the one she actively hates. He isn't all that fat,
but he as sure as hell *looks* fat—probably because his
fees are so overweight. And on top of that, his way of
condescending to Ginny ("Private investigating is a man's
job.") sends her blood pressure through the roof. Hiring
his help was probably costing her a pound of flesh. I had
to stare at her for a while before I recovered my brains
enough to ask, "Why him?"

"Because he knows money." She was practically spitting. "He can learn more in one morning about the personal finances of the people on our list than we could in a week. He's going to start with the full-time board members and the secretaries—try to find out if any of them are getting rich in private, or living on a lot more than what they get paid, or gambling with money they haven't earned, or rolling too high on the stock market—anything. He's got half the bank presidents in this town in his back pocket. I think he blackmails them."

After a minute, I said, "Lona can't pay you."

"I know that." She wasn't thinking about money. She was still steaming about Smithsonian.

"I can't either."

That made her look at me. "Who asked you?"

I got up, went over to her. Cupped her head with both my hands and kissed her on the mouth.

She didn't kiss me back. She just sat there and took it. When I stopped, she looked at me like the barrel of a gun and said, "The next time you do that, you better mean it."

Well, I meant it all right—my shoulders were trembling and my pulse was beating in my head so loud I could hardly hear her. But that wasn't what she was getting at. What she had in mind was something even more serious than the way I felt about her. We'd been through it before. She wanted me to quit drinking. Completely. Forever.

That was something I couldn't do. I wasn't worth it.

I went back to my chair and sat down—trying to hold myself so she couldn't see me shake. When I thought I could control my voice, I asked, "When is he going to call back?"

"When he finds something. Or this afternoon. Whichever comes first."

"And in the meantime?"

"We'll go talk to Dr. Sandoval. Then we'll go back to the school board and see what we can run down this time." Her composure was too perfect. I'd confused her and probably hurt her—which was something I had definitely not meant to do. While she got herself ready to leave, I spent a few minutes trying to think of a new way to curse myself.

She was still holding up her wall of businesslike professionalism as we rode the elevator down to the garage and took the Olds out into the morning glare. But after that she unbent enough to tell me what her plans were. They sounded reasonable, and if they worked, we could probably cross half the people off our list today. I let it go at that. I'd already pushed my luck too far with her.

The office of Dr. Camilla Sandoval was on the opposite side of the old part of town from where I lived. It was in a squat dull-red adobe structure that looked like it might have moonlighted as a bordello. Already the waiting room was full of mothers with babies in various stages of either stupor or hysteria. Most of them were either Chicano or Indian, and all together they gave a pretty good capsule summary of what life was like in the old part of Puerta del Sol. After half an hour in that room, Ginny and I had seen every degree of squalor, sickness, flamboyance, passivity, color, resentment, joy, hunger, love, and rage. A real education, if you can stand to hear babies squall— and see mothers hit them.

When Ginny told the nurse we had an appointment for nine-thirty, she just shrugged and gestured at all the people who were there ahead of us. It looked like it was going to be a long wait, and I didn't see any way around it. In this part of the world, the Anglos have spent the past hundred fifty years or so barging in line ahead of Chicanos and Indians and I didn't want to see any more resentment in those faces than was there already. But in situations like this Ginny has a thicker skin than I do. She stood it for that first half hour, then she dug some paper and a pen out of her purse, wrote a long note, and gave it to the nurse. Her way of asking the nurse to take it to the doctor didn't leave the woman much choice. Three minutes later, Dr. Sandoval called us in to see her.

She was a chunky little woman who looked like she'd been born too small to be a football player and too big to be a fireplug. If she was married, she didn't advertise it by wearing a ring. In fact, she didn't wear any jewelry at all. Her manner was tough, but it was a particular kind of tough—the kind that can look pain straight in the face and make it hurt less without being hurt herself (or without showing it, anyway). By the time she asked Ginny and me to have a seat in the square cubicle she used for an office, I liked her.

She sat down behind her desk and studied us for a second. Then she picked up Ginny's note and slapped it with the back of her hand. "Nine junky whores," she said, "thirteen or younger. Seven of them dead. What do you want from me? Do you think they were my patients?"

"Dr. Sandoval"—Ginny matched her tone evenly—"we're private investigators." She flipped the photostat of her license onto the desk. "We've been hired to find the two girls who are still alive. I don't think you know anything about them. That's why we want to talk to you. We want to ask you some questions about the people you work with on the Board of Education."

That was confusing enough to short-circuit some of Dr. Sandoval's hostility. She didn't exactly retreat, but she eased back a bit. "I don't understand."

"I know it's complicated," Ginny said, "and I can't tell you very much without violating the confidence of my clients. But I can tell you this. We have reason to believe these girls were kidnapped. We have also reason to believe that the kidnapper has some kind of connection with the school board. We'd like you to give us background information about some of the people who work there."

Now the first surprise was over. Dr. Sandoval was starting to fume. "This is insane. Do you understand what you're saying? Perhaps you don't know what the school board does. It exists to help children—to provide them with an education. Not all the members are idealists, of course, but they all believe in education. We all believe in children. What you suggest is inconceivable."

Ginny didn't falter. "Criminals come in all disguises, Dr. Sandoval."

"I repeat. It is inconceivable."

"Then you believe Paul Stretto is pure as the driven snow?"

The doctor hesitated. Not a long hesitation but nevertheless a hesitation, and when it was over she answered the question with a question. "If you're right," she asked, "why aren't the police involved in this?"

"Dr. Sandoval," Ginny drawled, "it wouldn't surprise me a bit if you have cops on your doorstep before the day's over. They're involved, all right. The only difference is that they're trying to catch a pusher. We're trying to find two little girls."

"I see." She scanned both of us, and after a minute she looked like she really did see. "I have patients waiting. Please be as quick as you can."

Ginny's gaze didn't shift an inch. "Paul Stretto?"

"Mr. Stretto is a politician. I doubt that he has so much as glanced at a textbook since fifth grade. He is on his way to an exalted career as a public servant." Her mouth twisted sourly around the words. "I can't believe that he would risk his future by involving himself in kidnapping."

"Maybe he has friends who just ask him for information."

"How would I know that?"

"Have you heard any rumors?"

"The rumor," Dr. Sandoval said, "is that Paul Stretto wants to be president. Of the United States."

"All right," Ginny said. "How about Astin Greenling?"

"That man is the salt of the earth." No hesitation at all. "His life has been very unhappy, but he burns himself out every day struggling to provide the children of this city with a decent education. Every year when the levies are voted down, the budget cuts always come out of curriculum. He'll have heart failure some day if he doesn't stop trying to raise the quality of education with less money every year."

"You say unhappy? In what way?"

"His wife has leukemia." Dr. Sandoval's tone made it clear she didn't intend to say anything more than that about Astin Greenling's unhappy life.

Ginny nodded. She was thinking the same thing I was. Treating leukemia costs money. Reams of money. But she didn't say anything about it; money was Smithsonian's job. Instead, she went on down the list. "What can you tell us about Martha Scurvey?"

The doctor frowned, took a moment to decide on an answer. Then she said, "I don't like her personally. But since she was elected budget vice-chairman last year, our accounting procedures have started to climb out of the Dark Ages. And she seems to have a talent for procurement—she gets lower prices for our supplies. I have to respect that—and it takes a little pressure off Astin."

"How long has she served on the board?"

"Just a year." Dr. Sandoval was sardonic. "For some reason, a lot of people don't seem to know that the full-time members of the Board of Education are elected by the city at large. As far as I know, she's never been elected for anything before."

I sighed to myself, and mentally crossed Martha Scurvey off the list. She hadn't been on the board when the first four girls disappeared. Ginny went right on, not wasting the doctor's time. "And Julian Kirke?"

"Him we hired—he wasn't elected at all. The board decided to get into this business of computerizing the files—which, incidentally, I've been fighting every step of the way. It's expensive, and I think the money should be spent on the children. But quality education doesn't have as much prestige as computers. Machines have more dignity than human beings." I was liking her more and more all the time. "But that's beside the point. When I was out-voted, the board started looking for someone who could handle the nuts and bolts of this grand system. After a few months, they found Julian. He is a data-management expert and had a good job with NCR, but they weren't promoting him fast enough to keep him happy. I think he's got some kind of power fetish, but that doesn't keep him from doing a good job. The fact is, he's making this whole thing less expensive than I thought it was going to be."

"How long ago did you hire him?"

"Two and a half—maybe three years."

"All right, Doctor," Ginny said briskly. "Just a couple more questions. How much do you know about the secretaries who work under Mr. Kirke?"

"Very little. That's his department, and it doesn't have much to do with me. I get the impression he's pretty hard on them—for that matter, he's barely civil to me—but they do good work. At least our correspondence looks professional now. Finally."

I wanted to think about that for a while. At the moment, I didn't know whether Kirke was a perfectionist or just a cantankerous sonofabitch. But it was going to have to wait. Ginny was asking, "How many people have access to those files?"

"In theory, everybody in the school system. They aren't supposed to be secret—they're supposed to help the schools run better. But things haven't reached that point yet. In practice, it's probably just the people who work there full-time. When the rest of us want to know something, we ask Julian or one of the secretaries."

Ginny glanced at me, looking for more questions. But I didn't have any. This was her type of investigation, not mine. If it'd been up to me, I would've told Dr. Sandoval exactly what we were looking for and asked her for some kind of intuitive answer. Her intuitions I would've trusted. So I shook my head. Ginny got to her feet and started thanking the doctor.

For a woman who didn't seem like she was rushing us, Dr. Sandoval got us out of there in a hurry. About a minute after we stood up, we were past the resentment of all those mothers and into the Olds. By then, the doctor was probably examining her next patient.

I pushed my sunglasses onto my face, but they didn't help much. While Ginny started up the Olds, I muttered at her, "That was fun. What did we get out of it?"

She jerked around to me. "That's a cheap shot."

I looked away—I couldn't face her. "I know. I just said it because I'm feeling useless. It's my niece we're trying to find—and you're spending money like it was water and working your tail off and my contribution is nil."

"Stop feeling sorry for yourself," she snapped. "What we got out of it is that now when we go to talk to these people we'll know something about who we're talking to."

"Will that help?" Trying to sound neutral.

"Damn right! It'll help us put some pressure on. Maybe we can get our kidnapper to make a mistake."

I couldn't argue with that. It was something to do. It might even work. So I just sat there while Ginny stamped down on the accelerator and took the Olds squealing out of Dr. Sandoval's parking lot onto the highway.

Chapter Twelve

I knew that Ginny and I were headed for a showdown—which I wasn't looking forward to, because it was a guaranteed no-win situation for me. In this day and age, there's no way to talk about shame and guilt without making it sound like self-pity. That's why people who have any integrity keep their goddamn mouths shut. A nice trick—if you can do it.

But the fireworks weren't going to start yet. We didn't

have time for them—we were working. On our way back to big Central High and the school board to take a crack at one of Ginny's plans.

When we got close to the school, we started hunting for a phone booth. Ginny's idea was to begin with Kirke. She didn't have anything particular against him—she just wanted to take advantage of the way he treated his secretaries. I had to admit it was a good idea. If he felt the pressure, it might shake him up a bit. And if he didn't, he might pass that pressure on to somebody who did.

When we found a phone, Ginny said, "I'll give you ten minutes."

"Should be enough. How long can you keep him?"

She got out of the Olds, and I slid over into the driver's seat. "I'll try for half an hour," she said, "but I can't guarantee it."

I put the car in gear. "That's OK. If he catches me, it'll just make somebody more nervous."

She said, "Right," and I drove off.

I parked in the Central High lot, and went into the building. Ten minutes didn't turn out to be too much time. It was between class breaks, and the halls were full of kids, half of them seemed to be trying to run into me. On top of that, with all the kids coming and going every which way I missed a turn and had to ask directions. And the whole time I had to fight this crazy impulse to stop what I was doing and just go hunting for Alathea. Just seeing so many young girls almost her age made me feel more desperate than ever. I was keeping an eye on my watch and saw that it had taken me more than eight minutes to get to the door with the sign on it saying, PUERTA DEL SOL BOARD OF EDUCATION/PAUL M. STRETTO, CHAIRMAN/JULIAN Z. KIRKE, SECRETARY.

I went down the hall and tucked myself around a corner where I could watch the door without much chance of being seen. Then I waited.

Exactly three minutes later, Kirke left the office. He looked a little more awake than he had the day before, and he was moving fast. Not hurrying, really—just going like a man who knew where he was headed and wanted to get there in a straight line. Ginny knew how to get results over the phone.

When he disappeared around a corner, I gave him a

minute for second thoughts, then went to the door and let myself in.

The front room hadn't changed—it still reminded me of the department of police. But it was busier. Several kids stood at the counter occupying the attention of five secretaries, but the one I wanted wasn't one of them. She was sitting at her desk and there was a harried look on her face. She was the one Kirke had chewed out in front of Ginny and me the day before.

I caught her eye, and she came over to the counter. I said, "Sondra?" She nodded. My face didn't register with her, so I said, "My name's Axbrewder. I was here yesterday."

"Oh, yes—I remember." For a moment, her expression relaxed, and she turned pretty—the way she was born to look. She leaned toward me and said softly so the kids couldn't hear, "You're the private detective." Word gets around.

"That's right, Sondra." I took a stab at trying to look charming, but for some reason my smile didn't feel right, so I dropped it. "I'd like to talk to you."

Judging from the way she turned her eyes up at me, I'd say she was at least giving my smile credit for good intentions. "What about?"

"I can't tell you here. Can you take a break or something? I'll buy you a cup of coffee."

At that, her face closed like a shutter. "I can't."

"Oh, come on." Axbrewder trying to sound persuasive. "Kirke won't catch you. My partner has him, and she won't let him go for at least half an hour. And if he does come back sooner, I can cover you." Trying anything. "He'd look better with his nose sticking out his ear— don't you think?"

Well, I was right about one thing, anyway. Kirke had been leaning on her hard. Too hard. Even timid people have limits, and Sondra had just reached hers. Her smile looked brittle and vaguely feverish—but it was a smile. "Where shall we go?"

This time, my own smile was a lot more genuine. "How about the cafeteria?"

"OK." She went to her desk and got her purse, then said to one of the other secretaries in a determined little voice, "I'm going to take my break now." A minute later, she was guiding me down the hall in the direction of the cafeteria.

I kept my mouth shut for a while. Just walked beside her, and let her feel as indignant and defiant and maybe scared as she wanted. But when we were sitting at a table in an oversized mausoleum they call the cafeteria with cups of coffee in front of us, I got started.

"How long have you worked here, Sondra?"

"About a year." She was so preoccupied with the risk she was taking she seemed to have forgotten I had some particular reason for wanting to talk to her.

"A year," I repeated, crossing her off my list. "How do you like it?"

She grimaced. "It's a job. I don't have much choice —I've got to work somewhere."

"But you don't get along with Kirke."

"Who does?" Defiance had the upper hand at the moment.

"What's his problem?"

Bitterly, she said, "He thinks secretaries shouldn't make mistakes. He thinks secretaries shouldn't be human."

I scanned her with what I hoped was an appreciative gleam in my eyes. "He's a little confused."

She rewarded me with another smile. If her color hadn't been so high already, she might've blushed.

I took a slug of my coffee, fought down an almost overwhelming desire to throw up—what could they have made the stuff out of, Clorox?—then asked carefully, "Sondra, how much do you know about this new filing system Kirke is working on?"

"Not much." She must have been used to the coffee— it didn't seem to faze her. "He only lets three of us touch it—and I'm not one of them. Just Mabel, Joan, and Connie. The rest of us only do ordinary office work—letters, transcripts, reports, stuff like that."

"What do you do if you need something in those files? Say you need to look up the records for a kid who goes to Ensenada Middle School."

"Usually I ask Mabel. Or Connie, or Joan, if Mabel isn't around."

"I see." I pushed my coffee away. Just looking at it made my stomach queasy. "Besides them and Kirke, who knows how to use the files?"

"Well," she considered, "there's Mr. Greenling—he's

nice—and Mrs. Scurvey. Mr. Stretto never touches anything. If he wants something, he asks Mr. Kirke for it. I think that's all."

"None of the other people on the board?"

"No." She was sure.

"What about people from the other schools? What if the vice-principal of Mountain Junior High, for instance, wants to know something?"

"They ask for it, and Mabel or Connie or Joan, or maybe Mr. Kirke, gets it for them. Those files aren't easy to use. They're sort of . . . in-between, you know? You don't just look in a file cabinet alphabetically and pull out what you want. They're getting ready to be put in a computer—which is different from just having them handy. Mabel says they're all in pieces, and cross-indexed every which way. Besides"—her tone went sour again—"Mr. Kirke doesn't like other people to touch them."

"That figures." I paused for a moment, trying to guess how far I could go with her without losing her spontaneity. Then I said, "Would you mind telling me a little more about Mabel and Connie and Joan?"

"Like what?" She must've felt giddy with courage—she sure as hell wasn't feeling suspicious.

"Well, take Mabel. What's her last name?"

"Allson. Mabel Allson."

"What's she like? Is she married?"

"I like her. Of all of us, she's the only one who ever stands up to Mr. Kirke. I think it's because she doesn't need the job. Her husband is a bank president—Flat Valley Savings and Loan, I think. She works because she likes it."

"How about Connie?"

"Connie Mousse." Sondra giggled. "We call her the Moose. She's a frustrated old maid. She hates everything. She works here because she likes hating it. If she had a husband, she wouldn't need the job—she could hate him instead."

"And Joan?"

"She's Joan Phillips. We get along OK, I guess, but I don't feel close to her. All she ever talks about is her fiancé. Jon—what's his name—Jon Gren, that's it. I ought to know all about him by now. He's a second-year intern at University Hospital. They're going to get married when he graduates."

She said some more—but all of a sudden I wasn't listening. I was thinking, *intern.* Who else besides pushers know where to get drugs? Doctors, that's who. Not Camilla Sandoval—it'd be too risky for her, we're talking about a hell of a lot of junk and all the records would be in her name. But how about a second-year intern in a major hospital? If he knew what he was doing, he could rip off any drug he wanted by the pound.

"Sondra," I said, "you're a delight. I haven't been delighted in a long time, and I've been needing it. But we're just about out of time." I fished out one of Ginny's cards, and handed it to her. "You can get me with that number. If there's ever anything I can do for you, call. Day or night—it doesn't matter. Especially give me a call if Kirke hassles you about talking to me. I'll make a pretzel out of him."

She smiled bravely. But the mention of Kirke brought back her fear again, and there was a hint of the old despair behind her smile.

"I mean it," I said. "Nobody pushes my friends around."

"All right, Mr. Axbrewder," she said brightly. She was determined to carry it off. "I'll keep that in mind."

It wasn't until we were on our way back to her office that I remembered that there was something else I had to ask her. "Just one more thing, Sondra. People like Mabel, Joan, Connie—how long have they worked here?"

"I'm not sure—longer than I have. I know it's been a long time for Mabel. The Moose has been here forever. And Joan—I don't know, maybe a couple of years."

I thanked her again and we went back through the school board door. The whole time I'd been with her, she hadn't once asked why I'd been asking her all these questions. But when she sat down at her desk, her face was white and her hands were trembling.

Up until then, I think I'd been underestimating just how scared she was of Kirke.

It was a little hard for me to understand. He wasn't back yet, and unless somebody ratted on her, there was no way for him to know she'd been out talking with me. But she seemed to think he'd know, just know.

Then he came back—stalked into the office so quickly that he almost hit me with the door. We glared at each other for a second. There was a hot red spot in each of his pale cheeks, and his chain-saw mouth was gripped tight—Ginny'd put pressure on him, all right. "I just finished telling your partner where to stick it," he rasped. "What the hell do you want?"

I smiled at him. "I'm waiting for her to join me. When she gets here, we want to talk to Mr. Greenling."

Kirke turned on his heel. The kids were gone now—he had a room full of women at desks to consider. But he homed in on Sondra as if she'd just sent up a flare. He had a good eye—there was something scared about the way she hunched over her work, not looking at anything except the paper in her typewriter and he spotted it. He went over to her, stood beside her. He didn't say anything—all he did was drum lightly on the desktop with his fingers. And watch her fall apart. The shaking of her hands got worse—her fingers got tangled up and in a minute she'd made a hopeless snarl out of what she was typing.

"When Miss Fistoulari gets here," he said, "take her and Mr. Axbrewder to see Mr. Greenling." He made it sound like a form of torture. Then he went into his private office and closed the door.

"Nice guy," I said to the room. It might as well have been empty—nobody even glanced at me.

"Thanks," I said. "I think I'll wait outside." I stepped into the hall, closed the door behind me. Mostly for my own protection—I couldn't stand the reproach of Sondra's hunched shoulders.

Before long, Ginny came down the hall. There was a fighting flare to her nostrils, but mostly she was just alert and ready—like she'd gone the distance with him, and he hadn't laid a glove on her.

"It better be worth it," I growled. "That man is a solid-gold bastard."

She considered for a moment, then shrugged. "We'll find out."

"What did you get out of him?" I asked.

"Not much. I don't know whether or not he's tough—but he's certainly hostile as all hell. At first, I couldn't figure it out—I wasn't hassling him in the beginning. But then it hit me. He hates women. According to him, he left his job at NCR because his boss was a woman. 'All women are bitches'—that's a direct quote." There was a fighting light in her eyes. "That was when I cut into him."

"I guess you did," I said. "He's taking it out on his secretaries."

"That's their problem." She was in no mood to sympathize. "If they don't like it, let them stand up for themselves."

For a minute, we stood there scowling at each other—or rather scowling past each other. Then she asked, "How about you?"

I shook myself, made an effort to get my insides into some semblance of order. Then I told her about Mabel, Connie, and Joan—and Jon Gren. She wasn't as impressed as I'd expected with the news about Joan Phillips' intern boyfriend. "First of all, you're assuming that if somebody is leaking those files, they're leaking to somebody they know personally. Maybe so, but maybe it's pure business—they're just doing it for money."

"At the moment, that doesn't matter," I said. "The point is, it gives us a place to work." She nodded, and I went on, "Anyway, our list is down to five—three secretaries, Kirke, and Greenling—and it isn't even lunchtime yet."

She looked at me sharply. "You're feeling better."

"Because I'm making a contribution."

"Glad to hear it." Her tone was sardonic, but I knew she didn't really mean it that way. Sardonic was just her way of keeping herself distant, objective. She was working—she didn't have time to worry about my poor dismal ego. I wanted to kiss her again, but I knew better. "Who do you want to tackle next?" she asked.

"We have an appointment with Mr. Greenling." Axbrewder playing at formality.

"Let's go."

I opened the door for her—just to remind her I wasn't Julian Kirke—and followed her back into the office.

Sondra's face had that swollen almost-crying look, and she wasn't willing to meet my eyes. But she came over to us right away and guided us down the back hall to Astin Greenling's office. In a minute, we were standing in a room that would've made a perfectly comfortable broom closet if it hadn't been crammed to the ceiling with files and textbooks. In a tired voice the curriculum vice-chairman offered us seats. When I sat down, my back was jammed against a bookcase and my knees were pushing the edge of his desk.

He looked vaguely more rumpled than he had the day before, but other than that he seemed pretty much the same. He gave the impression he was too obsessed with and exhausted by his work to get dressed in the morning without help. No matter what Dr. Sandoval said about him, he belonged on the list. He looked like a moral wreck. There aren't very many people in the world who are so good they wouldn't sell their own mothers into slavery—if you got them tired enough and desperate enough. Especially if they need the money for some "good" reason.

But he didn't make any effort to put us off, didn't tell us anything about how busy he was. He didn't say anything at all. He just sat behind his desk and looked at us with those exhausted eyes, waiting for us to tell him why we were there.

Ginny was quiet for a few moments—deciding what approach to use. Then she said, "When Mr. Stretto showed you those notes yesterday, the only thing you had to say was some inane comment about 'penmanship.' Didn't you understand what you were reading?" The hard-headed approach.

Greenling made an aimless gesture with his hands. "It doesn't have anything to do with me." He didn't sound hopeless—for him hopeless was so long ago he didn't remember what it felt like anymore.

"I disagree." To hear her, you would've thought she'd already made up her mind about this case. "There are only five people in this entire school system who could have kidnapped those girls. You are one of them."

"Kid—?" If she had suddenly ripped off her clothes and jumped him right then and there, he couldn't have been more surprised. "Kid—?" He couldn't even get the whole word out. Probably his reaction would've been the same in any case, innocent or guilty. It's amazing how hard it can be to tell the difference in this lousy world of ours.

"That's not all," she went on. "Of those five people, you're the only one who has a motive."

"Motive?" He was gaping like a fish. "I—? Motive?"

"You need the money. For your wife."

Wife was the magic word. It transformed him. Not all at once—he had to struggle with it for a minute. I watched him with a kind of nauseated fascination while

terrible things went on inside him. He looked like an
alcoholic going through withdrawal. Then it was over.
His eyes were bright, and all the lines of his face were
sharper. In a tight voice, he said, "Get out. My wife is
dying. Get out of here."

Ginny isn't insensitive, just committed to her work.
Which is why she's such a good detective. She didn't
flinch. "How are you paying for it, Mr. Greenling?"

But he didn't flinch, either. "We have security guards
in this school. I didn't want them—the money for these
things always seems to come out of curriculum—but now
I'm glad we have them. Get out!"

Ginny studied him for a moment. Then she got to her
feet. She'd done what we had come for—she'd turned up
the heat. There wasn't any point in trying to call Greenling's bluff. And right then he didn't look like a bluffer.
"We're going to find those girls, Mr. Greenling," she said
evenly. "Whoever kidnapped them we're going to nail
to the wall." Then she left the room.

I stayed where I was. Sometimes it works—sometimes
when people get mad at her they're willing to talk to me.
Innocent people, usually. When she was gone, I said,
"Come on, Greenling—save yourself some grief. Just
tell me how you're paying for it."

He picked up his phone, pushed a button. When a
voice answered, he said, "Connie, get Security. Now."

I didn't argue with him. It was his play—he could call
it any way he wanted. I wedged my way out of his closet
and closed the door behind me.

Ginny was waiting for me in the hall. I said, "Nothing," and she nodded. But she wasn't really paying attention. She was on some other trail—she had a hunting
look in her face. After a moment, she said, "Did you see
it?"

"See what?"

"Over on the right side of his desk. He had a stack of
paper—probably for notes. White stuff. Half sheets. They
looked like they'd been torn along one edge."

Chapter Thirteen

I said, "I don't believe it. That man is as innocent as the day he was born. Even if he has something to be guilty about, he's still innocent."

She looked at me—not challenging, just questioning. "What makes you say that?"

I was about to answer, *Because I've been there and I ought to know.* But I couldn't say that to her—not the way things were going today. So instead I said, "He's got too much dignity." It was lame, but I didn't have anything better to offer at the moment.

Ginny said, "Dignity covers a multitude of sins. I'd rather have proof."

"Yeah? I thought you were the one who said we didn't need proof."

She grinned quickly. "That's true. But I wouldn't turn it down if you offered it to me."

I loved that grin. "What're we waiting for? Let's go find some."

"Right." She went about three steps down the hall, then knocked at a door with a sign on it saying, MRS. MARTHA SCURVEY/BUDGET VICE-CHAIRMAN.

From inside, a woman's voice snapped, "Go away. I'm busy."

Ginny opened the door, stuck her head in, then looked back at me with a sudden ferocity in her grin. She gestured for me to follow her.

"I told you to go away!" the woman said angrily.

When I got into the office—which was about the same size as Greenling's, but a hell of a lot neater—I found out why. The air was thick with sweet gray smoke. Martha Scurvey was sitting stiffly behind her desk with a hash pipe in her hands. Probably she didn't want anyone to come in until the air-conditioning cleared the air. Or maybe until she smoked a cigar to cover the odor.

"I'll tell you what, Ms. Scurvey," Ginny was saying. "You give us a little of your time, and we'll forget what that stuff smells like." I could hear the grin in her voice.

"That's blackmail." Martha Scurvey was angry enough to pluck chickens—but she was also under complete control. A dangerous combination. She must've had a lot of charm on tap, or she wouldn't be sitting where she was—but at the moment it didn't show. The only thing she showed was stainless steel. I wondered where she picked up the hash habit. Offhand, she didn't look like the kind of woman who needed it.

"Not at all," Ginny said smoothly. "Just persuasion. The only thing we're interested in is a little talk."

Ms. Scurvey didn't want to talk. She wanted us to get the hell out of her life. But she knew how to concede without losing face. With a gesture that might've looked gracious if her eyes had backed it up, she offered us chairs. While we were seating ourselves, she stashed her pipe, pouch, and matches in a briefcase, which she then locked. Then she leaned her elbows on the desk, and said, "I prefer Mrs., not Ms. I'm a married woman and proud of it."

That sounded as phony as a three-dollar bill. How she felt about her marriage was irrelevant—what she was trying to do was get on top of the situation. Ginny let her try. "Certainly, Mrs. Scurvey. We're not here to give you any trouble. As far as we know, you're in the clear."

I had to admire her—Ginny plays control-games as well as anybody. Mrs. Scurvey had been snookered, and she didn't even know it. "In the clear?" she asked. "I don't understand."

After that, I stopped listening for a minute. I was distracted.

In a neat stack off to one side of her desk, Mrs. Scurvey had a pile of white writing paper. A handy size for notes—full sheets torn neatly in half. From where I sat, the paper looked like good twenty-pound bond.

I had a childish urge to nudge Ginny and point, but I resisted it. Instead I shifted my weight, sneaked a couple deep breaths, and went back to paying attention.

Ginny was saying, ". . . your opinion of Mr. Greenling?"

Mrs. Scurvey looked at her hands, checked her fingernails. "He's conscientious—very conscientious—but hopelessly out of date. His ideas of education have yet to reach the twentieth century. I'd love to do a strict cost-analysis of his department, but he won't let me touch it. I have to take his word for everything. At present." She made it clear Astin Greenling wasn't going to have the power to turn her down much longer.

"Do you know about his wife?"

"He doesn't talk about her, and I don't ask. I've heard she's ill. That's more than I want to know."

"What about Paul Stretto?"

"Paul is a forward-thinking educator with a keen appreciation for economic reality. He's brought this school system a long way toward facing the facts of life and doing the job it's supposed to do."

I was glad Ginny didn't ask what kind of job that was. The smugness in Mrs. Scurvey's tone made my scalp itch—I didn't like what it implied about her relationship with Stretto. Fortunately, Ginny wasn't interested in theories of education. Instead of pursuing Stretto, she asked, "How do you feel about Julian Kirke?"

"Personally, I think he's odious. Professionally, he does great work. His new filing system will save us thousands of dollars a year—once he gets it into the computer."

"Do you see him socially—know anything about him?"

Mrs. Scurvey gave Ginny a withering stare and said, "No." Kirke was probably too low for her—he wasn't chairman of anything.

"Who works on the files with him?"

"Three of his girls," she said stiffly. "Mabel, Joan, and . . . and Connie? I think that's her name."

"What do you know about them?"

"What should I know about them? They're his girls— ask him."

"Do they ever do any work for you?"

"Just routine typing."

"They don't help you with the files?"

"When I want something out of the files, I get it myself." Mrs. Scurvey was running out of endurance. Her tone would've curdled milk. All of a sudden, I could see she didn't smoke hash because she liked it—she smoked it because she needed it. She was brittle inside, and didn't want anybody to know.

Before I could think about it, I asked her. "How long has your husband been dead, Mrs. Scurvey?"

Milk, hell. She practically curdled me. "That's none of your business."

Which told me what I wanted to know. Now she made

sense to me. Her high-pressure approach to her job, her relationship with Stretto, the hash—she was running away from grief. I half wanted to ask Ginny to leave her alone. A married woman, and proud of it. It's a hard life when you lose everything that used to tell you who you are.

But Ginny was almost through anyway. "Just one practical question, Mrs. Scurvey. What's the phone setup around here?"

"The phone—? I don't understand."

"If I wanted to call you, could I reach you directly, or would I have to go through one of the secretaries?"

"Through the secretaries."

"And when you want to make a call?"

Mrs. Scurvey sighed. "Through the secretaries."

"So they can make calls that you don't know about, but you can't make or receive any calls that they don't know about. Right?"

Mrs. Scurvey was hugging herself with her arms. "Are you finished?"

"Yes, I'm finished," Ginny said. "Just let me make a note of that." Before Mrs. Scurvey could stop her—if Mrs. Scurvey wanted to stop her—she reached over and took a sheet off the stack of white paper. She got a pen out of her purse, scribbled something on one end of the sheet, then put it and the pen back in her purse. "Thanks for your time. We're sorry we troubled you. Come on, Brew." Thirty seconds later, we were out of the school board offices and walking down the halls of Central High.

I wanted to see that sheet of paper. But Ginny didn't seem to be in any hurry to look at it, so I asked her, "What was all that about the phones?"

"Just fishing," she said. "Whoever we're looking for doesn't work alone. One way or another, I think there's got to be at least two of them. It's hard for me to picture somebody who works here moonlighting as a pusher successfully. There are too many things that could go wrong. So I figure we're looking for somebody who gets the information, then passes it to somebody else. It's the somebody else who handles the girls."

I stopped her. "They wouldn't be stupid enough to call each other at work."

"That depends." She pushed open a door and we went

out into the glare of the parking lot. The asphalt was swimming with heat. "Greenling or Scurvey wouldn't, because their calls go through the secretaries. But that doesn't tell us anything about the secretaries."

When we reached the Olds, she put her purse on the hood and took out the sheet of paper.

Sure enough, it was twenty-pound bond. Neatly torn along one edge. The watermark matched all the other notes.

"Damn it," Ginny muttered under her breath.

"For sure." I couldn't figure out what Martha Scurvey was doing with paper like this. She wasn't supposed to be one of our suspects—she'd only been on the board a year.

But Ginny was cursing something else. "I should have grabbed a sheet from Greenling too. I wasn't thinking." She stuffed the note angrily back into her purse. "I swear to God, Brew," she rasped, not looking at me, "some days I don't know what I use for brains."

The frustration in her voice surprised me. I guess I tend to get so involved in my own inadequacies I sometimes forget she's human, too. Judging from the sound of things, finding this paper in Martha Scurvey's office must've broken one of Ginny's intricate logical chains. Ruined a theory or two, and left her feeling stupid. "Don't complain to me," I said quietly. "I'm the guy who lost the notes, remember? I didn't even see that paper on Greenling's desk."

"Yes, well," she said, jerking open the door of the Olds, "that's a big consolation."

That crack irked me. But I didn't snap back. Reciprocity—it was my turn to stay cool. I got into the passenger seat, watched her while she took us out of the parking lot and we headed in the direction of her office. When I got tired of looking at her scowl, I said, "So who cares about your brains? It's your body I'm interested in."

For a second, I thought she was going to let go of the wheel and clobber me. But then all of a sudden the scowl broke. She threw back her head and laughed.

"Ah, Brew," she sighed after a minute, "if I ever figure out what to do with you, you're going to be in big trouble."

"Take your time," I said. "I can wait."

We chuckled together, and while it lasted I felt better. About a mile from the Murchison Building we stopped for a quick lunch. As we were eating, Ginny looked at me abruptly, and asked, "How did you know Mrs. Scurvey's husband was dead?"

"Intuition," I said. "She doesn't have any kids, but she is having an affair with Mr. Paul M. Stretto. I don't know how I knew. It just came to me."

"Are you sure you didn't figure it out from the name on her door? It didn't say 'Mrs. George-or-whatever Scurvey'—it said 'Mrs. Martha'."

"That," I said flatly, "never occurred to me."

She shook her head. "You're not a well man. You ought to see a doctor. Maybe there's some kind of treatment for it."

I didn't try for a come-back. Her eyes were focused somewhere else, and her voice had an abstract sound—she wasn't even listening to what she was saying. She was groping for something—some kind of link that would tie this case together. I knew better than to distract her.

When we were finished eating, we went on to her office.

While she called her answering service I started a pot of coffee. But after that I didn't have anything to do except sit and watch her think some more. I didn't mind at first—Ginny thinking is Ginny making progress—but after half an hour or so I started to get restless. I was just about to interrupt her when she reached a decision. Without warning, she came back from wherever it was she'd been, and pulled the phone toward her. "The hell with him," she muttered. "I can't wait any longer."

There was a kind of suppressed violence in the way she dialed, and when she started talking her face was knotted in a grimace—but she managed to keep her voice tolerably smooth. Once she got to Smithsonian himself—past the people who fronted for him—she put the call on the speaker so I could hear him too.

Even over that tinny amplifier he had the kind of voice that makes you want to wash your hands. Oily and sticky. You'd have to be a bank president to like it. "What's the matter, Fistoulari?" he said. "No patience? I told you I'd call at three. You can't crack this case without me?"

Ginny picked up a metal letter opener, set the point in the blotter on her desk, and slowly twirled it with her fingers. "Of course not, Lawrence." Somehow, she kept the acid out of her tone. "You know I'm helpless without you."

"That's probably true." He couldn't have sounded more self-satisfied if he'd just been propositioned by Miss America. Ginny stopped twirling the letter opener and began slowly pushing it into the blotter. The expression on her face said, *Why am I talking to this fruitcake?* "Under the circumstances," he went on, "I won't keep you hanging. I have most of the information anyway. The only one I'm not satisfied about is this Stretto character."

"What have you got on him?"

"Nothing you want. For a politician, he looks pretty clean. But I always double-check politicians. He keeps a much higher profile than he can afford on Board of Education money—but right now it looks like it comes out of his campaign organization. Rumor is that it's clean money. Maybe it was born clean, and maybe somebody washed it. I'll know later on—probably by tomorrow."

Well, it was still possible Stretto was supplying files to somebody who supplied him with money. But I didn't believe it. He'd been too quick to call the commissioner.

"How about the others?" Ginny asked.

"Scurvey and Kirke are clean. Martha Scurvey is a society broad"—the letter opener was starting to bend —"and she probably has more cash in her purse than she gets paid in a year. Her husband was Matthew Scurvey, the computer biggie. He left her enough to buy her own public school, if she wants it." He paused, then said, "It's possible she's one of Stretto's private contributers."

"I already know that," Ginny said. With malice aforethought. But she kept her voice bland.

"Yeah?" Smithsonian growled. He didn't like it when people already knew what he was telling them. "Then maybe you already know about Kirke, too."

"Not a thing. I can't get close to him."

"Well, then." Smithsonian mollified. "He's clean. He lives within his means—which aren't that much, let me tell you. His apartment has a certain amount of class, and he drives a car that isn't cheap—it's a Citroën-Maseratti. But his bank financed the car. Take the payments on that—plus rent and taxes—out of his pay, and you still have enough for food, with something left

over for a trip to Mexico every once in a while. Unless
you're trying to support a little chickie on the side. He
isn't. Absolutely no money he can't account for."

Ginny absorbed that for a minute. So did I. I hated to
cross Kirke off the list, but at the moment I didn't see
any way around it. About the only thing I was sure of
in this mess was that whoever was kidnapping these girls
and pumping them full of junk was making money out of
it. Considering what can happen to you if you're con-
victed for kidnapping, it had to be a *lot* of money.

Then Ginny asked, "What about Astin Greenling?"

"Ah, Mr. Greenling," Smithsonian said, "the man with
the sick wife. I took a good look at him. Medical expenses
cause more crime in this country than anybody knows
about. You can bet he doesn't pay his bills with his sal-
ary. And the kind of hospitalization the Board carries is
chickenfeed. So I was a little surprised to find that in fact
Mr. Greenling does pay his bills. How—you ask? I'll tell
you how." Smithsonian was enjoying himself. "That
sucker is up to his ass in loan sharks."

"Loan sharks." Ginny sat up straight, tossed the letter
opener aside. I could almost see her thinking, *How does
he pay them back? Maybe he pays them with something
besides money. Maybe he pays them with information.*
"How long has that been going on?"

"About two years." Smithsonian chuckled. "I don't
know why they haven't broken his arms yet."

"After two years? How do you think he's handling it?"

"Hard to tell without actually talking to him. Probably
every time one gets nasty he goes to another one and bor-
rows enough to save his skin for a while. If that's what
he's doing, he's digging himself a hole they're going to
bury him in."

"All right, Lawrence," Ginny said. "You're giving me
exactly what I want. Now I've got some more names for
you."

"More?" he barked. "You think you're my only client?
I don't have better things to do than this—"

Ginny cut him off. "I'll pay. Whatever it is. Just send
me a bill."

"Believe it, Fistoulari. I'll send you a bill." He paused
to give us a chance to feel like we were being threatened,
then said, "So tell me the names."

"Mabel Allson," Ginny said promptly. "Connie Mousse.

Joan Phillips. They're all secretaries for the board. And Jon Gren"—she spelled out the names for him—"Gren is Joan Phillips' fiancé. An intern at University Hospital."

"Do not call me," he said heavily. "I'll call you. To-morrow—around noon." He paused again—probably waiting for Ginny to tell him how wonderful he was. When she didn't say anything, he hung up with a bang.

She switched off the speaker and we stared at each other for a minute. Or rather I stared at her, and she looked through me into empty space. I stood it as long as I could. Then I got up. "Let's go."

Her gaze didn't shift an inch. "Where?"

"Back to the school board. Or over to Greenling's house—talk to his wife. Somewhere. We can't just sit here."

She wasn't listening. "I've missed something. There's something here—something that gives it all away. But I can't pick it up. Damn and blast! What's the matter with me?"

I said, "You're trying too hard."

I don't know why I bothered. It didn't register with her at all. "I'm going blind. It's right here in front of me, but I can't see it."

I didn't see it either. So I took a deep breath, and said, "Acton."

That reached her. She looked up, and her eyes came into focus on my face. "What did you say?"

"Acton."

"What is that—more intuition?"

"No. I'm just trying to shake you up a little. You're in a rut—you've got Greenling on the brain."

She leaned back in her chair, put her hands behind her head. "You still don't believe he's the one?"

"Who, me? Do you think I'm crazy? Of course he's the one. Who else could it be?"

Her eyes narrowed—I almost couldn't see the fighting gleam in them. "All right, ace. Maybe I'm in a rut. She's your niece—what do you think we should be doing?"

"I think we should go try to shake down Jon Gren."

"Wonderful. Try it with my blessing. Only there's one thing you ought to keep in mind. Hospitals don't keep heroin around. Morphine, yes—heroin, no. He's just Joan Phillips' fiancé—that's all you've got on him."

What could I say to that? "Well then, let's go talk to

Mrs. Greenling." Trying not to sound defensive. No point in telling her she'd just shot down the only theory I had.

She sighed. "That may be a good idea," she said, getting to her feet. "So why do I feel like you're asking me to go hurt a sick woman?"

That probably would've made me mad—after all the things I'd done in the past three days, and Alathea still missing, I was in no mood for her to turn finicky. But I was saved by the phone.

She snatched it up. "Fistoulari Investigations." While she listened, all the blood drained out of her face and something else took its place—something that looked like murder. Then she said, "Hang on. We'll be right there." She put the receiver down.

If I hadn't known better, I might've thought it was me she wanted to kill. In a tight voice, she said, "That was Lona. She's over at University Hospital. The cops just brought in Alathea. She's still alive—but she's in a coma. O.D."

Maybe she wanted some kind of reaction from me— maybe there was something she wanted me to say. I didn't know, and I didn't care. I was already on my way out to the elevator.

Chapter Fourteen

I hit the call button for the elevator, hit it again, pounded the damn thing—finally, the lights of the floor indicator started to move. They were slow, slow. By the time the doors opened, Ginny was running down the hall to catch up with me.

"Sorry," she muttered under her breath as she scuttled into the elevator beside me. She must've thought I was holding it for her. "Had to call my answering service."

I ignored her. I was thinking, coma. Alathea. In a coma. Bastards bastards bastards.

"They'll get her out of it," Ginny said. "Doctors know a lot more about these things than they used to. She'll be able to tell us everything we want."

"Leave me alone." I looked at her, just enough to let her see I meant it. "That isn't what I need."

For a second, I was half afraid she was going to ask me just what it was I did need. But then the elevator opened into the basement, and we were both hustling toward the Olds.

I wasn't driving, I didn't have anything to do, I was helpless. The sun shines cheerfully, the traffic takes its own sweet time, and the man who designed the sequencing of the stop lights is a maniac—and there's nothing anybody can do about any of it. I just sat staring through the windshield with my hands clenched on my knees, trying to hold myself together while Ginny wrestled with things she couldn't change. I'd forgotten my sunglasses.

She made good time. She must have because I was still in one piece when she slammed the Olds into a parking space in the University Hospital lot. We hit the asphalt together. But when I started to run, she caught my arm, held me back so that we walked toward the entrance together.

I let her do it. When Ginny gives orders, I obey.

University Hospital is a tall building built in two square sections. For five stories the sections have a common wall, then the east wing goes on up for another five stories. They built the place out of red brick and when the sun catches it at the right angle, it looks like blood. The emergency entrance is on the ground floor of the west wing, and with all the security guards they have around, it looks more like a top-secret military installation than a place where urgent hurts are treated. At least during the day. At night, with lights in all those windows, it looks a lot more comforting.

We went in, asked a guard for directions, and got ourselves pointed toward the waiting room. That was where we found Lona.

She was standing at a window looking out into the parking lot. There was a lot of sun-glare from the chrome and glass, but it didn't seem to bother her. When Ginny said, "Mrs. Axbrewder," she turned around to face us. I wanted her to take a step toward us, hold out her hands, do something that would give me permission to put my arms around her. But she was too much alone for that— her pain cut her off from everything. She stood there small and brittle, with her mouth clamped shut because there was nothing she could say or even cry out that would relieve the pressure inside her. It was as clear as daylight we'd failed her, failed Alathea. When from somewhere she found the strength or maybe the generosity to say, "Thank you for coming," I almost groaned out loud.

"How is she?" Ginny asked softly. She felt as much a failure as I did—I knew that. The difference was she was able to keep it from interfering with more important things.

"I don't know," Lona said. There was a quaver in her voice she couldn't control. "I haven't seen the doctor since he came out to talk to me—before I called you. He told me what he was going to do—I had to give my permission because she's under-age—but I didn't understand it. He wouldn't let me see her. He said"—she didn't look at us, never lifted her eyes above my chest—"he said she's an addict. There are needle marks all over her arms."

"It's not her fault, Lona." What else could I say? "Somebody did it to her. She was forced into it."

Very carefully, she said, "I know that."

Lona!

"How did they find her?" Ginny asked. "What happened?" She wanted to know if the cops had caught the bastard who was responsible. Hell, I wanted to know. But she was moving slowly, gently.

"I'm not sure. I don't understand it. I got a call—from Lieutenant Acton. He was one of Richard's friends. He said that she had been found. He said she was wandering around somewhere—out on Canyon Road, I think —trying to get a ride back into town. Somebody saw that she looked sick and called the police. I don't know who it was. When they found her, she was already unconscious. In the dirt at the side of he road."

I wanted to throw up. She was only thirteen. Things like that shouldn't happen to children.

"Did he say anything else?"

"He told me she was here. He said I should come down here right away, because the doctors needed my permission to treat her."

For a minute, I had an impulse to grab the Olds and head for Canyon Road—out toward the mountains east of the city, where only the richest of the rich people live— and start banging on doors until I found wherever it was Alathea'd come from. It was a crazy idea, of course.

Maybe she'd just been dropped off so she could get herself killed by the traffic. Which didn't make sense, because there isn't that much traffic out there. But the impulse was crazy anyway—there were a hundred ways and reasons for her to be on Canyon Road—and I fought it down.

"Is there anything we can do?"

"No, thank you." Her eyes didn't leave the buttons of my shirt. "I'm all right." If she'd been any more all right, she would've been hysterical. "You don't have to stay if you don't want to."

Ginny's eyes were full of tears, but she didn't let them fall. "That's OK. We'll stick around," she said.

If that meant anything to Lona, she didn't show it. She just turned away from us, went back to staring out the window.

Then we waited. Just waited. Which is what makes the famous Chinese water torture so unbearable. It isn't the dripping of the water—after a while, your forehead just gets numb. No, it's the waiting between drops that does it. Drives you completely bananas. Other people came into the waiting room, left again. Two angry-anxious mothers told each other what their kids had done this time. A man fumigated the room with a cigar the size of a .45 while his aged father had an ankle X-rayed. A guy and a girl who'd been in a minor car wreck came in and took turns sitting around while they were checked out for whiplash. Compared to waiting, sobriety is easy.

It was almost four o'clock when a doctor finally showed up, asking for Mrs. Axbrewder.

Lona whirled as if she'd been stung. Her face was so full of questions she couldn't get them out—she just stared at the doctor and ached, dumbly begging him to say something.

"She's stable," he said. "Physically. She needs care, but she should be all right. I'm having her taken up to a room. You can visit her there in a few minutes."

Relief blurred Lona's face—she looked like she was about to give way when the doctor's tone sharpened. "But I have to tell you, Mrs. Axbrewder—we haven't been able to rouse her. She's still in a coma, and we can't reach her."

Ginny was standing beside Lona, had an arm around her shoulders. "How do you treat that?"

"We take care of her body, and wait. Maybe she'll pull

out of it tonight. Maybe tomorrow—maybe next week. Maybe—I have to say this, Mrs. Axbrewder—Maybe she'll never pull out. It depends on what kind of damage has been done to her brain. Permanent coma is rare, but it sometimes happens. When the dose is too much, or too soon, it can be like an eraser on a blackboard—the conscious part of the mind gets wiped out. Not often. Usually it's just a small part of the mind, and after a while the person recovers. Wakes up. Of course, it's complicated by the fact that she'll be going through withdrawal. All we can do at this point is keep her body fairly healthy—and pray."

Lona had her hands in her hair, pulling it away from her face. A woman in danger of going over the edge. Ginny gripped her hard. "Have you ever had a case like this before, Doctor?"

"No. But I've read about them. What I read is that things like this are most likely to happen when the addict resists the drug for some reason. The mind fights the body as hard as it can for as long as it can, and then there's a backlash."

That meant something—it was trying to tell me something. But I was too full of pressure to get a hold on it. The doctor told us what room Alathea would be in. When Ginny and Lona left the waiting room, I followed them in the direction of the elevator.

Then another question occurred to me. I turned, ran after the doctor, caught up with him at the nurses' station. "Did you do a complete physical on her?"

He looked at me sourly. "I don't know who you are. What's your interest?"

"My name is Axbrewder. Alathea is my niece."

He considered for a moment, then nodded. "I examined her. What do you want to know?"

It stuck in my throat for a second. Then I got it out. "Is she a virgin?"

He grimaced. Disgusted at me—or at the question. Or at the answer. "Not by a long shot."

I tried to swallow the acid in my mouth, but it wouldn't go away. Clenching my fists at my sides, I went to catch up with Ginny and Lona.

Ginny was holding the elevator for me. She had the same question in her eyes. I said, "Goddamn it to hell.

Yes." When she let the door close and punched the floor button, she looked mad enough to chew steel.

Alathea's room was on the eighth floor of the east wing. We found it without any trouble—the halls are laid out square and the doors all have nice big numbers on them. But when we got to her room, another doctor stopped us from going in. He was about as tall as Ginny, with longish red hair curling around his ears, more paunch than he needed, and bloodshot little eyes. He had freckles so bad they looked like smallpox. His white coat was buttoned up to his neck. There was a stethescope in one of his pockets, and his right hand gripped the handle of a black medical bag. He smiled blandly at us. "I'm Dr. Stevens. Now that she's out of Emergency, I'm responsible for her. You can see her as soon as I'm finished. It'll just take a minute."

Ginny nodded for Lona. We stood around in the hall while Dr. Stevens went into Alathea's room and closed the door.

He didn't take a minute—he took three. It felt like thirty, but we were in no position to complain. When he came out, he gave us his smile again. "Don't worry," he said. "She's going to be fine." There was something about him I didn't like—he had the look of a man who had just told a dirty joke—but it didn't seem important. With his hands in his pockets, he went down the hall away from the nurses' station. We went into Alathea's room.

It was a semi-private room. Alathea was in the bed near the door. A curtain drawn halfway across the room between the beds kept us from seeing who else was there. Past the second bed was the window. The afternoon sun came slanting in through it across a long section of the floor.

Alathea looked like death. Her face was a sickly paraffin color and the scrubbed white of the hospital gown only made it worse. The sheets were tucked up to her armpits. Her arms were bare—I.V. tubes ran up to bottles hanging from poles at the head of the bed. Around the slashes of adhesive tape that held the I.V. needles in place, there were other red marks like insect stings—tracks of them mapping the veins inside her elbows. Violation as bad as any rape. Lona went close to her, gripped her hand, and started to cry. After that, I couldn't see anymore. I was blind with tears.

I shambled over to the window, trying to control myself.

For a couple bad minutes, I couldn't seem to do it. But slowly my anger came back, and my eyes started to clear. I hit my knuckles on the windowsill until I could see straight again. Then I looked around.

The room was on the west side of the building and the window was right over the roof of the west wing, three stories below me. It had been fixed up as a recreation area, with stubby trees growing out of little plots of earth, big umbrellas for shade, and lots of wrought-iron tables and chairs. The place was full of people—nurses, men and women walking jerkily around or sitting in wheelchairs, children, visitors. They looked like they belonged there, catching a little sun to warm their bones. They all belonged—patients, nurses, doctors, visitors. Ginny and Lona. Only Alathea didn't belong. And me. She didn't deserve it, and I hadn't earned it.

There was a faint breeze coming in through the window. The window was double glass, insulated for the sake of the air-conditioning. But the hospital was saving money —the air-conditioning wasn't on, and the window was cranked open a crack at the top.

I turned my back on it, glanced at Alathea's neighbor. An old woman, as shriveled as a mummy—asleep and snoring. It surprised me to find I had pity left to spare for her. She looked like she'd outlived herself long ago.

I wiped my face with my hands, and went back to Alathea's half of the room.

Lona wasn't crying anymore. She sat in a chair beside the bed and held Alathea's hand as if both their lives depended on it. Ginny was still with her, standing behind her and gripping her shoulders with both hands—trying to squeeze some kind of strength into her frail body. I watched them for a minute or two, hunting for a way to tell them I was leaving.

I didn't get a chance. The door swung open, and Stretto came into the room.

He looked like a campaign poster.

"I came as soon as I heard." Maybe my ears were tricking me—I could've sworn his voice echoed in the room. Professional grief. Somehow, he got past Ginny without actually pushing her out of his way. "Mrs. Axbrewder, I'm terribly sorry. All of us at the board are just heartsick." He got her hands away from Alathea, took hold of both of them himself. From where I stood, he looked like he was asking her to vote for him. "In a way, I feel responsible. If Ms. Fistoulari hadn't alerted us, we would never have known there was trouble. We should have realized it ourselves months ago, and taken steps to prevent it from happening again. I promise you, Mrs. Axbrewder—I will use every resource at my command as chairman to make sure this kind of thing stops."

God save me from politicians. I wanted to slug him. But Ginny was in better control of the situation. "I'm glad to hear it, Mr. Stretto." The lash of her voice cut all his blather to pieces. "Now I'd like to hear how you knew she was here."

Which was a very good question.

But he was innocent the way only a politician can be innocent. "The police called me. Since you and I spoke yesterday, I've been doing my best to get action out of them. I even spoke to the commissioner." He was still campaigning. "Told him in no uncertain terms my opinion of the way this case has been handled and it appears he made my feelings clear to the officer in charge—a Detective Acton. Acton called me earlier this afternoon—no doubt trying to compensate for his former inadequacy by keeping me informed."

Acton, huh? That name was starting to crop up a little too often. I wondered just how many people he'd told about Alathea.

First things first. "Mr. Stretto," I said, "how many people did you tell about Alathea's being here?"

He started to answer, but a knock at the door interrupted him.

I went over to it, yanked it open.

Tred Hangst stood outside.

I started to say, What the hell is this—open house? But he caught my arm, jerked me out of the room. Or tried to anyway—people as short as he is can't actually move me around by brute force. I let him get me into the hall. After I'd closed the door behind me I took a good look at him.

If he'd had any sleep—or food either, for that matter—since I last saw him, it didn't show. There was fever in his eyes, and his hand on my arm trembled no matter how hard he held on to me. "Tred," I said, "what the hell's wrong?"

"Her answering service told me where you were. I've been looking for you all afternoon."

"Looking for us? Why?"

"Why the hell do you think?" He was more than just feverish. He was hostile and excited. "Because you hot-shots have been wrong about this thing from the beginning. That's why I gave up on you. Ever since I left you, I've been talking to people."

"So have I. I didn't get anywhere."

"Hotshot!" he spat. He was also desperate. "You were talking to the wrong people. You and Fistoulari never figured out why Mittie was kidnapped."

I was in no mood to play games with him, but I didn't let it show. He was stretched to the breaking point, and I didn't want to tighten him anymore. I figured he had something to tell me—something he was going to say as soon as he found a way. I gritted my teeth, and didn't touch him. "That's true."

"You've got drugs on the brain. You're so hung up on heroin you can't see what's going on."

"Tell me, Tred." Softly—softly. "What's going on?"

"Prostitution!" The word made him so mad he turned purple. "She wasn't kidnapped by a pusher. She was kidnapped by a pimp! He just uses drugs to control girls, make them do what he wants. What his customers want. They're all sick!"

He fell into a fit of coughing—or maybe it was sobbing—and for a long minute he couldn't go on. It wracked him pretty hard. When he got his breath back, a lot of the hostility was gone. "It's killing me, Brew." He sounded faint. "There are actually men in this city who want to screw thirteen-year-old girls. They want to screw—or worse—my daughter."

I couldn't stand it any longer. I caught hold of the front of his coat, yanked him off the ground until his face was level with mine. Through my teeth, I hissed, "What did you find out?"

It didn't scare him—he was past being scared. He didn't get mad, either—he was too tired. "I'm sorry, Brew. I keep forgetting about your niece. I didn't get much—just a description of the guy who lines up the customers. He's the one you go talk to if you want . . . want to . . ."

I put him down, straightened his coat. "Tell me what he looks like, Tred."

Dully, he said, "Tall guy. Red hair—curly. Freckles. His name's supposed to be Sevin Rinlassen."

But I wasn't listening to the name. I was concentrating on the description.

For a second, I was paralyzed. Frozen while images of a man with red hair and freckles played inside my head. I saw him go into Alathea's room. Dr. Stevens! I saw him come out of the room, walk away down the hall. There was something wrong, something I should've noticed before.

His hands—they were empty!

Then I moved. Snatched open the door, charged into Alathea's room. "Ginny!" I barked, "he left his bag!"

Lona and Stretto stared at me as if I was some kind of lunatic. But I ignored them, focused on Ginny. "That doctor was a fake. He left his bag in here."

It took one more second to reach her. Then she whirled, started hunting.

She dived under Alathea's bed, and came up holding a black medical bag in both hands. Carefully, she put it on the edge of the bed, snapped it open.

We were all watching her—me, Tred, Stretto, Lona. We all saw what was in the bag.

Three sticks of dynamite and some kind of detonating mechanism. The mechanism was ticking.

Lona fainted. Stretto caught hold of the bars at the end of the bed as if he was going to join her. I ignored them both, concentrated on Ginny. I don't know anything about detonators and neither does she. The one thing I did know is that you don't try to disarm a bomb if you don't know what you're doing. This whole scene didn't seem real to me. I couldn't believe it. Things like this don't happen right in the middle of the afternoon.

"Ginny," I said. Even to myself, I sounded like I was strangling. "Tell me what to do."

She stood up straight, closed the bag, snapped it shut. Carrying it by the handle, she walked out into the middle of the room.

"Tred," she said evenly, "go to the nurses' station. Tell them we've got a bomb in here. Get them to call the cops. I'm not going to take it out of this room. Tell them to get the people out of these rooms—start next door on either side, and work away. I don't know how much damage this thing can do. Go!"

He went.

"Stretto!" She had his number now. Her voice cut into him, and brought out the decisive man who'd let us see his files. "Take Lona. As far away as you can—the opposite side of the building."

He didn't hesitate. He scooped Lona up in his arms, started for the door. By the time he reached the hall, he was running.

"Brew, get the window open."

The window. Great idea. Toss the bomb outside where it couldn't get Alathea. I practically threw myself at the glass.

It was built into a heavy frame; it opened and closed with a crank. But the crank wasn't there.

I reached up to where the window was open a crack at the top and hooked my fingers over the edge of the frame. At the same time I braced my feet against the sill, and ripped the damn thing out of the wall.

That was when I remembered the sun roof.

I turned to Ginny, panted, "You can't. There are people down there."

She didn't flinch. "I don't know when this thing is going to go off."

I whirled back to the opening, leaned out and yelled, "Get away! Go inside! Get off the roof!"

A couple people looked up at me. The rest didn't seem to hear a thing.

"Brew!" Ginny snapped. "Get Alathea out of here. Then this woman. Tell the nurses to clear out those people."

I jumped at Alathea's bed, tried to move it. It was on wheels, but they were locked. I spent precious seconds kicking off the latches. Then I had the bed moving. The IV stands were built into the frame and the bottles clinked against the poles, but the needles in her arms were safe. Heaving my weight against the bed, I guided it through the doorway and out into the hall.

I was too occupied to be surprised when I saw Tred and Stretto coming toward me. "Take her!" I shouted at them. "Tell the nurses to clear that goddamned sun roof." They caught hold of the corners of the bed, and I turned and rushed back into the room.

Ginny was at the window. She was kneeling, bent over below the sill. Her right arm was hooked over the sill. She was holding the bag out the window, using the wall to protect herself.

"You'll kill yourself!"

"What do you want me to do?" Her voice was flat and fatal. "Drop it? Keep it in the room? If it goes off inside, it could kill everybody above and below."

I didn't argue. I went to the old woman's bed, started kicking off the latches.

By the time I got her out the door, a nurse appeared beside me. She was pale with fear, but she wasn't letting that stop her. "I'll take her," she said. Voice shaking. "She's an old woman. If she wakes up with all this going on and doesn't see a familiar face, she'll be terrified."

I gave the bed a shove for momentum, and let the nurse have it.

Scrambling on all fours to keep my head below the level of the sill, I went back to Ginny. When I reached her, I said, "Let me take it. You're too important to waste."

She fixed her eyes straight at me. "Get the hell out of here. I don't want to lose you like this."

For a moment, I didn't obey. I couldn't—couldn't leave her like that. But I didn't have any choice. If we both got killed, who was going to nail the bastard who caused all this?

"For God's sake, Ginny," I said. "Use your other hand."

I watched while she carefully shifted positions, got the bag into her left hand. Then I started to crawl away.

I was halfway across the room when the dynamite went off.

The concussion knocked me flat. I thought my eardrums were going to rupture. Then all of a sudden the air was full of dust and sunshine and silence. Hunks of plaster dropped from the ceiling. The wall above and below the window was cracked—there were cracks running along the ceiling—but everything was intact. I didn't know if any brick had been blasted off the wall outside onto the sun roof, but I couldn't hear any screaming.

Ginny lay beside me. She was covered with white plaster-powder from head to foot. For a moment, her eyes were open. Her lips said, "Brew," without making any sound. Then her head rolled to the side.

Her left hand was gone. What remained of her forearm

was just mangled meat. But her heart was still beating. Blood pumped out of her stump onto the floor. It looked like all the blood in the world.

I couldn't think of anything else to do, so I clamped my hand around her arm just below the elbow and squeezed with all my strength until the bleeding stopped. Hung onto her like that until help arrived.

PART IV

Friday Night/Saturday Morning

Chapter Fifteen

When the doctors took Ginny to surgery, I stayed where I was—sitting on the floor in the gutted room with my back against one wall just staring through the dusty air at nothing. The doctors had wanted to take me down to Emergency, examine me for possible concussion, shock, whatever. But I'd refused. Probably I was in some kind of shock—but it wasn't something they could do anything about. I didn't want them to touch me. I sat with my back against the wall, staring at nothing. Like a drunk.

Before long the door opened and Tred came into the room. He stood close to me, but I didn't have the strength to raise my head, so all I saw of him was his old jacket and his stale shirt and his ratty tie. For a couple minutes he just stood there. His awkward hands twitched once or twice, but he didn't say anything. Then he managed to force out a few words. "Stretto left."

I didn't answer. If there was an answer somewhere in the room, I didn't have it.

"Before he left"—Tred sounded like somebody'd gone over his vocal cords with a rasp—"he gave me a message for you. He said he wants you and Ginny to vote for him. The next time he runs for something."

Vote for him. Dear God in Heaven.

"Brew." He was pleading with me, but I couldn't seem to do anything about it. "Brew, get up. We've got to find Mittie." He didn't seem real enough to move me. The only thing I could see in the dust and the late afternoon sunlight was blood pumping out of Ginny's forearm.

But then I saw something else too. Thin silver streaks that fell and splashed on the floor. They made me look up. Tears were oozing from his face like booze-sweat. He had the power to move me after all.

They all had power—Stretto, Acton, Ginny, even Tred —they were all able to make other people feel fear or grief or respect. The bastard who put Alathea where she was sure as hell had power. The only exception was Axbrewder. He didn't have any of his own, so he lived off other people's. And when he couldn't get that, he got the best substitute he could find—out of a bottle. I didn't seem to have any choice about it. I was on my feet.

"Brew," Tred said, "you look terrible." He was trying to smile.

That finished the job. I was functioning again. *"I* look terrible? How long has it been since you had anything to eat?"

He shrugged. Food was irrelevent. "We've got to find Mittie."

"We're going to. As soon as I know Ginny's all right. But while I'm waiting I'm going to take you down to the cafeteria and put food in you if I have to shove it down your throat."

He tried to smile again. "Sure, hotshot. But before you do anything you might regret, you ought to take a look at yourself."

The mirror in the bathroom had survived the blast. When I looked in it, I saw what Tred was getting at. I was so thick with plaster powder that I looked like a spook. White powder made the rims of my eyes and my gums look red as fever.

I slapped at my clothes a couple times, and spent a minute coughing. Then I ran water in the sink, washed my face and hands, dried them on some paper towels. I still looked like I'd just climbed out of a ruin, but at least I was clean enough to be fairly presentable. With Tred behind me, I left the room.

A second later, I remembered something, and went back. After hunting around the room for a minute I found Ginny's purse. I fished out the keys to the Olds and took the purse with me.

After all the confusion, things in the hospital were

starting to get back to normal. Cops were pouring in, but at the nurses' station, some people were already doing paperwork again. I told them where I was going, and asked them to get word to me as soon as Ginny came out of surgery. Then I took Tred down to the cafeteria and bought us both supper.

Not because either of us was hungry. I had as much trouble as he did choking down whatever it was the hospital called food. But we had a long night ahead of us, and I didn't want us to collapse. A long night—and the only part of it I was sure of was the part where I was going to have to knock heads with Detective-Lieutenant Acton. I chewed away at some kind of cardboard-and-sawdust sandwich until it disintegrated in my mouth, and whenever Tred pushed his plate away I pushed it back in front of him. And all the time I couldn't help thinking the two of us together made a pretty poor substitute for Ginny Fistoulari.

But if we had any alternatives, I couldn't figure them out. I was in the middle of repeating my threat to force-feed Tred when a man the size of a small tank appeared in the doorway and in a voice like a bulldozer with the cutout open said, "Axbrewder."

Acton. When he saw I was looking at him, he beckoned for me with two middle fingers of his right hand. "I want you."

Tred looked back and forth between Acton and me with something like nausea in his face, but I didn't give him a chance to ask any questions. "Stick with me," I whispered. Then I got up and left the cafeteria.

Acton was waiting for me in the hall. As I came through the doors, he started to say something—but when he saw Tred following me, he changed it. "This is private, Axbrewder."

I stopped in front of him, looked at the dull glare in his eyes, at the way his jaws were clamped together. "No way," I said. "I need somebody who can tell the judge you hit me first."

His fists came out like pistons, caught hold of my jacket, rammed me against the wall. "Listen, Mick," he growled, "I'm the law, remember? I can have you locked up so fast it'll make you piss in your pants. I said this is private."

I didn't struggle. I didn't even want to. I just stared him

straight in the face. When he started to feel hesitant because I wasn't resisting, I said, "My partner got her hand blown off. My niece is in a coma. Do you really expect me to just walk away from it?"

He held me for another ten seconds. Then he took a deep breath through his teeth, and backed up. "All right," he said. Still deciding what to do with me. "Tell me something. I was in the medical superintendant's office a little while ago, and this goddamn sonofabitch Stretto came in. He damn near accused me of setting that bomb myself. According to him, I'm implicated in what's happening to all these girls. Now where did he get an idea like that?"

I shrugged. Trying to stay calm. But all of a sudden my heart was pounding—all of a sudden I felt I was going to be able to get something I needed out of Acton. "He almost got killed," I said as evenly as I could. "Now he wants to blame somebody. You're as good a scapegoat as anybody."

"How do you figure that?" He sounded like he needed a lump of granite to chew on.

"The bastard who set the bomb knew Alathea was here. Who knew besides you, me, Stretto, Ginny, and Lona? Five people—and you're the only one who wasn't there."

I had him now—that was the kind of argument he could understand. He chewed his lip for a while. When he said, "I didn't even know what room she was in. Who did you tell?" he wasn't challenging me anymore. He was working on the case.

I said, "Nobody," and waited.

He chewed for another moment, then spat, "Damn it, I did. I didn't talk to Stretto at all. He wasn't in when I called. I left a message for him with one of his secretaries."

"Which one?"

When he finally met my eyes, he looked like he was actually angry at himself. And just like that I knew what was going on with him. He was such a belligerent cop because he didn't have any other way to let out his frustration. For almost two years now he'd been trying to figure out what was happening with these missing girls—and all he'd got was nowhere. Their deaths—and the manner of their deaths—made him sick with rage, but he hadn't accomplished a thing. So he took it out on people who made him look bad to himself. When he said, "I didn't get her name," I wasn't even disappointed. I was relieved. Because now I knew he was going to answer my questions.

"Never mind," I said. "We already knew it has to be somebody who works for the school board."

His anger jumped into focus on me. "How the hell do you know that?"

I took out the piece of paper Ginny'd taken from Martha Scurvey's office and handed it to him. While he checked it out, I told him where it had come from.

That made a difference to him. "Now maybe we've got something." He put the paper away in his pocket. "All those other sheets—we've had them analyzed. We can prove they were all made by the same company—but we already knew that from the watermark. We haven't been able to prove they came from the same ream. Too many minute variations in the composition of the paper. Except for the last two. The lab-boys are ready to swear those two came from the same sheet. Fiber-tear, composition, everything matches. If this piece comes from the same ream, we'll have some proof we can use."

I could almost see the wheels turning in his head—get a warrant, search the school board offices, track down the source of these torn sheets of paper. Embarrass Stretto as much as possible in the process. It was a good system; it might even work. But it would take time—and I didn't have time. Mittie didn't have time. So I took hold of myself, and asked, "Acton, why did you have to scare people like the Christies? You didn't think they were pimping or pushing for their own daughters. What were you trying to do?"

He didn't look at me. But he answered. "Ah, screw it. I was trying to make something happen. Push here, and hope something cracks over there. What I wanted to do was keep it all out of the papers. Sort of trying to send a message to whoever was responsible. If I kept sensational stuff like that out of the papers, the people who knew what was going on would know I was still after them. I was just trying to make the bastards nervous."

I wanted to ask him why he thought that was a good enough reason to make parents who were already miserable feel even worse, but I was afraid he'd stop talking. So instead I said, "It was worth a try. Tell me how you found Alathea."

He still didn't look at me, but now it was for a different

reason. "I didn't actually tell Mrs. Axbrewder the whole truth about that. Some guy saw her out on Canyon Road and called in. I told Mrs. Axbrewder she looked sick. The fact is, she was wandering down the middle of the road buck naked. And bleeding. The guy who called said he thought she was trying to hitch a ride. When the doctor saw the cuts and scrapes on her, he said it looked like she'd crawled through a broken window or something."

I was staring at Acton, but I didn't really see him. I was thinking. Naked. Crawled. Something I'd been trying to figure out earlier came back to me. The timing. Every one of those kidnapped girls had been missing for two or three months before turning up dead. Except Alathea. She had only been gone for ten days. Why?

I knew why. Because she had escaped. They didn't fill her up with junk and then leave her to die like the other seven. She escaped. For a while, she managed to fight off the junk—she broke a window where they were keeping her, and crawled out, and went down Canyon Road, trying to hitch a ride until it was too much for her and she passed out. Which put her in a coma.

Just thinking about the poor kid trying so hard to do something nobody could do, struggling to climb out of a hell she hadn't chosen and couldn't refuse, made me want to scream. But I didn't. Instead, I said, "This time you'd better put a guard on her room."

"You damn well better believe it," Acton growled. "Anybody who wants to get at her now is going to have to fight off half the department."

I said, "Good."

Then I asked Tred to tell Acton everything he knew about Sevin Rinlassen.

Acton had already heard the bomb was planted by some clown pretending to be a doctor, but he didn't have the details. I made Tred spill them all. He hated doing it —hated having to say such things out loud—but I didn't leave him any choice. I wanted to cover every bet I could think of.

When Tred had told him everything, Acton went one way to put out an A.P.B. and I went the other. Tred followed me as if he was being sucked along in my wake.

I didn't have any very clear idea of where I was going. First I wanted to see Ginny. After that I'd try to figure out what came next.

I got lucky—I caught up with her while she was being wheeled from surgery to recovery. The aides objected, but I made them stop long enough for me to take a good look at her. She was still unconscious—dead to the world, pale, breathing gracelessly through her mouth. The stump of her left forearm was strapped up in tight white bandages, and the rest of the arm was in a cast to keep the bones from shifting. Helpless as a kid. I could've kissed her, and she never would've known the difference.

It only took a minute—I was too tense to stand there long. I put her purse beside her, so when she woke up she'd have her .357 handy. I found out from the aides what room she was going to be in when she came out of the recovery room. Then I let them take her away.

With Tred still trailing behind me, I left the hospital— feeling like a murderer that just hadn't managed to find the right victim yet.

Chapter Sixteen

The sun was setting in a bloodlike red wash as I drove the Olds out of the parking lot, and while Tred and I cruised down Paseo Grande toward the Murchison Building, darkness slowly thickened in the air. It was night when we parked in the basement garage and rode the elevator up to Ginny's office.

I had taken her keys. After unlocking the door, I snapped on some lights and we went into the back room. The smell of very well-done coffee reminded me I'd left the pot plugged in. I offered Tred a cup, then poured myself one and sat down at Ginny's desk to drink it. It tasted like burnt sweat-sock squeezings and motor oil, but I sipped at it anyway as if it was some kind of liqueur.

For a couple different reasons, I didn't want Tred to ask me any questions. He hadn't said anything since we'd left Acton, and I didn't want him to start now. For one thing, I didn't have any answers. And questions would just interfere with what I was trying to do. Sitting in Ginny's office, at her desk—drinking her coffee—I was trying to screw my brains to the point where I could think like she did. I didn't have any red-hot flashes of my own, and I knew I wasn't going to get any if I tried to force them.

So instead I was making an effort to look at things her way. Six hours ago, she'd been sitting right in this chair and she'd said, *It's right here in front of me, but I can't see it.* She'd had all the pieces she needed to put the puzzle together—she just hadn't been able to put them together in the right way. Now she was in the hospital, doped up with scopolamine or sodium pentathol, and I had to do it for her.

Which wouldn't have made sense to Tred, even if he'd been in the mood to give it a try—which he wasn't. He stood me as long as he could, then he said in a strained little voice, "Let's go."

I drank some more coffee, almost gagged. "Exactly where?"

"After Rinlassen. He's our lead. We can get somebody to tell us how to find him."

"It's too early," I said. "Pimps don't even start thinking about business until after ten."

"For God's sake!" he protested. "We've got to do something. They're doing it to her right now!"

He was probably right about that. Now would be a good time for them to shoot her up if they wanted her to be compliant later on—say between eleven and two. But reminding me about things like that only made it harder for me to stay calm. "Goddamn it, Tred!" I began, "do you think—?"

I stopped. An idea hit me—an obvious idea, something I shouldn't even have had to think about. But it felt like more than that. It was just something Ginny would've done automatically—but for some reason it felt like more than that.

I grabbed the phone and called her answering service.

When the woman answered, I said, "This is Axbrewder. Ginny Fistoulari is out of circulation for a while. I need to know if there're any messages for her."

Ginny—bless her foresighted or at least tolerant heart —had kept my name active with her answering service. In a bored voice, the woman said, "Some man's called four times in the last two hours. Didn't leave a name. He wants her to call him back at this number."

She read off the number. I grabbed a pen, scrawled the number on Ginny's blotter. Thanked the woman and hung up.

"What is it?" Tred asked.

I was already dialing. "Do you believe in intuition?"

"Intuition?" he rasped. "What the hell are you talking about?"

"In that case, maybe what you ought to do is pray." The number rang. I shut Tred out of my mind, concentrated everything I had on the secrets hidden in that phone line.

Somebody picked up the phone. A burly male voice said, "Yeah?"

"I was told to call this number." I held the receiver against my head so hard it felt like it was bending.

"Who d'you want?"

"I don't know. They want me. All they left was this number."

"Your name?"

"Fistoulari."

The man must've covered the mouthpiece, because I could hear him shouting but I couldn't tell what he said.

A minute later, another man was at the phone. "Fistoulari?"

It wasn't much, but it was all I needed. "No. I'm her partner—my name's Axbrewder. I was with her when you pulled your little doctor-act at the hospital."

There was a long silence. Then the voice snarled, "Well, aren't you the clever one? How did you know it was me?"

"I'm good at voices."

"Goodie for you." He paused. "Where's Fistoulari?"

"That little toy you left in the room blew her in half." I wasn't about to tell him the truth. I didn't want him to go back there, take another crack at her.

"Too bad it didn't get you, too."

"Too bad for you. Kidnapping, dealing, and prostitution isn't bad enough. Now you've got murder one. You're as good as dead, punk."

"Yeah, well"—his voice changed, became softer and greasier. "That's what I want to talk to you about. I heard rumors that bomb didn't do everything it was supposed to. I shouldn't have let him talk me into it in the first place. But that little whore can identify me. I want to deal."

"Deal, hell." I was gripping the edge of the desk to keep myself from shouting. "You killed my partner. Why should I deal with you?"

Tred was standing in the light across the desk from me.

He was chewing on his moustache, and his hands were clenched into fists at his sides.

"Because"—oil and lechery—"I can give you the man who's responsible for all this on a silver platter. I'm just the errand boy. He's the one who kidnaps the girls. He's the one who gets the junk, and pumps it into them until they're ready to do anything to get more. Anything, Axbrewder. He's the one."

I took Ginny's battered old letter opener in my free hand, bent it double, and threw it across the room hard. It took a sizable hunk out of the plaster. "Convince me."

"No problem. But I don't want to give you time to trace this number. I want to meet."

"That sounds like a good idea. Then you can just shoot me, and there won't be any witnesses left."

"Suit yourself," he snapped. "I'll be in that abandoned Ajax warehouse down at the end of Trujillo—about an hour from now. That's a good place for me, because I'll be able to tell if you bring anybody with you—like maybe the cops. If you do, you'll never find me."

The line went dead. I was left with what felt like a perfect set of my fingerprints indented in the handle of the receiver.

Tred hadn't moved a muscle. He was staring at me, dumb with pain and urgency. I didn't want to say anything, but I forced myself to for his sake. "You got most of it. That was Rinlassen. He wants—he says he wants to deal. Trade us his boss for some kind of immunity. Either he's telling the truth, or he wants to set me up."

Tred had to struggle to find his voice. "What're you going to do?"

"What the hell can I do? I'm going to meet him."

"He'll kill you."

"No," I said. "You're not going to let him."

While he absorbed that—or tried to, anyway—I dialed the answering service again. When I got the woman, I said to her, "Listen, this is an emergency. Call the police —get a message to Detective-Lieutenant Acton. That's A-c-t-o-n. Give him that number you gave me. He can track it down—I can't. Tell him I just talked to Rinlassen —R-i-n-l-a-s-s-e-n." I hung up before she could try to think of a reason not to do what I told her.

"That's going to do a lot of good," Tred said.

I shrugged. "It's worth a try." Got to my feet. "I can't

tell Acton where we're going—Rinlassen says he can spot it if I don't go alone. If Rinlassen sets me up—or gets away from us—maybe Acton can nail him by staking out that number."

Tred didn't answer. At the moment he looked as bedraggled as a wet chicken, but the dull glare in his eyes said as plain as words that Rinlassen wasn't going to get away from us.

"Come on," I said softly. "It'll take us quite a while to get down to that warehouse."

Tred just turned on his heel and walked out of the office. I unplugged the coffeepot, snapped off the lights, locked the door, and followed him to the elevator.

While we rode down, I said, "It could be that he really does want to deal." I wanted to be sure Tred wouldn't go off half-cocked. "He's not stupid—he's playing it pretty cagey. He knew about Ginny and me—this partner of his must've told him we were prying into their business. So when he saw us at Alathea's room, he knew he had a chance to get us all. After he sets the bomb, he gets out fast—he doesn't want to take any chances."

The doors opened, and we walked out into the basement toward the Olds. "But then he doesn't have any way to find out what happened. So he starts trying to call Ginny—a smart move. If somebody returns his call, he knows he's in big trouble, and he better start trying to find a way to get off the hook." I unlocked the Olds. We climbed in. "If nobody calls back, he figures he's in the clear. No witnesses who can tie him to the kidnappings. He can go back to pimping for his partner, and his partner'll never know the difference. Neat."

Tred wasn't paying any attention. He was staring out through the windshield into the night, and tears were streaming down his face again. I locked my jaws to make myself shut up, and I concentrated on just driving for a while.

But silence wasn't what he wanted, either. By the time we were down in the valley, working our way south along the river, he was talking himself.

"She's all I have left, Brew." He was gnawing on his moustache the way a drowning man clutches at straws. "You probably don't know what happened to us—things like that don't happen to hotshots like you." He was bitter, but it wasn't me he was bitter at. "We were happy—

she and her mother and me. I was a cop then—pounding a beat back in the days before they decided to do everything with squad cars—and we had a little house over on Los Arboles, and we were happy, her mother and me. Mittie wasn't born yet. Except her mother didn't like me being a cop on the beat—she wanted me to be a detective. But they had rules back then that said I was too short to be a detective. When Mittie was born I quit the cops to go be a detective for myself. So she'd have a father she could be proud of.

"But it didn't work out like that. People don't hire you for what you can do, because they don't know what you can do. They hire you for what you look like. You're built like a tree, and Ginny looks like a steel trap, and people just naturally go to you when they've got something important. They come to me when they've got something grubby. Domestic surveillance." His bitterness was so thick it practically fogged up the windows. "Prove that so-and-so is cheating on so-and-so, so that so-and-so can get a big fat divorce settlement. You know something, Brew?" he chuckled sourly. "They almost put me out of business when they invented no-fault divorce."

For a while, he went back to staring out the window. I hoped maybe he wasn't going to tell me any more—I was in no shape to handle it. But he wasn't finished. A couple minutes later, he continued, "Her mother wasn't impressed. I wasn't doing what she thought detectives did—I wasn't solving murders, rescuing kidnapped babies, breaking up drug rings. When Mittie was three, her mother ran off with an insurance salesman." His tears were running again. But he had a curious kind of dignity about it—it didn't make him sob or lose control. His voice didn't even shake as he said, "I raised her myself. She's all there is."

It took me long enough, but I finally figured out why he was so desperate. He was afraid the bastard we were after was going to feel the heat and decide to go out of business. Hide under a rock somewhere.

After destroying the evidence.

As long as Alathea stayed in a coma, Mittie was all the evidence there was. If that bastard knew Alathea was still alive, he might've already killed Mittie.

I took a tighter grip on the wheel, and pushed down

harder on the accelerator. Because there was nothing else I could do.

Even then, it took us damn near an hour to get down on Trujillo in the vicinity of that abandoned warehouse.

After that, I didn't rush it. When we were still half a mile away, I pulled over to the curb and stopped.

I asked Tred if he had a gun.

He didn't.

I took out the .45 and handed it to him. While he checked it over, I flipped the switch for the courtesy lights so that they wouldn't come on when I opened my door. Then I said, "Here's what we're going to do. You're going to hide down under the dash. When I get to that warehouse, I'm going to park in the darkest place I can find. I'll get out, and leave the door open. I'll go into the warehouse wherever I can find a door at the front. Give me a couple minutes. Then sneak out and get around the back somehow. Come in looking for me. Keeping me alive is up to you—there's going to be precious little I can do about it myself. This is his territory."

Tred didn't say anything. He just snapped the cylinder back into the .45, and ducked down under the dash.

I put the Olds in gear and drove the rest of the way down Trujillo.

The city fathers don't spend much money on streetlights down in that part of town—the whole place was as black as pitch. But the warehouse was silhouetted against the skyline and my headlights picked out the rest. The building stood behind a high steel-mesh fence, but the gates were gone. There was no other way in—which was one good reason why Rinlassen had chosen it as a meeting place. But that wasn't the only reason. It was a three-story building and the first two floors were constructed of battered steel siding. The top floor was lined with windows on all sides. He'd probably been up there for the past half hour, watching so if he saw anything he didn't like he could get out of there fast.

The moon wasn't up yet, so there wasn't any place to park that was darker than anywhere else. I coasted up to the front of the building, positioned the Olds so Tred had a good straight run to the east corner, doused the headlights and stopped.

"At least two minutes," I whispered. "I'm going to be moving very slowly." Then I opened the door and got out.

I stood where I was for a minute so Rinlassen could see I was alone, then walked over to the door beside the cargo entrance.

I put my hand on the door and pushed.

It squeaked bloody murder. As a way of demonstrating my good faith, I let Rinlassen hear me shut it behind me.

Then I was standing alone in darkness as thick as stone. Too dark even for me—when I waved my hand in front of my face, I could barely sense it moving out there.

But with the cargo entrance beside me, I figured I was standing in a pretty big open space. Holding my hands in front of me just in case, I started walking straight forward. Very slowly. My heels made an echoing sound on the concrete, but I didn't worry about it. I wasn't trying to surprise Rinlassen—I was counting on Tred for that.

And wishing like hell I had Ginny covering me instead. I wasn't worried about Tred's determination, I just didn't know how much sense he had left.

If he didn't have enough, that made two of us. Probably Ginny would never have let me get myself into this situation in the first place.

Then a voice barked, "That's far enough!"

I froze.

For about a minute while I stood there, I thought I heard faint scuffling noises in the distance.

After that, a light snapped on.

It just about nailed me to the floor. I was right under a powerful bulb with a reflector that focused the beam into a circle on the floor maybe fifty feet across. With me in the center. Surrounded by a secret and dangerous darkness that my eyes couldn't penetrate.

Very neat. Rinlassen could've killed me with a popgun.

But he must've had something else in mind (at least temporarily) because he didn't shoot. After a couple minutes, I heard heels on the concrete. Then Rinlassen materialized in front of me on the edge of the circle of light.

He had a big automatic in his right fist.

He came a couple steps forward into the light—no more. Not counting the automatic, his big advantage was he could get out of the light a lot faster than I could.

I didn't even try to move. I didn't want to give him any excuses.

He knew how to hold a gun—it never wavered. He was grinning, and his voice sounded like margarine. "All of a sudden, you don't look so tough, Axbrewder. How come that bomb didn't get you? I bet you wet your pants when it went off."

Part of me wanted to just forget everything and take him. "I came to get convinced, punk," I said. "Convince me."

He glanced around. "You alone?"

"I've got two cops in my pocket, if you'll just let me get them out."

"All right." He got down to business. "What do you want to know?"

"Who's your partner?"

"Ah," he grinned. "I'm not going to tell you anything you can use. I want to deal. You get the D.A. to give me immunity, and then I'll give you his name."

"We'll find him without you."

"No, you won't." He sounded very sure of himself. "You're not even close."

"You'll still have to convince me. I've got to know something to take to the D.A."

"That's why I'm here. What do you want to know?"

I took a deep breath. "I want to know why you used a goddamn bomb. Why didn't you just needle her to death? You've done it before."

"Not me, pal," Rinlassen said flatly. "He handles the junk—I never touch it. I don't even know where he stashes it."

That got me nowhere. I wasn't thinking straight—that wasn't the kind of question I needed to ask. *Come on, Axbrewder!* I snarled at myself. *Don't blow it now.*

"All right," I said. Holding onto myself hard. "How many girls are you going to admit kidnapping?"

"Nine," he said promptly. "But I didn't have anything to do with that, either. Getting them was his job. Just like doping them was his job."

"What was your job?"

"Well," he grinned, "the main thing was rounding up customers. Mostly I just made myself available. When some john who liked his white meat young found me, I made the arrangements—and took him out to where the action was.

"Other than that, I just took care of them. Fed them. Got the right kind of clothes for them. A lot of johns like to see a kid in fancy stuff—peek-a-boo bras, lace panties open at the cunt, stuff like that." He was grinning so hard I could barely look at him.

I said, "Keen. You're a nice man, Rinlassen. But I'm going to need something more solid. Tell me"—I almost faltered, almost gave it away. I saw a pale shadow in the darkness behind Rinlassen. It was Tred. All I could see was the white of his face and hands. He had the .45 in both fists, pointed straight at Rinlassen's back. It was all I could do to keep going—"you kept each one of those girls for maybe three or four months, and then ditched them. Why?"

Rinlassen shrugged. "We got a lot of customers, but most of them are regulars—know what I mean? After a while, they want fresh stuff."

"Yeah," I growled. "You kept one girl long enough to break in a new one before you got rid of her. So how come you killed Carol Christie so soon after you picked up Alathea Axbrewder?"

"Axbrewder," he said. "She some relation of yours?"

"No."

"Yeah, well," he said, "that Christie chick was trouble from the word go. Something funny about her metabolism —my partner had a hell of a time trying to get the right dose. Half the time she wasn't dopey enough—and the rest of the time she was all the way out. It was just an accident she got killed when she did."

"An accident," I said. "I bet it broke your heart." I imagined I could see Tred's finger trembling on the trigger. Easy, Tred. Take it easy. "What made you decide to go for two kids this time? You never did that before."

"Just improving the quality of our service." Rinlassen was smirking so hard I thought my nerves were going to snap. "Give the customer more variety. Some johns like blond—some like brunette. Some like a little two-on-one. Also, we wanted to make up for the trouble we had with Carol Christie.

"It was a good thing we had two." I could hardly believe it, but he actually seemed to enjoy telling me all this. "That Axbrewder was a feisty little bitch. We were going to have to get rid of her anyway. Some of the johns were bleeding when they got done with her."

Well, by God, Alathea! Good for you!

"Hangst was another story." I hated that grin. Right then, there was nothing in the world I hated as much as that grin. "She was just what we wanted—in spades. Once she got the hang of things, she couldn't get enough of it. I'll tell you, Axbrewder." He lowered his voice—he was about to let me in on a secret. "Most of our johns don't like cherry meat. So my partner and I used to take turns popping those little dollies. Kind of work them into shape —know what I mean? Hangst was my turn. God! she was a juicy little cunt."

Tred was moving.

I shouted, "No!" but I couldn't stop him.

He took one step into the light.

Fired.

The first shot hit Rinlassen like the kick of a mule. I saw the slug plow out through the front of his chest.

Clenching the .45 in both hands, Tred kept pulling the trigger. I had to hit the floor—the slugs that missed Rinlassen ricocheted off the concrete and went screaming into the dark.

When I heard the hammer click on a spent shell, I raised my head, started to get up.

Tred was staring at the gun. Trying to realize what he'd done.

I got my feet under me, went toward him.

Then it penetrated. His face broke open. He dropped the .45—it landed with a clatter on the concrete.

Without a sound, he turned and went running into the darkness. Before I could even try to catch him, he was out of sight and gone.

Chapter Seventeen

I chased his footsteps for a few seconds, but once I left the light I was blind. Sooner than I expected, I ran into a sheet-metal wall that rattled like thunder when I hit it. After the din died down, I couldn't hear Tred anymore, anywhere.

Cursing uselessly, I went back to the corpse.

Well, I had to admit Tred had done a thorough job. Rinlassen was about as dead as he could get without actually being cut up into bite-size pieces. At least three of the slugs got him—two in the chest and one in the head (there was a hole I could've put my fist through where his face used to be). Probably it would've made me sick if I hadn't already been too furious to give a rusty damn. Let him rot in his own blood. I just wanted to get my hands on Tred.

But Rinlassen dead was as much of a problem as Rinlassen alive. Maybe more. Now I had a body on my hands. A body that had been killed with my own .45. If the cops caught me, I was going to have one hell of a time explaining all this.

In fact, explaining was going to be the easy part. Getting the cops to let me go would be a lot tougher. The best I could hope for was to sit in jail until they identified Tred's fingerprints on the gun.

The thought of the trouble Tred was in nagged at me, but I wasn't about to take this particular rap for him. And I wasn't about to let the cops lock me away, even for a few hours. So I couldn't afford to make it too easy for them to tie me to Rinlassen's corpse. They'd make the connection fast enough when ballistics checked out the bullets and the computer matched them up with the ones that killed my brother. I dug out a handkerchief and used it to pick up the .45. Instead of wiping it off like I wanted to, I carried it by the barrel while I groped my way out of the warehouse.

Out in the night, it was a relief to be able to see again. And an even bigger relief to find the Olds where I left it. In my usual brilliant fashion, I'd left the keys in the ignition. But apparently Tred hadn't been thinking about things like that. So I was still mobile—I still had a chance.

I got in, locked the .45 in the glove compartment, and drove out of the warehouse yard onto Trujillo without turning on my lights.

I didn't turn them on until I started to hit traffic, almost a mile back north in the direction of the city. But I still didn't know where I was going.

Everything was too urgent. Mittie was in danger for her life, if she wasn't already dead. The cops would find Rinlassen's body pretty soon—I'd left the light on because I didn't know how to turn it off, and before long a patrol car would see that light and go in to check it out. Ginny was lying in the hospital with her hand blown off. Tred was running around completely bananas.

I couldn't relax, couldn't clear my head. I needed inspiration, and I as sure as hell wasn't getting it. After a

while, I found I was pounding on the steering wheel with
my fist.

With an effort, I clamped myself back under control.
All right, ace. You don't know what to do. What would
Ginny do?

Good question. Concentrating on it was so hard that in
five minutes the wheel was slick with sweat—but eventually I dug deep enough to get hold of an idea. After which
I spent a couple miles looking for a phone booth—and
wondering just what it was I carried around in my skull
instead of brains.

Rinlassen had known Alathea was in the hospital.
He knew because his partner told him. How did his partner know? Through the school board, somehow. Acton
had called Stretto, left a message with one of the secretaries. So what I needed to know was basically simple.
Which secretary? Who, exactly, did she tell? How many
people got that particular piece of information?

Acton probably hadn't gotten that far yet. He was
probably still busy getting a warrant, searching the school
board offices. Talking to Stretto—maybe to Martha Scurvey. There was at least a good chance I wouldn't run into
him.

Finally I spotted a phone booth and pulled over to it.
I used the directory to get Julian Kirke's address and
then headed the Olds in that direction—out toward the
east side of town.

It seemed to take forever to get there, but actually it
wasn't more than about forty-five minutes. He lived in one
of those fancy singles apartment complexes that sits on a
lot about four blocks long, and has tennis courts and two
swimming pools as well as a "recreation center" for
dancing and other predatory activities. The apartments
all have terraces and balconies with wrought-iron rail-
ings, arched entryways, redwood doors. Inside, they probably have mirrors on the ceilings of the bedrooms. The
surprising thing about these places is they aren't all that
expensive. The "swinging singles" usually aren't rich.

This particular complex was called Encantada Square.
After a little trouble, I was able to find Kirke's apartment.
It had a modest little card that said JULIAN KIRKE in a slot
above the doorbell.

When I rang the bell, I was trembling. I didn't think I
could handle it if Kirke wasn't in. The way I was feeling

if he wasn't in I'd probably jump to the conclusion he was out somewhere murdering Mittie. Then I'd probably sit down on the floor inside his nice arched entryway and start to cry.

At the time, I had absolutely no idea how I had ever managed to function at all back in the days before I met Ginny. I missed her so much I was in danger of blubbering.

Then the door opened, and Kirke stood there in front of me. He kept one hand on the doorknob. In the other, he held a drink I identified almost instantaneously as scotch on the rocks. He wasn't wearing a shirt. I could see he was a lot stronger than he looked with all his clothes on—he had the kind of muscles you get from lifting weights. I could also see the bruises I'd made on his upper arm.

Two or three different varieties of surprise and anger twitched across his face as he looked at me. I took advantage of them—brushed past him and walked into his apartment.

His living room was designed to look nicer than it really was. Sunken floor two steps down—soft, supposedly seductive colors—a thick cheap carpet—plastic potted plants here and there—a picture window with a clear view of the next-door neighbor's picture window. And not much in the way of furniture—just one recliner, a stool, and a sofa big enough to sleep three or four swingers at the same time. I stood there in the center of the room for a minute and tried to figure out how to handle Kirke. I had too many priorities—protect Alathea, get information, stay out of jail, find Mittie alive. And nothing but terrible consequences in all directions if I failed. I was looking for some really devastating way to curse my lack of inspiration when Kirke broke the silence.

"Mr. Axbrewder," he said. "What an unexpected pleasure." He sounded like a beaker of sulfuric acid he was planning to throw in my face—but hadn't done it yet. Civility and sarcasm were doing some kind of balancing act.

"Yeah." I turned to face him. He stood at the top of the steps—which gave him a chance to look down on me a bit. He was holding his drink as if he knew what it could do to me. His anger and surprise were gone—he was under control. Master of the situation. "That's the story of

my life," I said. "One unexpected pleasure after another."

He studied me for a moment. Then he said, "You've
had a rough day. You need a drink." He started toward a
sideboard-bar behind the sofa.

"I don't need a drink," I snapped. My nerves were in
worse shape than I thought. "I need some answers."

He waved his glass at me. "You sure?"

"I don't drink while I'm working."

He shrugged and sat down side-saddle on the back of
the sofa—the perfect host, showing me he didn't need to
be in a position where he could look down on me. He
sipped his scotch.

I waited.

By then, you would've thought I was ready for anything
—but he still managed to catch me off guard. "I heard
what happened to your partner," he said. "Too bad. It
must be rough on you."

"My partner?" I asked stupidly. I had the horrible
feeling I was completely out of my depth.

"Getting her hand shattered like that." He looked
thoughtfully into his glass. "Messy. But it shows one thing,
Axbrewder. You're smarter than I thought. Most of the
big tall he-men I know have this irresistible compulsion
to protect helpless little women. You don't have that problem. I admire that. Let them take their chances, like anybody else. Of course"—civility slipped a couple notches
—"your partner isn't much of a woman." He took another swallow of scotch. "She should've been born a
man."

I must have been staring at him like a lunatic, because
the next thing he said was, "Are you sure you're all
right?"

"No. Ginny is the brains of this team." Why was I
telling him that? "Without her, I'm in lousy shape." I had
to fight to make myself shut up. It was like trying to cork
a bottle you're holding upside down.

"What can I do to help?" he asked. Sounding civil again.

But the sneer on his face would've turned butter rancid
at fifty paces. Suddenly, everything went cold inside me
and I was calm again. Mad enough to knock down walls
with my bare head—but calm. The muscles of my face
and shoulders relaxed. "Answer a few questions," I said
evenly.

"If I can." He was looking me straight in the eye.

"How did you know about Ginny?"

"Stretto called me this evening—told me all about it. I guess he needed somebody to brag to. But politicians aren't supposed to brag, so he had to use your partner as an excuse to bring in all the brave things he did. By now he's probably called most of the school board, the mayor, and half the City Council."

I groaned. "Wonderful. With help like that, I'm going to need a goddamn Ouija board to crack this case."

"Why? What's the problem?" he asked. Mildly interested.

"Oh, hell," I said. "Why not?" Not looking at him. I didn't want to help him figure out I was trying to set him up. "This is an 'information' case, Kirke. It all comes down to who knows what when. How did they find out. Like, how did Stretto know Alathea was in the hospital in the first place?"

"That's easy. Some cop called—a Detective Acton."

"Did Stretto talk to him?"

"No, he wasn't in. Acton left a message with one of the secretaries."

"Which one?"

"Sondra."

Sondra. The innocent one. "She gave the message to Stretto?"

"No. She gave it to me. I run that office."

"Were you alone?"

"Are you kidding?" he chuckled sardonically. "Nobody's ever alone in there. Half the office was listening."

"Like who?"

"Let me see," he mused. "Mabel, Joan—and Connie. I'm sure of them. Maybe there were a couple others."

"And what did you do with the message?" Keep it going, Axbrewder. Don't give him time to think.

"Gave it to Stretto, of course."

"As soon as he came back in?"

"Sure."

"Was he alone?"

"No. Greenling was with him."

"Who did they tell?"

Kirke paused for a moment, stared at me. Then he said, "How the hell should I know?"

I sighed. "Yeah. Well, you see my problem. Somebody

on the school board is leaking information to the bastard who set that bomb. But finding out exactly who is starting to look impossible."

He asked, "Are you sure it's the school board?"

I went on looking out the window. The man in the next-door apartment was lying on his sofa reading his book. "I am. The cops aren't."

He considered that for a minute. Then he said, "I know what your trouble is, Axbrewder. You're too tense. You need to relax—get your mind off it for a while."

I turned around. "How am I supposed to do that?"

He got to his feet. "Change your mind. Have a drink. I have some scotch here that'll make you kiss all your troubles good-by."

I glared at him. He sounded like he was making fun of me. "I told you—" But if he was—if he knew about my drinking problem—he didn't show it. He sounded almost sincere. I made an effort to swallow my anger. "The problem is, I'm an alcoholic. I have a hard enough time staying sober as it is."

His jaw dropped. "You're kidding."

"No." Maybe I was just getting paranoid—I could've sworn he was sneering at me.

"Oh, come on. A man like you? I don't believe it."

"Believe it," I growled. I was in no mood to put up with this. Abruptly, I started for the door.

He caught my arm. There was something in his face too earnest to be a sneer. "Come on, Axbrewder. That woman's been putting you through the wringer—now she's got you believing you can't even have a few drinks. You're no alcoholic. She just tells you that to keep you in line." He was really trying to persuade me. "Stick around. We'll put our feet up, and have a few drinks, and tell each other secrets. I know some things about the school board that would give you hives."

He was making me sick. I said, "No, thanks," peeled his hand off my arm, and stepped past him toward the door.

Right then, all the decisions I hadn't been able to make were made for me. Something inside me shifted, and I knew what I had to do.

When I reached the door, I turned to face Kirke.

He was still watching me. His hand was out, offering me his glass. He was trying to smile.

I said, "I had a talk with a guy named Rinlassen tonight."

He didn't even blink. The way he said, "Oh, yeah?" you would've thought we were talking about the weather.

"He's the guy who set the bomb. Unfortunately, he got shot before he could tell me anything useful."

That made him at least look curious. "Did you shoot him?"

"No. But I wish I had."

Then I left the apartment. Slammed the door behind me. I got out of there before my shakes made me start to stutter.

When I reached the Olds, I had to hold my head in my hands for a minute. Cursing. I'd done what I could for Mittie—that was the easy part. If Kirke was the bastard I was after—*if*—by telling him about Rinlassen, I'd given him one less reason to be worried. One less reason to destroy the evidence—if he hadn't already done it. And if he wasn't the one, I hadn't hurt anything.

The easy part. Just a gamble that might reduce the odds against me. That wasn't why I was shaking.

I was shaking because I was afraid.

Because now I knew what I was going to have to do. I was going to have to go talk to el Señor.

Chapter Eighteen

The idea would never have crossed my mind if old Manolo hadn't suggested it. When he'd whispered his advice in my ear—his breath smelling of anisette and secrets he couldn't or wouldn't tell—I'd thought he was just politely telling me to go to hell. But now I knew better. Old Manolo understood things better than I did. He'd known what a chance to crack this case might cost me in the end.

Which only made me feel worse. El Señor was the kind of man who could sink a drunk like me without so much as making ripples. He didn't like Anglos, and he didn't like private *chotas*. If he wanted to, all he had to do was wave one aristocratic eyebrow, and I'd find myself holding cement together in the foundation of some new building, or little bits and handfuls of Axbrewder-burger would be fertilizing apples up in the North Valley. Oh, el Señor was a gentleman—sort of. He didn't bother himself with people who didn't bother him. But off-hand I'd say the easiest way to commit suicide in Puerta del Sol is to go ask el Señor a couple questions about his business. Some of the cops who tried it haven't been found yet.

Of course, I didn't have anything as threatening and maybe pointless as "law-enforcement" in mind. All I wanted was to protect Alathea. Do something for Lona and Tred. Rescue Mittie. Nail the sonofabitch who was responsible.

But I was an Anglo and a private investigator. I was scared. El Señor had more reasons to kill me than talk to me.

And I was alone. That was the real crusher. I've done worse things with Ginny either backing me up or leading the way, and they weren't this bad. Because she was there. Now she wasn't. And the bastard who had crippled her was going to try one of two things to protect himself —destroy the evidence, or kill the people who were on his trail. And I was the only one left who could even take a crack at stopping him. If el Señor decided to stir me into a ton of concrete or feed me to the apples, then somebody else was going to die tonight, too. Somebody I cared about.

But the things that had me so scared were the same things that made me put the Olds in gear and drive away from Encantada Square. For a while, I doddered along down the road, driving like an old man—but I drove. And after a few blocks the cold air and the night helped me start to pull myself together. Night was something I could understand. At night people do things for reasons that make sense to me. I took the long way around to give myself time to recover—but I went where I had to go.

El Señor's headquarters is an old movie theater not far from where I live. Or it used to be a movie theater before he had it completely rebuilt inside. All he left was the facade, the marquee, and the ticket window. Now the place fronts as a nightclub called El Machismo. It's one of those places where people go—mostly Anglos, but certain kinds of Chicanos and Indians show up, too—when they have too much money and not enough sense to know the man who feeds them their kicks has nothing but contempt for them.

When you remember el Señor gets a good part of his

loot by catering to the pains and weaknesses of the people who live in the old part of town—"his" people—you might think his headquarters would be down in the old part of town itself, an area that would help shield him from things like the law. But his location suits him. From that converted theater he can go fishing for rich Anglos as easily as he can run numbers, extort loans, sell drugs or bodies for his own people. Puerta del Sol is full of society dudes and broads, money-punks of all flavors, who think going to El Machismo at night is "exciting," but who wouldn't be caught dead going into the center of town.

I parked the Olds in the lot across the street, gave the attendant a couple bucks so he wouldn't lose my keys, then spent a minute standing on the sidewalk—hesitating. The marquee was lit, and the big letters proclaiming, "El Machismo" were the color of cheap lipstick. On a good night, going in there was like meeting an old whore. This time I felt like I was on my way to arrange for me and a few other people to become cadavers.

But I went in anyway. Crossed the street. Paid my cover charge at the ticket window. Pulled open the blackout doors, and went in.

After wading a few yards along a deep carpet the color of lava, I reached the maitre d'. He looked like a matador in a tuxedo. His eyes flicked over me, and he pigeonholed me somewhere down around not-worth-the-trouble. When he asked, "Table for one?" he sounded so bored he was almost snoring.

"No, thanks," I said. "I don't want food—I want action."

He lifted one eyebrow. "Action?"

He was part of the screening process. He was supposed to be able to tell the difference between people who just wanted dinner and entertainment and people who were after something spicier. He was supposed to be able to spot *chotas*. Either way, I didn't look good to him.

But I was in no mood to argue with him. I glared down at him, and said, "I want to see el Señor."

At that, he actually blinked. Both eyes. "El Señor?" he asked evenly. "Who is el Señor?"

I grimaced. "Call the manager. I'll talk to him."

He couldn't hold back a grin. "As you wish." He picked up the phone on his desk, dialed. When he got an answer, he spoke Spanish, thinking I wouldn't understand. "With me," he said, "I have an Anglo who wishes to have speech with el Señor. Possibly he is from the police. I think you wish to learn about him a little before you throw him out."

He listened briefly, then hung up and turned back to me. "One moment," he said in English.

A moment was all it took. Then a door beyond him opened, and a man came out.

From my point of view, he wasn't tall. But he was built like an armored car. His arms were so heavy they made his sleeves look like sausage casings, and there was no way in the world he was going to be able to button his jacket across that chest. He didn't even make an effort to hide the gun tucked into his waistband. Under his nose, he had a hair-line moustache, and his eyes bulged like a frog's.

I recognized him by reputation. Muy Estobal. Rumor had it he was el Señor's bodyguard.

He looked toward me. "Will you accompany me, señor?" He sounded like a piranha inviting me to lunch.

I shrugged, and followed him.

We went through the door he'd come out of and he led me down a long hall to a small office with a door so heavy I half expected to see a combination lock on it. When he closed it behind us, it made a permanent-sounding little *thunk*. It wasn't the only entrance—but that didn't make me feel much better.

Muy Estobal didn't sit down. Didn't offer me a seat. Moving so fast I couldn't stop him, he spun around and hit me in the stomach.

I doubled over, reeled back against the wall. For a long minute, I couldn't breathe. Little suns danced around the air in front of me. My guts felt like I'd been shot with a howitzer.

While I was helpless, he checked my empty shoulder holster.

"Now," he said, "you will tell me your name."

With a gasp, I got my lungs working again. "Axbrewder," I panted. Staying doubled over.

"What are you?"

"Private . . . investigator."

"What do you wish with el Señor?"

"None of your business."

His right fist jumped at my head like a cannonball. But this time I was ready. I slipped his fist past my left ear. Straightened up. With all the strength of my legs and back and shoulder, I hit him an upper-cut that flipped him over the desk behind him.

I vaulted after him, landed practically the same time he did. Before he could try to move, I clamped one foot down on the back of his neck. I held him that way while I helped myself to his gun—a snub-nosed Smith & Wesson .38. Then I let him up.

When he reached his feet, glaring as if he couldn't decide how he wanted to murder me, I said, "Now it's my turn, *pendejo*. I want to talk to el Señor. Ask him a couple questions. I'm not here to cause trouble. No hassle— *comprende,* Estobal? I have a problem of my own, and I think he might give me a little help. A couple answers. If I don't get to talk to him, *then* I am going to cause trouble. For a start, I'm going to break your neck." He didn't so much as swallow. "Are you listening, *pendejo?*"

He spat. "Yes."

"Good." I took a deep breath—but I couldn't hold it. My stomach hurt too bad. I broke open his .38, took out the cylinder and dropped it in my pocket. Then I put the gun down on the desk. "Take me to el Señor."

Giving up the gun probably did more to convince him that I meant my speech about not wanting to cause trouble. He picked up his .38 without taking his eyes off me, shoved it back into his waistband. Then he opened the other door to the office, and stalked out.

I followed him. Close enough so he couldn't break away and far enough back so he couldn't turn and hit me again.

But he didn't try any tricks. He led me down another hall, and out into a large room where the people approved by the maitre d' did their gambling. The air was thick with smoke and the noises people make when they're throwing their money down a drain and calling it a good time. Roulette, craps, blackjack—all as illegal as hell in this state, and every one of them nothing but a cheap shot disguised as magic, a chance to make something out of nothing. There were house players scattered around the room—handsome studs and luscious broads daring the customers to believe the obvious fact that el Señor wouldn't be in this kind of business if there was any way he could lose. But most of these fine folks couldn't see the dare; the magic already had them by the throat. If you told them putting their money in the toilet was gambling, you wouldn't have been able to stop them from emptying their pockets and flushing the stuff away themselves.

But that wasn't the only thing going on. Estobal moved fast across the room—but even keeping up with him, I had time to spot at least one man and two women who didn't have the vaguest idea they were tossing away every cent they had. They were so wired you could've hit them over the head with a brick, and they wouldn't have known the difference.

The really screwy thing about it all was if you'd taken a poll in that room, every one of those suckers would've told you they were more *alive* right then than any other time in their lives.

But it was none of my business, and I didn't have time to get up on my white horse about it. Estobal was holding a door open for me. When he closed it, we were in a short little hallway—maybe ten feet between doors—and there were two other goons with us. They didn't look at me, didn't wave guns, didn't even talk to Estobal. They didn't have to; we all knew what they were there for.

Estobal opened the other door and I followed him with the two goons on my heels. Into an office that made Ginny's look like a phone booth. It had a full bar (complete with barkeep), a couple Olympic-size sofas, and a desk you could've played tennis on. The carpet was like a trampoline. I half expected to see potted sequoias in the corners.

Aside from the barkeep, the only man in the room was sitting behind the desk. He was a dapper grandee from his manicured fingertips to the ends of his van dyke beard and moustache. He couldn't have been more than five foot six—that desk should've made him look like a dwarf. But something about the way he sat there looking at me made him seem a lot bigger. Somehow, he fit in that office. It was his, and he liked it the way it was.

El Señor.

Estobal marched up to the desk. He didn't say anything —he just took his gun out of his pants and put it down on the blotter so el Señor could see the cylinder was missing.

In Spanish, el Señor asked, "What is the explanation of this?"

I answered for him. "I am the explanation. I am named Axbrewder. I do the work of a private investigator. I wish to have speech with el Señor."

I was hardly finished when I heard the cocking of pistol hammers. I didn't need mirrors to know the goons behind me were ready to blow me in half.

"*Chota!*" Estobal spat.

Trying not to sound like I was desperate—or even like I was in a hurry—I said, "I wish to speak with Hector Jesus Fria de la Sancha."

El Señor's eyes narrowed. For a moment, he studied me. Then he leaned back in his chair. "Please to be seated, Señor Axbrewder." His fingers made a delicate gesture at the goons, and suddenly they were standing back against the wall. As I sat down, Estobal stamped out of the room.

After half a minute, el Señor asked quietly, "How does it transpire that you have knowledge of my name, Señor Axbrewder?"

I answered him in English. Trying to shore up my position by exerting at least that much control over the conversation. "What difference does it make? The people who told me don't have anything against you. And I don't want to give you any trouble. I'm here for myself. Leave it at that."

He steepled his fingers, gazed closely at the way the pink tips touched each other. "Already you have given me trouble. You have humiliated my Estobal. Now he will be either unsure of himself or else very angry. Either one, his value has been made less."

"He'll recover," I muttered.

"Nevertheless." El Señor was not accustomed to being contradicted. His English had a mechanical accuracy more threatening than any amount of rage or screaming. "Your presence here casts doubt upon my Estobal. It casts doubt upon my personal safety. Now you say that you are here for yourself. You presume a great deal upon my benevolence, Señor Axbrewder."

I said, "No." At that point, I didn't really care whether I contradicted him or not. "I'm too familiar with your reputation for benevolence. What I'm counting on is your sense of honor."

He considered me closely, then said, "I think I do not like the tone in which you address me."

"Señor Fria"—I was hunched forward in my chair, half protecting my sore guts and half pleading with him— "let me tell you why I'm here. Then you'll understand my tone."

He unsteepled his fingers, rested his arms on the arms of his chair. "Very well. Begin."

Begin, hell. It wasn't that easy—there were so many things I had to explain before I could get to the point. I felt a sharp urge to get up and start pacing around the room, try to relieve the tension. But I didn't—I didn't want to make the goons nervous. I just sat there racking my brains. After a minute, I said, "I'll tell you what happened to my niece."

Carefully, I told him Alathea's whole story—her disappearance, the note, Lona's concern, her decision to hire Ginny and me, Alathea's reappearance, her condition, the bomb in the hospital. And all the time, I watched el Señor's face, studying it for any kind of surprise or sympathy to tell me where I stood with him.

But his smooth neat features didn't show a thing. When I stopped, he said, "Some word of this bombing in the hospital has come to me. A very bad thing. What has it to do with me?"

"I told you—she's in a heroin coma. At thirteen she's been forced to become a junky and a whore, and she's in a coma."

Abruptly, he leaned forward, placed his hands flat on the desktop. "Señor Axbrewder," he said softly, "I do not sell heroin to young girls."

"I know that." I did my best to make him believe it— my life depended on whether or not I could make him believe it.

He didn't move a muscle. "Continue."

"Señor Fria," I said, "seven young girls age twelve or thirteen have been kidnapped in the past two years. They disappear—their parents get phony notes. Then somehow they get hooked on heroin, and they turn into whores. And three or six months later they end up dead. My brother's daughter was number eight. Number nine is still missing."

"Again I ask—what has it to do with me?"

"Heroin." I wasn't afraid anymore—I was past that.

My voice was as soft as his. "Every nickle bag in this state has somebody's name on it, and you know all the names. The man who kidnaps and rapes and dopes these girls gets his heroin from somewhere. You know who he is. I want you to tell me who he is."

"Go to the police. Let them find him."

"They will," I rasped. "But not tonight. They're not that fast. And he knows they're getting close. Tonight he's going to kill number nine, and get rid of the body. Destroy the evidence."

"I see." Again, he leaned back in his chair, considered me from a distance. Then he said, "Perhaps I know the man. It is possible. Tell me, señor—why should I deliver him to you?"

"You're a man of honor. What he's doing is terrible."

"He is an Anglo. The girls are Anglo. Honor means nothing among Anglos."

"Anglo, Chicano—it doesn't make any difference. They're only thirteen. Some of them are twelve."

"You also are Anglo. You are a *chota*."

Through my teeth, I said, "Señor Fria, I'm her father's brother."

Something about that reached him. He was silent for a long minute, looking at the ceiling. When he spoke again, his tone was softer. "I myself have two daughters. If I were dead or in prison, and some evil were done to them, my own brother would pay any price to punish that evil."

With one hand, he gestured at the bar, and two seconds later the barkeep set a bottle of tequila down on the blotter. With two glasses.

"We will drink together," el Señor said. "Then I will give thought to this thing you ask."

Right there, it all collapsed. I stared at the bottle while everything inside me went numb. Stared while he poured hefty jolts into both glasses. Took one himself. Pushed the other across the desk to me.

I didn't touch it.

"Drink, Señor," he said softly.

My hand tried to move, but I didn't let it. I just sat there, and stared at the glass, and didn't touch it.

"Señor Axbrewder." Soft and ugly. "I give nothing without price. You are known to me—you are what the Anglos call 'alcoholic'. You are yourself an Anglo and a *chota*. You have intruded upon myself, and humiliated my Estobal. This is the price."

I didn't touch it.

"Do not insult me," he said. Soft and ugly and fatal.

I wanted to say something, wanted to appeal to him somehow, make him understand. But I didn't have any words for it. There weren't any words. If I took a drink, it wouldn't do me any good to know the name he was offering me. I wouldn't be able to do anything about it.

I got to my feet. "Sorry I bothered you," I muttered. "Should've known better."

El Señor made a cutting gesture with the edge of his hand. His goons hit me before I could get away from the chair. Maybe I could've taken them if I could've moved, but I didn't get the chance. They caught my arms, jerked me back down into the chair. One of them knotted a fist in my hair, hauled my head back. It all happened too fast. I was gasping and couldn't help myself.

El Señor came around the desk, picked up the bottle, and started pouring tequila down my throat.

Then I went blind with tears while the stuff burned its way into my guts.

Chapter Nineteen

The goons turned me over to Muy Estobal, and Estobal turned me out of El Machismo.

He was very methodical about it. First he half carried me down a couple back halls until we reached a door that took us out into a dark alley behind the place. Then he searched my pockets until he found the cylinder to his .38. Then he started to pound on me.

Grinning like a barracuda.

One hit split my lips so bad I sputtered blood every time I breathed. Another blow almost cracked my jaw. A couple more continued the job he'd already started on my ribs. After that, he had to hold me up with one hand so he could go on punching me with the other.

I suppose I should've been making some effort to defend myself. I wasn't all that drunk, but everything had already fallen apart. It was all hopeless, and I couldn't seem to think of any good reason to exert myself. So I didn't; if Estobal wanted to beat me to death, that was his business. My brain was numb.

Numbness is a wonderful thing. I really wasn't feeling his fists much. Half the time I couldn't even see him, but I could hear him fine. He was panting like a locomotive, working himself up into a terrible lather. I could hear him grunt every time he swung; I could hear the thudding sound when he connected.

Then I heard something else. A voice—a woman's voice. It sounded dimly familiar.

It said, "Release him." In Spanish.

Estobal stared down the alley for a second. Then he braced himself to hit me again.

"I do not jest," the woman snapped. "This man is known to me, Estobal. I am much in his debt. For his sake I will risk many things to punish you. The police will be grateful for any reason to lock you in their prison."

Estobal pushed me away from him. I bounced against the wall, and fell on my face. "Do not seek to threaten me, girl," he rasped. "El Señor will be displeased."

"Then permit him to be displeased. If he seeks to harm me, all Puerta del Sol will laugh at the man who revenges himself upon a woman."

Estobal muttered some kind of retort, but I couldn't make it out. Then he was gone—I heard the door slam behind him.

A minute later, the woman was kneeling beside me. "Ay, Señor Axbrewder," she said in English. "Are you severely hurt?"

With her help, I rolled over onto one side. My chest and face were starting to hurt, and I had to hunt a long way through pain and alcohol to find her name. "Senorita Sanguillan," I said. At least, that was what I tried to say. "What're you doing here?"

I heard a tearing noise, and then she was dabbing my chin and mouth with something. It felt soft, like a piece of her slip. While she tried to clean me up, she answered my question.

"I wished to speak with you. Señor Sevilla—Manolo—who is known to you, is the father of the man who married the daughter of my mother's brother. When I revealed to him my wish, he gave me to understand that you had a great matter in your heart which compelled you to seek words with el Señor." She kept wiping at my face while she spoke, and it hurt off and on, but I was too fuzzy to care. "Hearing this, I came to this place and inquired of you. I was informed with some laughter that you had been admitted to speech with Muy Estobal." There was suppressed fury in the way she said his name. "Therefore I awaited you." Under her breath, she muttered, *"Pendejo."* I knew she didn't mean me.

Groaning, I tried to crank myself into a sitting position. It wasn't easy—I wasn't absolutely sure which way was up. But she got her arms around my shoulders and helped me. Her face was close to mine—she was studying me anxiously.

"Is it possible for you to rise?"

I said, "Theresa." The way my mouth felt, it was all I could do to mumble. "Why did you want to talk to me?"

She hesitated, then said, "Rise to your feet, and I will inform you."

I shook my head. "Just tell me."

She sighed. "Very well, Señor Axbrewder. But you must not think ill of me."

I wanted to tell her not to worry, but I didn't have the strength. Or maybe what I didn't have was the sobriety.

Facing me squarely, she said, "I have taken back the charges against the man who sought to harm me. I do not wish you to speak against him."

That was the last straw. It was all too much for me—nothing mattered anymore. I let myself fall back against the cement and closed my eyes.

"Señor!" She tried to shake me, but she didn't have the weight to move me much. "You must understand. Because of this Captain Cason, I have lost my employment in the Heights. He spoke, and I was sent away without reference. He is too strong for me. He desired me to take back the charges, and I agreed so that he would permit me to find some other place of work."

I didn't move. Why should I move? The only thing she could have offered me that would have meant anything was a bottle—and that never occurred to her. After a while, she gave up tugging at me; I didn't even hear her leave.

I must have blacked out. The next thing I knew, she was back. With help. Two young men—old Manolo's sons, if I understood her right. They got their shoulders under my arms, heaved me up, and lugged me off.

I dragged along between them for a couple minutes, but then the strain started to hurt my chest too much. I had to take some of my own weight to ease the pain. After that, old habits took over. By the time she got me where we were going, I was practically walking by myself.

Her place was a ramshackle old adobe tenement about three blocks from El Machismo. The walls had once been painted, but now they were so chipped and weathered the building looked like it had some kind of disease. Terminal futility. The young men levered me up a flight of rickety wooden stairs, and then she was home. The one room she shared with her mother and two sisters was never going to look clean no matter how often they scrubbed it—ordinary soap and muscle can't keep up with rats.

She sat me down in the middle of the room in the only chair. Her mother heated some water on a stinking oil stove while her sisters watched me from their blankets with frightened animal eyes. When the water was ready, the young men held my arms while Theresa scalded the cuts on my face.

The pain blinded me again. It wasn't until after my eyes cleared I realized somebody else had come into the room.

Old Manolo.

He looked at me with a face full of sadness. But I didn't pay any attention to that. I had something else in mind.

He had a bottle of anisette in his coat pocket.

It was almost full.

As soon as his sons let go of my arms, I lunged at Manolo and got my hands on his bottle.

Putting my mouth around the mouth of the bottle tore my cuts, and the alcohol burned them like the lick of a whip. I stood it long enough to get three or four good swallows. I've never liked the taste of anisette, but right then I didn't care about that. All I wanted was to get drunk. Drunker. Drunk enough to pass out.

I put the cap back on the bottle, stuffed it away in one of the pockets of my jacket. Then I looked old Manolo in the face. "I took your advice," I muttered stiff-lipped. "Went to see el Señor. Now here I am. If you've got anything else to tell me, you'd better say it now. While I'm drunk enough to stand it."

His old brown eyes never wavered. "Ah, Señor Axbrewder," he sighed, "This night I have heard many sad tales. The daughter of your brother's widow has been found without her mind. A bomb has taken the hand of your partner. The setter of the bomb is dead, and you have come no nearer to the author of all these evils. It is a deep regret to me that el Señor saw fit to withhold the knowledge you seek. I will never again give such advice as I gave you. I am an old man, and old men are foolish."

His eyes held me until I couldn't stand it anymore—I had to look down. I didn't want him feeling sorry for me. I was in bad enough shape without that.

"Señor Axbrewder," he asked gently, "what will you do?"

That was a good question. Since I didn't have an answer, I took another slug of anisette. It was starting to get to me—some of the numbness I needed was coming back.

"Will you not go to the woman your partner? She has the name of a wise and clear-sighted person. Surely she will wish to know what has befallen you."

Ginny. Just thinking about her made my heart hurt. But Manolo was a cunning old bastard—he knew what he was doing. It was a sneaky way to give me advice, but it worked. Ginny. That was it, of course. Things weren't bad enough yet—they wouldn't be bad enough until I went and told Ginny I'd screwed everything up. Then I'd be free to drink as much as I wanted. It wouldn't be my problem anymore.

Everything has to be paid for—even freedom. Humiliation is the price you pay for alcohol, one way or another.

I got to my feet, wincing at the way my ribs seemed to grind together. I shook off the hands trying to hold me and went past old Manolo to the door.

I was on my way out when I recovered enough consideration to turn around. Holding myself up on the doorframe, I said as clearly as I could in Spanish, "Theresa Maria Sanguillan y Garcia, I give you thanks. I think no ill of you, but only good. When a burden is too great to be borne, it must be set aside." Then I left.

I stumbled a couple times on the stairs, but the railing held me somehow.

After that things got harder. Walking made my chest hurt. And my balance wasn't good—every time I had to stop myself from falling, I jarred my ribs. But I had to do it, and I did it. Went back to the parking lot of El Machismo to recover the Olds.

Then I was driving. I concentrated on it hard—the last thing I needed in the world was a driving-while-under-the-influence bust. But I couldn't help making mistakes. Once I had the distinct impression I was going the wrong way down a one-way street.

I hung on to the wheel with both fists, and kept moving. A couple times when things got fuzzy, I stopped and took a swig from my bottle. Not much—just enough to hold me together. Eventually, I reached University Hospital.

It didn't occur to me that there would be a problem getting in to see Ginny until after I'd parked the Olds and got out to look around. Most of the windows were dark, which reminded me of the time. Naturally, the security guards and night-duty nurses weren't going to want me wandering around their hospital at this hour of the night.

But I was too drunk to let that stop me. Drunk as I was, I remembered Ginny's room number.

I went into Emergency. But instead of stopping at the nurses' station, I walked straight to the waiting room as if I had some perfectly good reason for being there. Then I sneaked over to the stairwell. The door to the stairs had a big sign on it saying, "Emergency Exit Only." I went in fast. Once I got past the door, the only thing I had to worry about for a while was meeting somebody on the stairs.

I didn't meet anybody. If I had, I probably would've gone to pieces.

When I got up to the floor I wanted, I looked out through the little window in the stairwell door. I didn't see anybody. Ginny's room was just two doors down from me on the opposite side of the hall. Getting in to see her was going to be easy.

Too easy.

I cracked the stairwell door a couple inches, made extra sure the hall was empty. Then I went across to Ginny's door. And stopped.

I didn't want to just barge into her room. Not only did I have strong feelings about her right to privacy, I also knew how fast she could be with that .357. So instead of pushing open the door and going in, I knocked, waited, knocked again. No answer.

I took the time for one more quick drink. Then I let myself into her room.

It was a semi-private room, like the one Alathea had been in, and the reading light over the head of Ginny's bed was on. The curtain separating the two beds was pulled almost all the way across the room, and there was no light on the far side, so everything past the curtain was dark.

Ginny was sitting up in bed. The head of the bed wasn't cranked up, and she didn't have any pillows behind her—she was just sitting there as if she was getting ready to answer my knock. But there was an I.V. hanging from a pole over her head, and the tube was plugged into her right arm. Which pretty well immobilized her—she couldn't have come to the door.

She was looking at me.

Staring at me. Her eyes on either side of her broken nose were as dark as if she'd been mugged. There was a look of horror in her face.

I didn't move. I couldn't. She paralyzed me.

Her voice cut through me like the flame of a blowtorch. "You're drunk!"

That staggered me. Rocked me back on my heels.

"You sonofabitch!"

I blinked at her like an idiot. Ginny? She didn't understand. She didn't know what had happened to me. I hadn't expected her to react like this. I wanted to explain.

She didn't give me a chance. "Get out of here, Mick." Just the tone of her voice made my ribs groan. "I don't want to have anything more to do with you. Do you hear me, Mick?" She spat that *Mick* at me as if it was the worst thing she could do without actually shooting me. "Get out of my life."

Mick. She called me Mick. Nobody calls me that—nobody. Not since Richard—. Not since I killed Richard. Rick and Mick. Nobody. I had to fight to keep from crying out.

"All right." My voice shook—I couldn't control it. "If that's the way you want it."

Nobody! It would've been better if she had shot me. No simple little hunk of lead would hurt like this.

But when I turned for the door, I caught a glimpse of her purse out of the corner of my eye. It was on the floor a few feet away from the nightstand. I was thinking, *Shot me*. Her .357. In her purse.

What was it doing there?

If she'd accidentally pushed it off the stand, it wouldn't have fallen that far away.

Then all of a sudden my skin was crawling with intuition. Something was trying to get through to me—something was trying to reach through the stuff in my blood, make sense to me. I struggled for it. I wanted to beat my head on the wall. I was too drunk—I couldn't think.

I had to think.

Why had she called me Mick? The pain was killing me. I couldn't stop it. I had to stop it. Had to think.

Ginny had gotten her hand blown off because she didn't want anything to happen to me.

Think!

Her purse was too far away from the nightstand. It couldn't have fallen there accidentally. Somebody must've shoved it.

Why?

To get it away from her. So she couldn't reach her gun.

Why?

Think!

She needed me.

I had to be sober!

But I wasn't sober. I was standing there like a lush, with a bottle of anisette in my pocket, and my hands clenched in front of my face. Seconds were getting away from me, and I couldn't bring them back.

Hands clenched.

Clenched the way I'd clenched them around Kirke's arm a couple days ago.

Why had I done that?

Because Kirke said Alathea was a little whore.

For an instant, I almost screamed.

And everything came into focus.

We hadn't told Kirke this case had anything to do with sex. We hadn't said a word about that to the school board. How had he known? Unless he was responsible.

Kirke!

That was why he'd tried to get me to drink with him. He knew I was getting close. He wanted to keep me there in his apartment until he figured out some way to kill me.

Then a horror of my own landed on me so hard I almost dropped to my knees.

Kirke knew Ginny was in the hospital. Stretto had told him what happened to her. He knew she was here.

I didn't know what to do.

There was a steel armchair with a green vinyl seat against the wall next to the door. I put my hand on it to hold myself up.

Then it all came together at once—intuition, rage, fear, love. I snatched up the chair as if it was nothing. With one sweep of my arm, I threw it at the curtain near the head of her bed.

It hit something behind the curtain. I heard a muffled groan. A gun went off—the slug plowed into the ceiling.

Ginny and I were already moving. She flipped out of bed, crouched down on the floor. I jumped over her, dove across the bed into the curtain.

The curtain had already been torn by the chair. It came down under my weight. I landed half on the chair, half on somebody who was twisting frantically, trying to get up.

The curtain hid him. I didn't know if he still had his gun, but I didn't care. I just hammered with my fists. The third time, I hit something hard that must've been his head—he slumped under me, stopped moving. But I didn't stop. I could hear Ginny shouting, "Don't kill him! He knows where Mittie is!" But the pressure was too strong, and I couldn't stop. I crashed at him with everything I had until I heard another gunshot in the room.

I rolled off him, got up.

Ginny was standing beside her bed with her .357 pointed at the ceiling. The IV tube had been ripped out of her arm. Blood was dripping slowly from her elbow.

There was nobody in the other bed.

I swallowed hard, managed to ask, "Kirke?" I hurt everywhere. My knees felt like mush, and I was lightheaded. I had to hold onto the bed frame.

Ginny nodded. Then she put her gun down on the nightstand. For a second, she looked like she was going to faint. But she fought it off. "Oh, God, Brew," she breathed. "I thought he was going to kill you."

Slowly, I was coming back under control. I reached down and pulled away the curtain—just making sure I hadn't hit him too hard.

His head was pretty well battered, but he was still breathing.

The whole room stank of anisette. One side of my jacket was soaked, and my pocket was full of broken glass.

Chapter Twenty

Acton got an address out of Kirke—I don't know how, and I don't want to know. All I cared about was that Acton took me—and about eight other cops—with him when he went to check out that address. It was a long way up Canyon Road toward the mountains. But Acton drove like a bat; we must've set some kind of record getting there. The sky was turning pale, but the sun still hadn't climbed up over the mountains when we reached the house. It sat in a little valley between two hills, so it was completely out of sight of its neighbors. A house only somebody very rich could afford. A nice place—a sprawling ranch-style, complete with everything except its own airstrip. But right then none of us felt much like admiring it. Acton and I broke the door down, and all ten of us went charging in.

We found Mittie. Alive. Hungry, strung-out, and frantic—but alive. One of the cops took her back into town to the hospital while the rest of them started searching the house.

I didn't do any searching. Once I knew Mittie was safe—safe in spite of all the stupid things I'd done in the past twelve hours—a lot of the tension inside me snapped, and I had to sit down.

After a while, Acton came and stood in front of me. He had his hands in his pockets, and his fingers were jiggling keys or coins or something.

I said, "You weren't surprised when you saw who it was." Which was true—when he'd got to the hospital and seen Kirke, he'd looked like he'd known it all along.

He said, "Naw. I spent half the night talking to the school board. Scurvey and Greenling both said they got their note paper from him. He's the board secretary—he's supposed to provide things like note paper. Tearing sheets in half is an old habit of his. Didn't prove nothing, but it sure as hell made me suspicious."

I nodded tiredly. Then I said, "You're going to have to find her father."

"Naw," he growled again. "He turned himself in about two-thirty this morning. Babbling something about killing the man who set that bomb. I wanted to talk to him, but right about then we got this call"—he was grinning sourly —"about a shootout at the hospital. So he's still sitting there in the cage."

"He used my gun," I said. "Didn't have one of his own. It's in the glove compartment of the Olds." Then I said the only thing I could think of to give Tred a hand. "He was covering me. Rinlassen had a gun on me and Tred was trying to keep me from being blown away."

Acton nodded—I could see he was going to accept that story without worrying about it. Another piece of tension faded, and for a few minutes there I almost went to sleep.

But then the cops started finding things. The note paper didn't give them any trouble—there was a stack of neatly torn half-sheets on the desk in the den. Same watermark as all the runaway notes. That—and all the fingerprints in the house—gave the cops the kind of evidence courts love. Nine counts of kidnapping and seven of murder.

And after some more diligent searching (your typical police search—it made the house look like it had been used as a test site for some new kind of high explosive), the cops found the heroin and the money. It wasn't a particularly big cache of junk—Kirke probably had to drive down to Mexico for a few days every three or four months to stock up—but it was enough. The money came out to over a hundred thousand dollars—it was all Kirke had left after paying for housing, junk, food, clothes, and Rinlassen. Obviously, he kept it in cash so it wouldn't show up in his financial records anywhere. Which explained why Smithsonian thought he was clean.

Acton rubbed his hands together. "This bastard's going to get the gas chamber."

A couple cops stayed behind to keep an eye on things

until the print-and-picture boys arrived. The rest of us piled into the cars and went back to Puerta del Sol.

Acton dropped me off at the hospital. The sun was up now and all that crisp morning light made me squint. But for once in my life I was glad to see it; nights like that last one I could do without.

It was too early for visiting hours, but the hospital staff didn't make me wait. By then, Ginny and I were celebrities around there—if "celebrity" is the right word for it. One of the head nurses made an exception for me and took me up to Ginny's new room.

This time when she saw me, Ginny smiled. It lit up her whole face.

I sat down in one of the chairs against the wall, and for a minute or two we didn't say anything. We just smiled at each other.

I didn't want to do anything else. But after a while I started to feel like I was in danger of making a fool of myself. "All right," I said. My voice was so husky it almost made me laugh. "All right. I can't stand the suspense. After what I've been through, I want to know how you figured out this case."

She looked beautiful to me. Even her broken nose was beautiful. "What makes you think I figured anything out?"

"You were right on the edge of it." That was something I was sure of. "The only reason you didn't get it then was because you were too tight. I'm willing to bet you had the answer right there in the front of your head when you woke up after surgery. You probably tried to call me, but there wasn't any way you could track me down."

She nodded. I was right, of course. Intuition didn't have anything to do with it. I just knew Ginny.

"I missed something obvious," I went on. "I'm going to go crazy unless you tell me what it was."

She leaned back against her pillows, looked up at the ceiling. Fistoulari thinking. "I missed it, too," she said after a moment. "It wasn't Stretto or Scurvey—we were pretty sure of that. You were sure it wasn't Greenling, and I was willing to believe you. So it had to be Kirke or one of the secretaries.

"So finally it all came down to the way Kirke ran that office. All those girls were kidnapped during the day—at different times during the day. By somebody who had some kind of tie-in that would make the girls go with him. Somebody the girls would at least vaguely recognize. Somebody who could make a good excuse for himself if he accidentally got stopped. So that pretty much excluded any fiancés or husbands. It had to be somebody who actually worked for the board.

"But each one of those little kidnapping operations must have taken a fair amount of time. From the office to whatever school it was. Pick up the girl. Drive out to that house on Canyon Road. Back to the office. That was what we missed. Kirke was the only one who could arrange that kind of time away from the office during the day. If one of his secretaries had disappeared for that length of time, he would've nailed her to the wall. The way he ran that place, he was the only one who could get away."

Well, I was right about that too—what I'd missed was obvious. Axbrewder the genius. Somedays I'm amazed to find I'm still smart enough to put my clothes on straight.

Ginny was looking at me hard. I didn't understand it until she started to say, "I'm sorry I called—"

I interrupted her. "Forget it. I was in a fog—you had to get through to me somehow." Then I grinned. "Besides, you knew Kirke didn't know my first name."

For a minute, she was blinking back tears, and I didn't know what to say.

There was a knock at the door. Ginny nodded, and I said, "Come in."

It was Lona.

She had a vaguely startled look, as if something she couldn't believe was happening to her. At first, she had trouble finding her voice. Then she said, "I wanted to tell you. I just talked to the doctor. He said"—she swallowed—"he said Alathea is getting stronger. Her vital signs are getting stronger—and steadier. He said that probably means she's going to come out of it. Maybe soon. He thinks she's going to be all right."

After that I couldn't see for a while. My eyes were running, and everything was blurred.

Ginny said, "I'm glad. She's a wonderful girl."

Lona said, "You didn't find her. You didn't bring her back."

When Ginny didn't answer, I knew Lona was talking to me. Blindly, I said, "I know. She saved herself."

For a moment, Lona didn't say anything. Then she said, "You caught the man who was responsible. That's what Richard would've wanted you to do."

I had to cover my face with my hands. When I got myself back under control, Lona was gone.

Ginny was smiling at me like the sun.

I got to my feet. She'd had a rough eighteen hours—she needed rest. And Tred was going to need me to tell the cops my side of the story. Maybe he was even going to need me to post bail for him.

But before I left there was one thing I had to do.

I walked over to Ginny, bent down to her. Gave her the best kiss I had in me.

It hurt my cut mouth a lot, but I didn't care. Because she wrapped her arms around my neck and kissed me back. Hard.

When we stopped, I was grinning like a crazy man. I was practically floating as I turned away, started for the door.

Her voice stopped me. "What're you going to do now?" she asked. "Go have a drink?" She wasn't angry, and she wasn't blaming me. There was none of that in her tone. Just pain.

"No." I faced her again, so she could see I was telling her the truth. No big promises or predictions—just the truth about how I felt. "I'm going to put that off for a while."